The Diary of Carlo Cipriani

An Outer Banks of North Carolina Novel

J. Willis Sanders

ISBN-13: 978-1-954763-10-4 (paperback)
ISBN-13: 978-1-954763-12-8 (hardcover)

BUGGS ISLAND BOOKS

Printed in the United States of America

Cover photo by Paul Swisher Jr.
Cover by Elaina Lee: For the Muse Design

Author's Note

This is the first in a series of three novels that take place on the Outer Banks of North Carolina. Those who know this amazing place understand how it begs us to return every so often, like the tide tugs at our hearts and souls.

The Diary of Carlo Cipriani starts in 1521, and is a fictional account of how the original Spanish Mustangs arrived north of Corolla. There's much more, of course, but why spoil a good story?

If the Sunrise Forgets Tomorrow occurs in the early days of World War II, when German U-boats were sinking ships off America's eastern coast at will. It takes place on magical Ocracoke Island, where four British seamen were buried after a U-boat torpedoed their ship. Although serious, it contains two of my favorite characters: twin eighteen-year-old sisters who made me both laugh and cry, sometimes within paragraphs of each other.

Love, Jake takes place at Nags Head. It is decidedly contemporary, with a character who experiences problems that few were aware of in the distant past. It also contains romantic heat not found in the first two, described tastefully instead of graphically.

Each has a certain flavor. Each has a specific voice. Each should appeal to lovers of the area in different ways. And who knows? More books about this unique place may emerge from my imagination yet.

Please enjoy, J.W.S.

Also by J. Willis Sanders:

The Colors of Eliza Gray

Verified Amazon reviews:

"Captivating! ... J. Willis Sanders has captured love in this story. Love of a father to his daughter, love between brothers and sisters, and true love struggling to find a way to a future together. I look forward to Sanders' next book."

"I can honestly say that "The Colors of Eliza Gray" had me hooked from chapter one! It had me wishing for a "happily ever after" for Eliza from the beginning. Every emotion is found in this book and J. Willis Sanders definitely knows how to draw his readers in! I had read half of it before I realized it and finished it up the next morning!"

"Enjoyed this book so much! Stayed up way past my bedtime to finish it. Romantic and inspiring story. Great descriptions enabling the reader to visualize the scenes. Highly recommended."

"You won't be able to put this awesome book down! Love, love of a father and their love!!!! Please write another about how their lives are going!!!"

Treasures Found, Treasures Hidden

Finding a treasure this intriguing—let alone hiding it again—doesn't happen very often. Neither does finding a treasure that could land a person in jail. My hobby relates, so I'll cover that as well, including how this lengthy preamble is necessary to explain the historical accuracy of what I found. "Amazing" doesn't begin to describe it, so I'll get on with it.

I discovered it on the east coast of the United States, north of Corolla, North Carolina, where the descendants of wild Spanish Mustangs, supposed shipwreck survivors, have not only survived, but have thrived on this strip of sand and gnarled trees, scrub vegetation and marsh, for hundreds of years. For anyone curious about the horse's background, DNA testing in 1992 and 2007 confirmed the Spanish origin of those horses tested, so it should be safe to assume they're all of Spanish origin.

As far as my hobby, I'm one of those people who scan the beach with a metal detector.

As to my "jail" comment, it's illegal to remove archeological finds from private land without the owner's permission. Since much of the land north of Corolla is owned by developers, I would likely be prosecuted if I reported my find. Regardless, I don't intend to keep it. I plan to send a copy of it to publishers anonymously, along with a note to send the proceeds to the Corolla Wild Horse Fund, plus how they can find out why when they visit their website. Then I'll return the treasure to where I found it and keep the manuscript for my wife and I to read as often as we'd like.

As to where I found this treasure, which explains its historical significance, I had driven my four-wheel drive pickup up the beach from Corolla and had walked behind the dunes in a grove of what's locally known as "live oak" trees. For readers who've never seen one, they're the old men of the Outer Banks. They're stunted and gnarled, and their limbs spread low to the ground, shaped by the prevailing winds into skeletal arms, hands, and fingers. If trees have character, these trees have character. Their normal growth pattern is to spread extremely wide, making them the perfect place to hang a hammock on a single low limb. Another surprising trait is how they only lose their leaves in the spring, as new leaves start emerging. They also grow small, sweet acorns that birds and deer and the horses eat.

In this grove of live oaks, when my metal detector warbled and chirped its electronic alarm, I set it down and started digging with a small shovel I carry when detecting.

Expecting the disappointment of an aluminum can from a litterbug, I was surprised to find several rusted pieces of metal about the length of my index finger. The size and shape suggested nails, but so much rust encased the metal, I couldn't make a better guess.

Thinking they were trash instead of anything significant, I set them aside to throw away. I scanned in wider circles and stopped at another, much stronger signal, which sent a fine tingle of anticipation up my spine. I dug about a foot deep in the sand, checked the signal again, and dug until I hit something that thudded with the hollow sound of a wooden container.

I was about two feet deep by now. Sand flowed back into the hole every time I shoveled, so I had to widen the hole before I could go deeper. When I had removed enough sand to uncover what I'd hit, I dropped the shovel and stared.

The slightly rounded wooden top, gray with age, resembled a treasure chest like in the movies and on TV. Four rusty iron bands ran front to back, curving to match the contours of what appeared to be a lid.

With my hands, I scooped more sand away from the sides. Two rusted hinges connecting the lid to the bottom, including a huge clasp secured with rope, saw sunlight for the first time in who knew how long. Instead of being red with rust, a patina of green covered the clasp. I knew brass, when aged, turns green, so this must be a brass clasp.

I dug like a beagle after a rabbit, throwing sand in the air while imagining a hoard of gold doubloons like those Mel Fisher brought up from the wreck of the Spanish galleon *Atocha,* sunk in a hurricane off the Florida Keys in 1622. On each end of the chest, I felt two rope handles. I continued digging until I could wiggle the chest in its sandy grave, then grabbed one of the ropes to lift the chest out. The rope broke and I fell on my rear. Rather than try the other rope, I dropped to my back and wiped sweat from my forehead with a gritty palm.

Using the shovel again, I dug to make a sloped side in the hole and was able to drag the chest out. It wasn't very large, maybe two feet by one foot by one foot deep. More clumsy than heavy, it couldn't hold any gold doubloons, unfortunately. Using the shovel, I broke the rope holding the clasp. It opened with a gritty squeak when I gave it a hard pull.

Inside were several quills from some sort of bird. The feathers had turned to dust, and the tips of the quills were black. Several corked bottles, stained the same shade of black on the insides, hinted at ink, so the quills must've been centuries-old writing quills. In a corner of the chest, a folded piece of yellowed cloth hid a rectangular shaped something. Beside it, another piece of cloth was rolled into a long, slender shape.

Unfolding the rectangle of cloth, which fell apart within my fingertips, revealed a leather-bound book. I took it from the chest and placed it in my lap. As I eased the cover open, the binding creaked at about an inch, so I stopped.

Inside, two locks of black hair, one curly and one straight, were each tied with a thin length of red ribbon. I couldn't read the first three of the five words written in a different language, but the last two must be a name: *Carlo Cipriani.*

Since the name sounded Spanish, the other three words must be Spanish. Lucky me, a friend of mine speaks Spanish, so a plan took shape to discover the author's secrets.

I eased the long, slender piece of cloth from the chest and gingerly unrolled it to keep the decayed fabric from falling apart. What appeared to be two pieces of a wooden flute, broken in two, complete with several holes and a notch for blowing, surprised me.

As curious as I was about the flute, I was more curious about the musician who played it, who must've also written the book. Why would anyone break a fine instrument like this unless the person was in an extreme emotional state?

I returned the cloth and flute to the chest, decided against keeping the quills and ink bottles, and buried the chest in the hole, where the author must have buried it countless years ago for a reason that I hoped to discover in his book.

Long story short, my friend said the Spanish words were *The Journal of Carlo Cipriani,* and all I'm thinking is if the chest and everything in it, including those intriguing locks of hair, possibly from two different women, are genuine, what a story Carlo had to tell.

Most of the pages of the journal were stuck together, so my friend and I searched online and learned how humidification would loosen the pages. We set up a down-and-dirty humidifier using a cool mist unit from a drug store, a wire rack for cooling cakes, and a large cardboard box. I suggested the box because I thought it would absorb excess humidity before it hurt the book.

A week later, we teased the pages of yellowed parchment apart with tweezers and found one page torn out about two-thirds of the way through. Squinting at the tiny print, my friend said the writing was too hard to read and to please find someone else.

Long story short again, I asked my high school Spanish teacher, also a history lover, to translate it. He loved it so much, he got a writer friend to add a creative touch. Since I can hardly write a thank you note, much less a book, the writer wrote this section, typed the translation, and I printed the book at home. After my wife and I read it, we anonymously sent copies to several publishers to see what would happen. They might question the name because we chose "diary" over "journal." The first recorded use of "diary" is well after Carlo's time, and we thought *The Diary of Carlo Cipriani* had a better ring than *The Journal of Carlo Cipriani.*

We also found it interesting how paragraphs weren't used during Carlo's time, making it hard to read for the translator. To ease this issue, the writer suggested using paragraphs, indentions, and more modern language for today's readers. I suggested contractions, but the writer said they weren't used in the 16th century, and historical accuracy should at least be attempted.

Three things of note: One is how Carlo, if the diary came from 1521 as dated, was educated to the point of writing. He covered this in the journal, so I'll let him explain it. The second is how he addressed each diary entry with "Dear Luisa." I could say more, but why spoil the story? The last noteworthy thing is how he wrote with a mix of third and present tense. When I saw that I could hardly believe it, because I thought present tense was more of a modern way of writing. Then again, after reading the entire novel, it's possible that Carlo's mental state had a lot to do with it. He never explained the different tenses, nor how he couldn't record his experiences while in the middle of them. Still, none of that kept my wife and I from turning the pages like nothing we'd ever read before.

So, if you're reading this book, that means we succeeded, and Carlo's story is out there for the world to enjoy.

Some readers may ask why I didn't trust this find to some government entity or museum? Well, the honest answer is how the romantic in me wanted the chest and everything in it to stay where Carlo had left it. After reading his words, you may agree, because he was quite the romantic himself.

Another question readers might ask is what will stop someone else from finding the chest like I did.

Not only did I take all the metal off before I buried it the last time, my wife and I bought the lot a short while later and hired a contractor to build a small house there. Now, no matter who descends upon the beach north of Corolla, North Carolina, carrying metal detectors and shovels, Carlo's memories will always be safe.

Thank you for your story, Carlo. I can't help but think I know you. If there's one thing my wife and I hope for, it's for you to have finally found peace at the end of your long journey.

For you see, Luisa, to be loved is one thing, but to be understood is everything.

Carlo Cipriani

September 11, 1521

Dear Luisa,

In my twenty-four years of life, I have experienced a thing or two that might have taken me from this world. However, never did I think one of those things would be drowning in the middle of the vast and wondrous sea.

The wind has ripped the storm sails at their seams. Men have taken them wet and sodden from the masts and are dragging them into the hold for replacement. Down here, flickering candles within glass holders hang from every other beam or so, illuminating some of the crew who heave until vomit splatters at their feet.

My stomach is empty, for I knew better than to eat the hardtack biscuits soaked in the gruel within the communal trough, where men line up each dawn to break their fast. Two days ago, like great black mountains rising from the blue-green depths, storm clouds burst from the southwest horizon, and nothing but fear has filled my belly ever since.

Near a niche I have claimed, with a convenient plank for a seat, a candle flickers a pool of yellow light into my lap. Rainwater leaks through the decking to wet my head, while saltwater seeps from the planking at my back, further wetting my stinking blouse and stinging my raw skin. With each shriek of wind, with each rise and fall of a wave, with each watery hand slapping at the ship as if it were nothing more than a worrisome fly, I stop writing to avoid ruining my letters, and it is then that my concentration fails, allowing the sour smell of unwashed bodies mixed with the vile odors of bile and urine to surround me. When calm returns, which is not often, I huddle over to place quill to page once more. Between my water-logged shoes, the ink bottle stands steadier than the rest of us poor souls. Thank God above for the stores of ink and quills I found yesterday, within a sealed chest tucked in a corner of the hold, for my few quills and single bottle of ink shall never last if I make it through this journey alive.

Within the other end of the ship, farthest from where the men collapse to sleep each night, our cargo of horses scream shrill, shrieking calls when the ship breaches a particularly huge wave and drops into a trough. I dare not see about Cantante. If I did, I would likely break my neck when the ship lists side-to-side and pirouettes like a swimmer caught within the swirling vortex of a whirlpool. Besides, his Spanish blood is similar to my own, with many a trial beneath his hooves, and he can abide the storm until it ends, although, like the storm of my life, it seems it never shall.

I began this journey without a single expectation, and whether I lived or died was of no consequence. I bought this journal with plans of winding away the hours of my voyage by noting whatever swimming, floating, or flying creatures I saw, but when the notion struck to chronicle what may well be my last days for you, Luisa, I gave up my indifference concerning my life. Now, if God allows, I shall return and place my words within your hands for you to always remember me by, and, if possible, to ask your forgiveness once you understand why I left Palos de la Frontera and all that was dear to me, including you.

The ship rises, rises, rises. I slam my journal closed, clasp it between my legs, and grasp the beam in preparation for the sickening fall into the trough of the wave—but we continue rising, as if sailing to Heaven itself. The bow gradually turns downward, the ship points toward hell, and the men carrying the new sail slide by me, cursing and raging, tangled within the heavy material. Something crashes at the bow, possibly wood splintering, followed by sea water rushing over my feet as we level. I cork the ink bottle, secure the quill within the pages of my journal, and wedge everything into a space between the plank and the wall of my niche. Time to leave my small hideaway and check Cantante, the truest friend I have upon this vessel.

The ship manages to remain level during my steps. When I near the storage area before the horses, their caretaker, Barros, greets me with a raised hand. "Carlo, I knew you would come. No worries, your Cantante is secure."

"And the rest?"

"One mare broke a leg and was screaming as if all the demons in hell were after her." Barros raises his hand, wet and shining with blood, and slices it across his throat. "She shall scream no more."

The candlelight from a nearby holder must reveal my revulsion, for Barros pats my shoulder. "Stop making that sour face. Grilled horseflesh for supper when this storm blows over shall set a smile upon your lips."

I do not tell Barros, but to me, eating horse would be like eating a member of my own family. I shall die before that happens, and anyone considering making Cantante a meal shall die with me.

Barros raises his huge head of curly black hair upward, eyes scanning the underside of the deck. "Ah, the storm is quieting. Let us see what damage the ship has taken."

We climb the sea-slick ladder and I hold in a gasp. The ship sits within calm waters. Around us, clouds form a circular wall reaching upward to clear blue sky. It is as if someone has drawn a dark curtain around a huge section of sea, except the curtain is roiling and boiling like smoke from a woods fire. As amazing as the sight is, it fills me with a fear that makes my guts clench. This storm has held us captive for two days, and when the other side of this circle of calm overtakes us, we shall be at the mercy of the wind and rain once more, a watery hell that may well send us to the bottom of the sea yet.

"Mother of God," Barros mumbles, crossing his chest. "In all my travels I have never seen such a thing."

I lower my eyes from the circular curtain of clouds. "How far do you think the storm has taken us off course?"

"I asked the navigator that very thing at breakfast. He said until he can see the full width of the stars and moon again, he has no idea. The storm is moving northeast and we were sailing southwest. Who knows where we are after two days, and who knows where we shall be after two more days, when the storm is done with us?"

Imagining the returning fury of the sea, I look out at the glassy surface.

And gape.

"Barros … the other two ships … where—?"

"Who knows, Carlo? At least we are not them because we know where we are."

"They are likely in hell," a high-pitched voice says behind us, unlike the gruff bass of Barros.

I turn to meet the hatchet-faced scowl of Sancho, the man who passes for our cook, although much of what we have eaten during our voyage, such as salted beef, fish, and pork, along with molded cheese and the rare vegetable or fruit, has gone to mush during the storm.

Barros breaks out into a huge, yellow-toothed smile. "Then, Sancho, we shall celebrate their passing with horseflesh. One of the mares broke her leg, and I eased her suffering for her."

Sancho raises his head upward. "It is like we are inside the burnt and blackened skull of some great one-eyed beast, and we are looking out at the heavens." At this extremely accurate description, I cross myself.

Sancho and Barros start to discuss their favorite methods of cooking horse, and I look away. By the wheel of the ship, the captain and his first officer direct men to their repairs. From the hatch, the storm sail is dragged out, secured to ropes, and hoisted upward to the spars. At the stern, a man leans over the rail, stands and runs to the captain. As quick as I can, dodging men at their tasks, careful not to fall on the sea-slick deck, I go to the wall beneath them to listen.

"Say it again, man," the captain says. "I cannot understand your babbling."

"The rudder, sir. It is bad cracked an' shall take no more beatin'. We are done for, sir, done for. No way we can control the ship when the storm—"

I risk a look upward. The captain has clamped his hand over the babbling mouth. "Say one more word and I shall kill you where you stand, do you hear me?" Widened eyes, an ashen face, and a single nod answers the captain, who removes his hand from the mouth. "Panic shall do us no good. Do the best you can and be quick about it." He pats the shoulder of the man. "And say your prayers while you do."

The man hurries toward the stern, and the first officer faces the captain. "Shall I give the order for lashing ourselves to whatever is still solid before the storm hits?"

The captain huffs a hard breath. "And let not a one of them have a chance by going down with the ship?"

"Apologies, sir, but they might rather go down with the ship than bloat and float to the surface days later, to have gulls and sharks and such feast upon them."

"Point taken, but giving that order shall panic them as much as telling them about the rudder." The captain steps closer to the rail. I press my back against the wall. "Have you seen that young fool, Carlo?"

"No, sir. He is likely with his horse in the hold. I never saw a man so attached to a horse in all my life. It is as if they were brothers."

"I should not have allowed him to join this voyage, but his story tugged at my heart. What a tragedy to have it end without him returning home to see his family and his daughter."

"Yes, sir, I agree. He never told me what happened to his wife, other than she died. Has he mentioned her to you?"

"Not a word."

"Well, he shall have his horse to accompany him to his death. Perhaps a tune with his flute shall be in order for his hoofed friend."

"Have you heard him play for the horse?" the captain says, wide eyed.

"I certainly have. The horse even bobs his head up and down in time with the notes. It is a sight to see."

Another man runs to the captain. "Sir, the planks in the bow are spreading and we have no more packing to stop the leaks."

"Then use rags, clothes, whatever. She shall hold together if we keep our faith. Off with you."

Despite the mention of my flute playing, and how Cantante loves it, the false hope conveyed by the captain at the hopelessness of our situation starts to drag me to my knees, but I find one last bit of strength to stand, resolve firming the bones and muscles within me.

Below, I take the candle from my niche and gather my meager belongings—the journal, ink, quill and, at the last minute, my clothing—then take everything to the chest where I found the ink and quills and put everything within. For the clothing, I stuff it amongst the ink bottles in hopes my treasures shall survive the storm on some far and distant land, even if I do not. I start to close the top when my flute, within a rolled-up cloth, catches my eye. I take it from the cloth and place it within my pocket. When the time comes, Cantante and I shall share one final tune.

Closing the chest, I stop, take the journal out, and open it to remove the curl of hair tied with a length of red ribbon, the last remnant of my beloved—

Her name clamps my teeth shut. No, not her name, but that horrible day, the worst of my life, which refuses to pass my lips. I wanted to hold the lock of hair, black and shining, to my cheek, to inhale my remembrance of her aroma after a bath, to recall the silky softness of her long tresses within my hands, but … I cannot.

With the lock of hair secure within my journal once more, I shut the chest, leaving the rope untied within the clasp. If I find the courage to play for Cantante before our fate descends, I shall return the flute and secure the chest so the last precious articles of our life may join their doom together.

September 15, 1521

Dear Luisa,

Before I attempted sleep, I could not bring myself to play for Cantante, for I would have broken down with tears and ruined my notes. Patting his sleek neck and scratching the white star centered within his forehead, I bade him goodnight and farewell, fully expecting our end to arrive within the black of evening. I then returned to my niche, rested my back against the damp hull, and fell into a deep and entirely unexpected slumber.

After waking to dim sunlight shafting through the storm-cracked decking overhead, the voices of men above, the pounding of mallets, and the thud of footsteps teases me up the ladder.

As my head rises into the yellow morning, the aroma of meat cooking meets my nose. Over by the rail, away from three men mending frayed ropes from the rigging, Sancho has made a firepit of ballast stones and is happily roasting a haunch from the mare, pierced through with a spit. Several ravenous men, all licking their lips, stand around him, and I imagine stories told by some of the crew about cannibals in faraway lands, followed with jokes about how human flesh has the same texture and taste as roast pig. Of course, this revolts me as badly as the idea of consuming horse.

I ask some of the waiting men about our position relevant to the roiling black cloud wall, and the general consensus, which matches my own observation, is the circle has grown larger and more powerful, witnessed by the speed in which the mass moves, like ashen sails billowing across the horizon. Those men who answered me also agree. We are about three-fourths of the way across the circle of calm sea, and most fear, like I do, at how we shall be engulfed as darkness falls, to be blindly broken against wooden beams, to drown within the murky depths or, like some who finger the blades tucked within their belts, to cut their own throats before befalling any of these fates.

Like some mountain ram leaping up a cliff, the head of Barros extends from the hold, black curls fluttering within the increasing breeze. He comes over and slaps my back. "Ah, Carlo, a good day to feast upon horseflesh, is it not?" He leaves me to sniff the smoke rising from the grease as it drips from the haunch and hisses on the coals of the fire. "What say you, Sancho? Is she ready to sample yet?"

Sancho severs a bloody piece from near the glistening bone and offers it to Barros. "Give it a try. After all, you ended her suffering for her."

Bile fills my throat. I turn away and leave to the satisfied sounds of Barros crunching gristle and smacking his lips.

No one works near the stern. I aimlessly stroll there in order to appear unconcerned about the least little thing in the world. Leaning quickly over the rail, black ponytail beside my cheek, I see the results of the first two days of the storm. Along the full length of the rudder, visible within the blue-green water, cracks and splinters foretell our fate. One wave shall be all it takes. The ship shall flounder, capsize, and burst from watery blow after watery blow, until her remains spread across the sea.

A short way from the smoke and fire, a few impatient souls, who must want their horse well done, dip hardtack biscuit within the communal trough, something else to remind me of pig. Knowing I need sustenance, I snatch a biscuit from a bowl, soak it with the watery gruel, and when it is soft enough to break open, do so to check for worms or maggots. "Why do that?" one of the men asks. "Meat is meat no matter if it be insect, fowl, walks upon hooves, or flies in the air. Eat and be glad about it."

I ignore him and check for wriggling white bodies regardless. Finding none, I shove a doughy morsel into my mouth, force the gooey mass down, and drink water from a skin beside the bowl of biscuits. More bites meet the same fate, leaving my throat feeling as if one of the dolphins that occasionally dart within our bow wave has taken a wrong turn into my gullet. As I raise the skin for more water, a blinding burst of light clears the wall cloud to our east, an artificial sunrise for our last day alive.

Along with myself, men shade their eyes and look upward. Shaking heads, crossed chests, and silent prayers with trembling lips follow. They then return to their various chores about the deck.

The day, restricted by the shortened path of the sun, including the movement of the wall cloud toward us, passes all too quickly, and the sun sets below the edge of the roiling mass, leaving us within dim yellow light again.

Tatters of horse hang from the haunch, nearly bare from grasping fingers tearing it from the bone. Sancho quenches the fire with buckets of sea water, and Barros and I help him return the ballast stones to their home beneath us.

Above deck again, hoping to glimpse blue sky one last time, I cringe at the flash of lightning and the resulting crash and roll of thunder bursting from the nearing wall. The whispering breeze transforms to intermittent gusts, demon-shouts of joy at our approaching demise.

At the same time, heads turn toward the wheel, where the captain lowers his hand. The cords of his throat work with an intense swallow. He removes his hat, revealing a receding hairline. Unlike most of us, who have let our chins grow bristly with beard, his face is clean-shaven, and I admire him for his fastidious appearance within the face of what is about to occur. I happen to be lucky on that score, as the men in my family do not grow heavy beards, although I do have a faint black stubble upon my chin and beneath my nose.

"Men, I have done you a terrible wrong, and it is my fervent hope to receive your forgiveness for it. Your work is most appreciated … most appreciated indeed."

The captain raises a finger to his eye. Although I cannot see the gleam of tears, I am certain he shall wipe them away, which he then does.

"Men, I mistrusted you with information. Our rudder is severely damaged, the bow as well. As you have seen, the storm is strengthening, and when it overtakes us, we have no chance whatsoever. Unless God grants us a miracle, we shall not last the night."

I expect incredulous expressions to fill the deck, but not a one does.

"No matter, Captain," one man says. "We shall kick this old windbag back to where it came from, right in the arse." He hocks and spits over the rail. "Ta hell with it, I say."

A general cry springs up, positive shouts and praises for the captain and the ship. He gestures toward me and I point to my chest, not believing he would call me to come to him for anything. Gesturing again, he confirms my guess by tipping his head to one side and mouthing, *yes, you.*

With shouts and yells still ringing within my ears, I climb the steps to join the captain, who leans close. "I have always wanted to see a young man play a flute and his horse dance. What say you?"

"Begging your pardon, sir, but is now the time?"

"Now is the time like no other. The men are in fine spirits, and I wish to keep them that way. Fetch your flute and go to your horse. I and what men care to listen shall be along shortly."

Apprehension tightens my chest as I clamber down the ladder. Following the light from the candleholders illuminating the innards of the ship, I watch for the huge rats inhabiting the darkness. Seeing none, I reach Cantante and look into the depths of his cinnamon-colored eyes.

"Well, my brother, do you think we can give the crew a smile before the storm hits?"

He lowers his head and extends his nose. Prickly hairs and soft muzzle nuzzle my cheek, and I laugh. "Oh, you like the idea to the point of flirting, is that it?"

Pulling away, he snorts, and a blob of horse snot splatters to my forehead. I wipe it away with my forearm. "Yes, sir, Cantante, sir. Apologies for mistaking your affection for attraction, sir."

Behind me, footsteps shuffle. I turn. As far as I can see, even back to the shaft of light entering the opening in the deck, pairs of eyes reflect flickering candlelight.

One man still moves forward, the captain, who joins me. "Like myself, those who have only heard of your prowess with both horse and flute are curious about it. Please honor us, Carlo."

I take the flute from my pocket, set my lower lip near the hole, and to my fear, cannot think of a single song. "Can anyone name a tune?" I ask. "My mind is as empty as all the wine casks in a port after a party of Spanish seamen have come and gone." This comment draws chuckles and nods, but no one offers a song.

Then, from behind the pairs of broad shoulders and numerous sweat-stained garments, the apprentice who tends the captain and his cabin, a lad of about fifteen I have heard, comes forward meekly. Dark hair falls about his slender shoulders as he nods. "Do you know— I mean, sir, do you know the song called *If I am Never to Return from the Sea?* I can sing it if you do."

At the mention of this melancholy ballad, I expect the captain or the men to admonish the boy. None do, so I raise the flute to my lips again and nod to the boy to sing.

Shock at his piercing tenor nearly stops me from playing, but I manage it regardless, matching the high and haunting melody that rises and falls like cresting waves upon the sea within a gale, tops brilliant with bubbles and foam. Instead of Cantante bobbing his head up and down, he sways it side to side slowly, almost reverently, as if he knows the seriousness of the song and our pending predicament.

The song is short—a verse and chorus only—and I nod at the boy to sing it through once more.

Oh, yes, my love, I left you in Spain.
Oh, yes, my love, I left you in pain.
But I shall try my best, God willing, you see.
To return in the spring, and soon be with ye.
Though if I ne'er return, ne'er return from the sea,
Please seek a new love, who seeks not the sea.
And keep me in your heart, for all eternity,
If I am ne'er to return, to return from the sea.

As the last notes fade, both from the boy and my flute, nothing more than the muted lapping of the waves upon the hull, the rigging tapping the masts and spars, and the breaths of what may well be our entire crew whisper within the dimness of the hold. Except for the shuffling of their feet, silently they disperse, until I am left with a curious stare from Cantante.

As if a mirror is before me, I look into my own black eyes reflecting within his. How do I not weep after all I have been through, with all of my failures and all of my guilt, of which this song has so aptly caused me to remember?

The ship lurches to one side. Thunder cracks and rumbles, vibrating the very wood beneath my feet. I run to the chest and place the flute within the folds of cloth beside my journal, secure the clasp with the rope and climb the ladder to the deck. The wall of clouds, which swirl and roil like an army of gray-shrouded riders circling us upon horseback, is almost here.

The captain is at the wheel, his first officer at his side. Some men lash themselves to whatever wooden protrusion they can find. Some stand and stare, accepting their doom. One lone soul takes his knife from his belt and raises it to his throat.

The bow pierces the wall cloud. The ship dances to the left and then heaves over at an impossible angle and rights herself again. I climb down the ladder while I still can and hurry to Cantante. Shining hair flies around Barros huge head as he cuts the ropes securing the horses within their stalls, intending, I suppose, to give them a chance to swim for their lives. He does the same for Cantante, hands me the knife, and points to another within his belt. "Put that in your belt and tighten it in case land is near."

I do as he says. "What makes you think land is near, Barros?"

"Just a hunch from an old horseman, Carlo. Best be prepared." He pats my shoulder and leaves.

Turning to Cantante, I dig my fingers into his mane and bury my face into his neck. "Our fate is almost here, my brother. I can think of no better friend with whom to meet it."

At this moment, Luisa, one of my fondest memories, which is one of the lonely sparks of happiness still remaining within both my heart and soul, bubbles to the surface of my mind. In it I play an innocent tune with my flute, one common for children. Sitting upon the fence beside me, you clap your hands and laugh at Cantante bobbing his head. You are two seasons old, head filled with loose black curls like your mama, all smiles and bright eyes, the love of my young life as a papa.

It is spring. Beyond the corral, the vineyards are greening. My own papa walks the rows, inspecting both leaf and branch with a love for the grapes and the land that only equals his love for his family. Mama brings us mantecados for an after-supper treat and you gobble several. Crumbs dot the pink bow of your lips, like the first flakes of our last snowfall that year.

Lighting flashes through the slitted decking above me, a fence of light lasting for a single blink of my eyes. Thunder blasts my eardrums. Although Cantante remains still, the muscles of his neck tighten beneath my hands. He snorts, snorts again, and snorts again. How the other horses do not panic, I do not know. Perhaps they see my magnificent brother, with his gleaming black coat, brilliant white star upon his forehead, and spirit as strong as any I have known, as a leader setting an example.

The wind increases to whistles within the rigging, then screams, then screeches. We list and spin. Guttural cries of anguish come from the men above, while soft voices pray somewhere within the dark behind me. It is at this moment that I remember the first officer telling the captain about bodies bloating and rising to the surface and all manner of sea creatures feeding upon them, which makes me tie the loose stall rope around my waist. Give me a grave at the bottom of the sea any day instead of gulls pecking my eyes out.

Waves thud into the bow. Wood gives way, cracking and groaning. Water rushes up to my ankles, to my knees, and stops.

I wait, wait, wait, and wait more. The ship slews sideways, and the weight of Cantante nearly crushes me against the stall, followed by burning daggers of pain driving into my chest. To test if my ribs have punctured my lungs, I start to wheeze as deep a breath as I can manage, when another wave hits and a wall of seawater fills the hold and what can only be a huge beam strikes my head.

Clinging to the tatters of my consciousness, I realize I have lost my grip within the long mane of Cantante. My world is a mass of water, timbers, and the hooves of horses slashing against me, until my very thoughts drift away from my dying mind.

September, 1521

Dear Luisa,

During one of my first classes at the Monasterio de Santa María de la Rábida, Father Cristobal enlightened my group of boys about the world of the dead. "It is not for the faint of heart," he said, placing both hands upon his desk and leaning toward us. "So make very, *very* sure you do not do something so terrible as to end up down there."

I had heard about hell, of course, so I expected scorching fires and the screams of the damned instead of sheer darkness, my head so filled with pain that I thought it would explode, my body tumbling over and over, the wind howling, lightning intermittently bursting within my vision, and thunder echoing within my skull.

Gradually, as I awake from my stupor, I realize I am still tied to the rope and am somehow draped across the timber and adjoining wall, enough to keep my head out of the water. Within the heart of the storm, the platform succumbs to each and every whim of each and every wave. One moment I ride a frothing crest, the next I wallow within a trough. How the wall never turns over, I do not know.

The leather tie securing my ponytail is gone and hair whips into my mouth and eyes. After each gagging breath, in which I am forced to swallow salt water, I spit out as much as I can. This is my hell for hour upon hour, until the winds abate, the waves cease their crashing, and the thunder rolls one long and ominous booming that I soon learn signals an end to my torture.

In a sudden burst of pinpricks, stars fill the gashes between the parting clouds, allowing enough light to see how I am completely and utterly alone, not even a single splinter from the ship to accompany me.

I work my way farther onto my wooden home, taking care to not tip it over. As rickety as it is, God has surely kept it right-side up and myself from drowning for some unknown reason. Stable enough to lie upon my back, I do so. Without warning, warm urine wets my crotch, and I understand one of the detriments of being an old man who cannot control himself, although the chances of me reaching such an age are slim.

Amazingly, I nap intermittently, the lapping of waves against my island of wood a serenade for my nerves. Within the heavens above, each time I awake, the position of the stars has changed. Then a huge moon, red and bloody, lifts from the horizon, and the man within it peers down at myself, as helpless a soul as ever was.

At daybreak, I awake to gulls screeching overhead. Not long after, I vomit sea water and bitter bile. The sun climbs upward. The heat grows unbearable. My groin and underarms sting from salt. The corners of my mouth crack open, the same for my lips. My tongue is a great dried slug, lacking a trail of slime with which to lubricate my teeth and the inside of my cheeks as it passes.

How long I float upon my make-do raft I do not know, for my consciousness ebbs and flows like the tides of the river Rio Tinto at Palos de la Frontera. The sun sets, the sun rises. Heat and humidity saturate my body with sweat. One nightfall, a shower of rain sends soft droplets of relief within the evening twilight, and I open my mouth as wide as possible to drink the precious moisture. The rain ends too quickly. Near to crying, I swipe droplets from my face and suck my fingers greedily.

The moon rises like a wheel of orange cheese, the edge nibbled away by mice. A chevron of large birds passes before it. Their calls, unlike any I have ever heard, honk again and again, one of the loneliest sounds I have ever known.

Within the night, the waves rise higher, and in the distance, they crash as if against land. Am I saved? Am I alive? Shall I dash upon some rocky shore and end my journey crushed and splayed and bleeding?

I roll over and grasp the edge of the wall with swollen fingers. Since my skin is wrinkled like a dried grape from my constant immersion within the sea, I fear it shall peel away to muscle, tendon, and bone.

The crashing grows louder. Beneath me, a wave rises and gurgles and crests, and my wall skims along, wind against my face. When I expect my wooden home to crash against unseen rocks, the dim moonlight illuminates a sandy beach. With my water-softened fingernails, I tear at the knot within the rope around my waist, but before I can untie it, the front of the raft is driven downward by the crashing wave and the raft turns over upon me. Searing pain burns into my right calf muscle, but I manage to locate the sandy bottom, work myself upward to suck in a breath, and drag the raft ashore.

Gagging and vomiting salt water that also burns my nostrils, I drop to my knees. Belly empty again, I roll to my back and suck in air as if my chest were a bellows feeding a forge. Between the pain within my calf, the ache within my chest from trying to catch my breath, and the salt water stinging my chaffed groin and underarms, it all combines to push me to the brink of unconsciousness. The roar of the surf goes quiet. The stars swirl within the heavens. A blackness darker than any night I have ever experienced descends upon me.

I see you, Luisa, playing with the doll you begged for at the market in Palos de la Frontera, one afternoon when we strolled along during late summer. Sweat beaded your forehead and glistened like dew upon ripening clusters of grapes within the vineyard. Coins and the doll exchanged hands. Taking it from me, you looked up with crinkling dark eyes and said, "Oh, thank you, Papa! Thank you so very, very much."

I long to hear your voice again, to kiss your tanned cheeks, to lift you into my arms and hold you close, to breathe in the very scent of your hair on that scorching day.

Where am I? What land has God dashed me upon? Are people here? Did any of the ship wash ashore so I might find a barrel of water or a bite of something to eat?

For a person to cry while asleep is possible, for I have done so, but even within the midst of my unconsciousness, I feel hot tears stream down my cheeks, past my ear lobes, and then their cooling touch upon the back of my neck. Not only shall I never see you again, Luisa, but my only brother, Cantante, lies at the bottom of the sea.

September, 1521

Dear Luisa,

The heat of day purges me from the cool of night. The sun glares down, making me slit my eyes to avoid the brightness. A breeze feathers sand against my face. Waves crash, but not so loudly. Perhaps the tide is low.

After several trembling attempts, I touch my head where it was hit when the wave burst the ship open and spilled her guts upon the sea. The place is swollen and tender. I prod it further to feel for a broken skull, and a burst of white-hot pain explodes within my head. My arm falls out to my side. I reap ragged breaths, raise my head to study my calf, and see what resembles the rusted head of a spike protruding from the bloodless wound—a spike that must have been used to secure the wall of the horse stall to the ship, and which, with rusted patina, spells certain death if I cannot remove it before my calf begins to putrefy.

As I continue to study the spike, my neck muscles spasm and my head thumps to the sand. Too late, Luisa, all too late. I am as helpless as you were, newly born and bloody from the womb of your mama.

How she would have adored you. You would have been her every sunrise, her every spring morning, her every lazy summer afternoon, her warmth beside the fire during long winter nights, when we would have sat and taken turns holding you while tickling your plump cheeks.

To imagine those days are my fondest dream turned nightmare. Why did I leave you? Why did I leave my own mama and papa and sister? My God in Heaven, what I have lost because of my heartache, and because of my own selfishness in trying to forget that heartache.

But I am certain Mama and Papa are caring for you, Luisa. Beatriz, no doubt, unless she has a young man by now, is spoiling you with hugs and kisses and walks within the vineyard, where she squeezes the juice from a grape between your lips, which you then smack and smile with.

I blink and blink again. The blue sky turns to fog. Another blink clears my vision. To my side, some sort of crab, not much bigger than the palm of my hand, comes toward me and stops. Stalked eyes twitch. Mandibles flick side to side. It scurries forward and backward to test my defenses, eight dagger-like legs a ghostlike blur. Losing interest, the crab picks at the sand with two tiny claws extending from near the mandibles and brings whatever tidbits it finds upward to sample. A grain of sand adheres to one eye, and it ignores it.

"Hello, my crusty friend," I croak, wondering if this stone with legs harbors enough fluid within the small body for a sip with which to quench my cracked lips and to refresh my parched throat.

The mandibles work. One eye stalk lowers like a fishing pole, then the other. Dagger legs ease forward an inch … another … another, and a winged shadow swoops over us. Thinking better of having me for breakfast, the crab scuttles into a nearby hole.

The shadow swoops again. Before I can focus upon the owner, wingbeats of air buffet my face. The shadow settles down. Wings shuffle into place. The gull cocks a yellow eye at me or, Heaven forbid, the moistness of my eyeball. "Shoo," I manage, probably sounding like the feathered demon before me when it squawks. It shakes the gray head, advances a step, and another shadow lands beside it.

This gull is much larger, with a hooked yellow beak perfect for ripping fish apart, as well as plucking the eyes from a nearly dead traveler.

I do not care for cursing, but my wretched luck makes me do so despite my aching throat. After tying myself to the ship to avoid losing my eyeballs to these feathered devils, it is about to happen, and I am too weak to stop it.

The smaller gull flaps and screeches at the larger gull. Beaks clatter. Wings beat both breast and body. The gulls back away from one another, coming to agreement that each can have one eyeball a piece, I am afraid.

The larger gull rounds my head for my left eye. The smaller gull advances toward me for my right eye. They stop and turn their heads to one side, lining me up for the strike, their own yellow eyes bright with greed.

The smaller gull strikes and slashes my cheek, missing. Hot blood wells from my skin. The larger gull comes closer and draws the huge white head back for the snake-like lunge. All I can do is close my eyes and wait.

"Hey, you!" a feminine voice yells, "Get away from there!"

Footsteps thud within the sand. The gulls retreat into the air. I can hardly see for the tears within my eyes. Someone bends over me. Dark hair hangs over tanned shoulders. Her face is tanned also. Kind eyes gaze into mine.

I can hardly believe it, Luisa. Your mama has come to take me home to Heaven.

September, 1521

Dear Luisa,

Night again. A small smokeless fire burns beside me, the crackling warmth a comfort I have forgotten ever existed. I am upon my back. Above me, tucked within the blanket of blackness, stars glitter and twinkle the same as at home.

Facing away, your mama lies on the other side of the fire. The spare yellow glow illuminates head-high vegetation of some kind around us. Beyond your mama, my raft leans against the trunk of strange, twisted tree, whose limbs have the general inclination of reaching away from me. A gust of wind whispers within the branches, causing them to quiver scant inches above the sand, like restless claws scratching within a cemetery for a spirit to strangle.

It is then that I notice what must be a sail within a pile at the base of the raft, a tangle of rope, and a three skins half rounded with water, which means the person lying by the fire is not your mama and I am not in Heaven. So, someone else must have survived the shipwreck and found me before the gulls plucked out my eyeballs.

Realizing my mouth, tongue, and lips are moist again, I raise to elbow, call to the person, and he rolls over. The lad who served as the apprentice for the captain blinks several times. "Ah, sir, you are awake. Do you know how hard it is to make a man sip water while he is unconscious?"

I sit up cross-legged and cringe at the wound within my calf. The spike is gone, and the hole is nicely stitched. "Fine work," I say to the lad.

"It is a necessity when tending to a captain who might encounter bandits and such."

I ask the lad his name, for I have never heard it.

"Mateo," he says. He nods toward the skins. "Water?"

After a lukewarm drink, which I am able to enjoy now that I am awake, I seal the skin and set it aside. "How did you stay alive during the storm?"

"The same as you, by tying myself to one of the horse stalls. I shall drag it to this rise in the morning so we can make a shelter. Winter shall come eventually, and we should prepare. Staying upon this high ground should keep us above the tides as well."

"Did you find food?"

"A sealed cask of salted beef. The seal broke and the seawater and the heat spoiled all but the center."

"Do you have any with you?" I ask, imagining solid food to chew and fill my belly.

"I landed south of here, about a mile. Some of the ship is scattered along that area. I was exploring when I found you, and keeping you alive was my priority."

I manage a smile. "Thank goodness for priorities. By chance is anyone else alive."

"The captain lashed himself to the wheel. I buried him two days ago." Mateo touches the dingy white blouse he now wears, which he did not have when he found me. "I took his blouse but only just now had the courage to wear it. I have not seen anyone else."

I gesture to the fire. "I see you have a flint and steel. How much wood is nearby?"

"Plenty of dried limbs have fallen from the trees. They look like humped over old men, do they not?"

"They certainly do." I pause, considering the wildest of hopes. "Did any horses make it to land?"

"Not that I know of. I am sure you miss Cantante. I loved how he enjoyed your music." Mateo tilts his chin to one side, toward the wall behind him. "You have not walked that way. I think this is an island."

I sit up straight. "Why think that?"

"There is ocean to one side and calm water to the other side. I can barely see trees there as well. This island reaches north and south, but it is nothing more than a blur. I put that wall against the tree to keep any tribes of people who may live there from seeing the fire. I doubt they can, the land is so far away."

Thankful for the industriousness of my savior, I lie down. "I suppose I better rest so my leg can mend. We have much work to do, dragging whatever we can find from the ship to make a better shelter than one wall."

"Rest or not, you must walk gingerly. That spike nearly went to the bone." Mateo lies down as well. "I have been having nightmares about the captain. I keep wondering who else might wash up."

No doubt Mateo means who else might wash up bloated and half rotten, eyes pecked out by gulls and hunks of flesh bitten away by sharks.

Shuddering at the thought, I close my eyes. The embers pop and then settle to their earlier occasional crackle. How I wish Cantante would enter our circle of light. With him at my side, I might have the will to live, but without his steadfast courage, my own courage shall likely melt like frost upon leafless grape vines as it turns to water at the first touch of sunlight.

September, 1521

Dear Luisa,

Mateo was correct about my leg. I could hardly move it when I woke, but he was up like a rabbit, adding sticks to the embers. He blows until they flame, adjusts a stick or two, and looks my way. "I went for some of that salted beef while you were asleep. I think it shall be better hung over the fire with a stick."

I ease up, gritting my teeth at the pain within my calf. The wound is somewhat pink, not red or putrefied or leaking pus, thank goodness.

Soon the aroma of sizzling beef makes my mouth water. As Mateo cuts a bitesize morsel from the stick, I slap my hand to my belt.

"I borrowed your knife," he says, offering me the morsel. "Eat slowly, or you shall get sick." He hands me one of the water skins while I chew the salty beef, savoring the glistening fat upon the crusted surface. Chewing a morsel himself, he then swallows water behind it from another skin. "Do you have a wife and daughter at home? You were dreaming about someone called Luisa and Juliana."

I notice Mateo no longer calls me "sir." Perhaps saving my life makes him feel we are friends and equals now, although I thought of us as equals before. Still, Luisa, the name of your mama trembles upon my lips, so I offer a compromise.

"Yes, my wife and daughter."

The words hang between us. More meat is consumed. More water is swallowed. Mateo wipes his greasy fingertips upon his ragged breeches and stands. "I shall see what else I can find upon the beach. You stay and rest. Your stitches might open otherwise."

My new friend leaves. I lie down, but soon tire of doing the same thing I have done since the ship sank. After prodding my stitches and feeling little pain, I stand and stretch my leg, put weight upon it and take a few tentative steps. I should be able to take a slow walk north and explore for myself while Mateo is gone.

The gnarled trees and dense brush encircle our small encampment. On my way to the beach, limbs and tangled vegetation snag my blouse and breeches. Tiny vines attempt to ensnare my bare feet, shoeless since the storm stole my pitiful excuse for footwear. I hear feathered fluttering within the trees, but do not see the winged inhabitants. Within the brush, a glimpse of brown fur, possibly a rabbit-like creature, bounds away. Tiny cloven hoofprints, similar to those of our red deer in Spain, cross a narrow trail. Being the son of a farmer who trades for food instead of hunting it, I know little about snares or traps or spears or bows and arrows. I shall ask Mateo about his capabilities when he returns, for our supply of beef shall not sustain us forever. Allowing myself a chuckle, I grin at the impossible prospect of turning cannibal and feasting upon Mateo, and then whisk the thought from my mind. Never shall I do such a thing to another human, for I shall die myself first.

Leaving the brush, I stop at the top of a dune to survey the wide beach, the pounding waves, the endless blue-green sea. Shells of all shapes and sizes litter the cream-colored sand, from spirals, to round and nearly flat, to bits and pieces wet and glistening within the morning sun. I turn to my right, toward the south, and shade my eyes. In the distance, the dark head of

Mateo is a spec bobbing up and down as he walks away. To the north, the beach extends as far as I can see, and then I have an idea.

Mateo believes we are on an island, so why not climb a vantage point from which to see if he is correct or not?

At our campsite again, I flex my leg while studying the limbs of the largest tree. The pain is little more than a dull ache, so up the tree I go, favoring my wound with each step.

At the top, I steady myself by grasping two narrow branches, and see Mateo is correct.

To our west, at the end of our woods, head-high strands of grass form a marsh wavering with the breeze. Beyond this blanket of green, a huge body of gray water stretches to a thin line of darker green, except taller than our marsh, which must mean it is a forest. I turn upon my quivering branch to see the ocean again. Nothing but the humped backs of wave after wave fills the horizon.

On the ground again, I pick my way through the trees and brush and reach the beach once more, where, beside more brush and trees bordering the sliver of sand, I trek north.

The day warms. Sunlight dapples the sea. Beyond the breaking waves thick with foam, pelicans chevron over crests, into troughs, and rise again, wingtips almost touching the shining surface.

In some places, instead of rising to dunes, the beach gradually slopes upward to brush and trees. Here and there the limbs and foliage give way to mounds of sand lined with clumps of coarse grass and slender stalks growing from them. At the tips of each stalk, some sort of flat grain resembling oats fills the end, waving in the breeze with a rustling whisper.

My calf muscle loosens, the soreness lessens, so I increase my stride. The warming sand is a tonic to my bare feet, as if sitting by the fire at home, wearing socks after a day of tending the vineyard near the end of the season, when winter is about to arrive.

Taking deep breaths, I marvel at the sweetness of salt air and the crisp hint of the coming winter. Mateo is correct about needing shelter, but having no idea how far north we are, we do not know when winter shall arrive. Regardless, we should—

I jerk to a stop, wincing at the stab of pain within my calf, and peer into more dunes beside another section of dense trees and brush. Did I hear a horse snort?

I climb partway up the first dune, favoring my sore leg. My feet sink into the sand, sending another stab of pain through my calf. I stop, listen again, and swear I hear the faint thump of hooves upon the sand from within the trees and brush. The sound goes silent, but the possibility of Cantante surviving the shipwreck sends me sliding down the dune, where I limp along until an opening allows me behind it.

Another snort, this one closer, draws me forward. To the left, I take what might be a game trail. Then, to my right, I glimpse a patch of brown hide. It darts deeper into the vegetation and I jog after it, dodging trees, ripping through vines, heart thudding, sweat beading my brow.

No more snorts. No more thumps of hooves within sand. No more glimpses of brown hide.

Behind me, the soft rush of wave and wind, along with the screeching of gulls, brings me back to reality. The horses are dead. Cantante is dead. The rest of the men are dead. Mateo and I are utterly and completely alone, low on food and water, and await the coming winter with nothing but a partial wall leaning against a tree for shelter within a dense patch of woods on a barren island.

I turn to go back to the beach, and the unmistakable touch of a clammy hand grips my ankle. "Carlo, is it … is it really you?"

September, 1521

Dear Luisa,

To say I expected to find another shipmate upon this island is the understatement of the day, but lying hidden within the brush, hand upon my ankle, Sancho peers up at me with slitted eyes.

"My God," he says, his voice a hoarse whisper. "It *is* you."

The hand falls from my ankle. I drop to my knees within the sand. "Sancho, how—"

"Water, Carlo. Pease, God in Heaven, do you have water?"

"Can you walk if I help you? I have water."

Sancho says to help him up. With his arm around my neck and mine around his waist, we half-walk, half-trudge back to the beach, where we stop and start a dozen times before I get him to the campsite and lie him down beside the barely smoldering fire.

As he drinks from a skin, I warn him to sip instead of gulp to keep him from getting sick. His thirst sated, he gives me the skin and sits up. "God above, I never thought to drink water again." He points to a slice of remaining beef on a stick above the fire. "Is that from one of those small deer within these thickets?"

I cut a piece and give it to him. "It is salted beef from the ship. Mateo found it and brought some here."

Chewing beef, Sancho stops to swallow. "So, the singing boy is alive. Anyone else?"

"Not that we know of. How did you manage to escape the storm?"

"By climbing within a cask nearly empty of salted fish. The smell was terrible. If I never eat another fish again in my life, it shall be fine with me." Sancho chews and swallows more beef. "How did you and Mateo stay alive?"

I tell Sancho how we tied ourselves to the horse stall walls, and he nods. "Very smart thing to do."

I then tell him how Mateo found and buried the captain, including how some of the stores from the ship washed ashore to the south, including how Mateo is there now, searching through it.

Sancho pauses eating to ask for the water skin. After a sip, he tips the skin toward me as if in a toast. "Perhaps Mateo shall find your flute. We could do with a song to celebrate living, could we not?"

Opening my arms wide, I gesture to the trees and brush surrounding us. "Not much of a place to live, nor with food unless we can make a snare for the rabbits or a spear for the deer."

Sancho spits into the sand at his feet. "I have been a cook since I started sailing. I know nothing of such things."

"We have to try, Sancho. What else can we do?"

He smiles a snaggle-toothed grin. "We can always eat each other like the cannibals do."

"Do not even joke about such a thing."

"Hush with yourself. You know I am joking."

Sancho lies down and closes his eyes. I tell him I am going to see about Mateo and leave for the beach.

In the distance, a dark head comes my way, and my mouth falls open. If my eyes do not deceive me, the stout form of Barros walks beside Mateo. As they near, Mateo waves, and my mouth falls open again. Within his hand he holds my flute, which means he found the chest with my journal and the quills and ink, which also means I can continue writing to you, my beloved Luisa.

The gruff chuckle of Barros reaches my ears. "Look here, look here, our flute player lives."

"As does our horseman, Barros. How did you manage— No, wait, I found Sancho to the north and brought him back to our camp."

"Imagine that," Mateo says. "I expected to live out my days upon this island alone. Now I have three friends to keep me company." He gives me the flute. "I found this within a chest floating within the surf, along with some quills and ink. Barros helped me pull it above the tide line because we knew it held your journal."

I take the flute. Although the sight of my instrument thrills me, sadness at never seeing Cantante dance to my music again makes me wonder if I shall ever play it again.

"Why the frown?" Barros says. "Oh, you are sad because you lost your dance partner. Never fear, I saw several horses far to the south."

This news ends my sadness and jolts my curiosity. "Several you say? Was one black like Cantante? He is the only one that is bla—"

"I am afraid not, but never give up hope. I was about to do that very thing when a wave tore the ship apart. I managed to cling to a piece of wreckage and arrive here." He pats the shoulder of Mateo. "And my savior brought me back from the sea of the dead with a fine drink of water."

"As he did for me."

"I only did what any moral man should do for his fellow shipmates," Mateo says.

We walk north along the beach, my flute within my grip as if I am holding your hand, Luisa. How I long to do that again one day, but I fear it shall never happen. All I can do now is to survive and hope a ship finds us.

At our campsite, Sancho is still asleep. I place my fingers to my lips and whisper to my fellows to let him rest.

Barros takes two packets of salted beef from his pockets. Mateo adds sticks to the fire and lets them burn down until the coals shimmer and glow, then skewers the meat on the stick over the heat. Grease soon drips into the coals, sending up the aroma of cooked beef fat.

A moment later, the nose of Sancho twitches. He sits up wide-eyed, to take in the vision of Barros sitting across from him. "How the devil did you get here, Barros? The last I saw of you, you were on your knees praying and crying."

Barros shares a huge grin. "I prayed for you as well, you old horse eater you. You should be happy I did."

Mateo borrows my knife, cuts beef and passes it out. "With four mouths needing food and water, we must find a way to secure both. None is left on the beach to the south."

I take a slice of beef from Mateo. "Not to mention gathering wreckage to build a better shelter than one wall leaning against a tree."

Barros chews and swallows. "If we can catch one of those nags, we can feast on horse."

"How many?" Sancho says.

"I did not count them."

At the mention of eating horse, I refrain from commenting about those I may have seen to the north. The last thing I intend is to give away their whereabouts to anyone who would slaughter them. Time to change the subject.

"We should be able to find shellfish or crabs," I say. "If not within the rough waters of the sea, perhaps within the calm waters behind this island."

"I have seen fish there," Mateo says.

Sancho screws his face into a scowl and explains how he shall not eat fish because of being within the salted fish barrel for so long, which elicits laughter from Barros. "Never say what you shall or shall not do, Sancho. You shall eat horse dung before you wither and die."

"I wish the ship had carried a cargo of pigs," Mateo says. "Roasted pork would please us all."

"And fish and shellfish have little fat," Sancho says. "Nor does this beef or any fish we might catch. We need fat for energy to get us through the coming winter." He points a gnarled finger at Mateo. "You are just about the right size to take the place of a yearling pig on a spit over the fire."

"You better smile when you say that," Barros says. "This boy is the most industrious of us all. I would as soon eat a red-hot coal from the fire as think of eating him."

"Pardon me for my ill humor, Barros, but facts are facts."

"What about the deer and rabbits within the thickets?" I ask. "Does anyone know how to set a snare or make a spear?"

Mateo lowers the water skin from his lips. "If we ration the water and beef, we have enough to last a week. I think we should drag what wreckage we can back here and build a substantial shelter."

"Who are you to tell us what to do?" Sancho says, sneering. "You are nothing now, not even the apprentice of the captain."

"I am only trying to help."

"What we need," I interrupt, "is a compromise." Three pairs of eyes dart my way, and I continue. "The strongest of us can work on the shelter while the others find water. We cannot live long without water."

"Agreed," Barros says. He points to my calf. "What happened there?"

"A spike from the stall pierced his leg nearly to the bone," Mateo says. "Luckily, my skills as an apprentice to the captain allowed me to stitch it closed." He leans close to me. "You should clean the sand from it before it putrefies. I know little about healing such things, but that shall surely kill any of us."

I stand and work my leg. "It is tender but not too much. I shall go to the ocean and wash it right away."

Making my way through the trees and brush, I see our comings and goings are creating somewhat of a path from how we have broken limbs and pushed vines aside. I ease down the dune and limp to the surf, where I gingerly wash my wound. Although I told Mateo it was tender, it is worse than that, and when I return to dry sand and gently squeeze it, a slight drainage seeps from the stitches.

After a quick shake of my head at my predicament, I rise and face the vast sea and her blue-green waves, which stretch to the cloudless horizon.

What a predicament indeed, Luisa. Only time shall tell how myself and my companions fare upon this island.

How I wish I had not left you and my family. How I wish I were in Spain again, to enjoy the simple pleasures of hearth and home. How I wish Ju—

God help me. God help me. How I wish I could do something as simple as thinking the name of your mama without the pain of her demise harpooning a hole into my heart.

I turn toward the camp, vowing to do all I can to return home one day, Luisa.

Do not give up hope, my daughter, and please pray for your papa with all the strength your earnest heart can muster.

October 1, 1521

Dear Luisa,

Over the following week, Mateo and Barros returned to camp with enough materials to complete our shelter, consisting of two horse stall walls, two hull walls, and a section of sail for a roof, raised to a peak with a length of rope in order to shed rain. Although our room is drafty and small, it is our hope that we shall stay warm and dry enough to maintain some semblance of normal.

Within my corner, where I sleep upon a piece of tattered sail like my fellows, I keep a make-do calendar by carving notches into the horse stall plank upon which I tied myself before the wave ripped the ship apart. Sancho looks my way each time as if I were insane. Barros says nothing. Mateo privately tells me it is a good idea to record our time here if it helps pass the days, and to ignore the stares from Sancho.

During our excursions south, we found a small keg of water, enough to sustain us for two weeks. Having combed the beach fully, we assembled the shelter instead of searching for more water. However, we must find another source soon, as well as a source of food.

During this time, much to my relief, no more is said about eating horses, or each other. We sit quietly at night, gnawing beef and sipping water. Our tiny fire crackles and pops, sending the slight haze of bitter woodsmoke upward, where it departs between the sail and the walls, like the ghosts of our shipmates now dead.

When our small portions are consumed, we simply sit, sometimes picking at a scab earned from our labors, sometimes looking upward at the stars through the openings within our walls, sometimes taking furtive glances at each other, no doubt to debate within our minds the unbelief of watching ourselves transform into bearded resemblances of our pasts, with bones more apparent, cheeks more sunken, clothes loosening to the point of cinching our belts further, and skin peeling from endless sunburns, all while we toil our days away from sunrise to sunset.

On this night it softly rains, and two buckets at the outside corners of our sail catch drizzling streams of water.

Mateo lies upon his back with his eyes closed. He is not asleep, for upon his sunken stomach, he laces his fingers over and over, occasionally steepling them, occasionally not. Barros leans on elbow, brown eyes reflecting the fire. Sancho has the nauseating habit of trimming his fingernails and toenails and then crunching and swallowing them, and it is all I can do to not scream at him to stop.

My dearest Luisa, you were born on a night such as this, except in the spring. I waited at the cracked front door while the screams from your mama bored into my ears each time they careened through our home. In the quiet moments, I opened the door wider, risking the rain to breathe in the humid night air that carried the faint and delicate aroma of grape blossoms, sweet and earthy upon the intermittent breeze.

My papa waited with me, saying not to worry and how all would be well. Mama kept a steady supply of boiled water and strips of cloth ready for the nun, who asked for them at what I thought was too often an interval. Standing by the fireplace, between glances at the bedroom door and shaking her head mournfully, Beatriz chewed her nails.

My poor sister grew up a worrier, and often voiced her concerns to me about my state of mind after you were born. Many is the time I chastised her for those words, for you came into the world a perfect example of love for me to cling to.

What I hope is the last crunch of a toenail comes from the clenched teeth of Sancho. He lies down upon his piece of sail and closes his eyes. Barros drops from his elbow to his back and rolls over. The hands and fingers of Mateo end their dance of lacing, unlacing, and forming a steeple upon his stomach. Soft snores soon follow, louder snores from Sancho, and pig-like snorts from Barros.

The fire burns lower. The rain taps the sail over our heads with dull monotony, like the fingertips of Father Cristobal rolling upon his desk while we students worked at our letters.

Forgive me, Luisa, but my mind wanders to things better left unwritten for your.

The moonlight glowing upon the olive-toned shoulders of your mama ... their smoothness beneath my lips as tempting as a naked swim within the sea ... the slight salt of that sensitive place within the hollow of her neck beneath her ear and her girlish giggle when I flick my tongue there ... the fullness of her breasts within my hands after she rolls me over and sits atop me ... the black curtain of her loose curls enclosing our faces as she leans close to kiss me ... her gasps of delight mixing with the chirp of crickets within the meadow near our home, not far from the blanket upon which we cling to each other.

Although these sweetest of memories stir me, tears burn within the vacant hollows of my skull.

I palm wetness from my cheeks, roll over to face the fire, close my eyes.

So many dreams of days long past drift within my memories, some I shall never forget, like red carnation petals adrift within a stream, some I wish to never recall, like dried leaves clattering along the cobbles leading to our home within the dead of winter, their crisp edges as razors against the beating muscle of my heart.

I sit up, alert and listening. Did something move near the entrance to our shelter, where a width of sail hangs with corners tied to keep drafts out?

I linger, then lie back down. Just spirits come for my haunting, nothing more, nothing less.

Across the fire, nearest the width of sail, Barros sits up blinking owllike. He faces the sail, waits, and faces me. "Carlo, did you hear something? It sounded like some animal snuffling outside."

"I am not sure what I heard. Perhaps it was just a gust a wind."

"You two be quiet so a man can get his sleep," Sancho growls.

Mateo sits up. "Whatever it is, it does not sound very large."

At the edge of the sail, where it meets the sand, a twitching nose appears and I point. "It is one of those rabbits I have seen."

Barros licks his lips. "Mmm, roasted rodent on a spit," he says, barely above a whisper.

Sancho pokes around the fire. "We have no stick big enough to kill it. Can you grab it, Barros?"

"Let me untie the sail before I try. If I miss and it runs, we can run after it."

"In the dark and in the rain?" Mateo asks.

"Stop being an old woman," Sancho hisses.

The nose still twitches. A tiny paw, brown and furred, appears, almost as if the rabbit is offering itself to us as a sacrifice.

Barros finishes one knot. His and the eyes of Sancho gleam with the thrill of the hunt. Even though this small creature is hardly worth the effort of feeding four full-grown men, I imagine a circle of cannibals eyeing their intended victim. Tragedy has not only left us lacking in decorum, it has turned us into savages, and I fear how far we shall descend into that savagery before we all have perished from our coming starvation.

Barros finishes the second knot. The twitching nose and brown paw recedes to a sliver beneath the sail. Barros slowly stands. Sancho tiptoes to his side. Mateo waves me forward, where we wait behind our fellow savages.

In a rush of grasping hands, Barros and Sancho burst through the sail into the rain. Curses and breaking brush follow as they crash into the thicket.

Mateo and I grin at each other, thankful we have much more sense than to let our empty stomachs transform us into such a menagerie of madness.

The crashing stops. Rain patters upon the sail. The surf pounds the beach behind us.

Mateo and I look at each other. Barros appears at the edge of the brush, widened eyes reflecting the dim light of our fire. "You better see this."

Their headlong rush into the brush has opened a gap. Picking our way along within the semi-blackness, we follow him until he reaches the marsh and the huge expanse of calm water.

Barros stops beside Sancho, who is squatting behind marsh grass while holding several of the thick, green blades aside. He motions us down and points. "You two have younger eyes than Barrows and me. What do you see across the water, within the darkness of the trees that we can see in the daylight?"

I stand slightly and focus over the marsh to where Sancho points. Beside me, Mateo does the same. Almost simultaneously, we both exhale a single word in an explosion of pent-up breath.

"Campfires."

October 2, 1521

Dear Luisa,

I slept poorly last night, which is understandable given our new neighbors.

We left the view of the campfires and returned to shelter, where Mateo added wood until our fire blazed to average proportions. Then we went back to where we saw the dim yellow glow of the campfires across the water and turned to see how visible our own fire might be through the trees and brush. Sighs of relief escaped us, for not the smallest sliver of light revealed what we now knew to be our hiding place from a native tribe living across the water.

Sitting cross-legged around our fire, none of us mentioned the obvious, which is how, from now on, we must be forever vigilant on our island, lest we are seen and draw those natives here to massacre us for whatever reason, such as simply thinking we are an enemy or to eat us.

Eventually we lay down, but each time I glanced at my fellows, worry creased the corners of their eyes.

The rain drizzled to an end. I dozed off and on. Now, through a slit within the highest plank beside me, the yellow light of dawn illuminates a sliver of cloudless sky. Another day to survive. Another day to dream of rescue. Another day to believe in the possibility of coming home to you, Luisa.

The morning continues to brighten, while the never-ending wind, which varies between a rare calm and a blustery gale, rustles the tree limbs, with an occasional gust whistling through the brush. Salt air rides in from the east, where the sea crashes her waves upon the beach. Gulls *scree-scree* overhead, winging their way to break their fast, and I am certain pelicans are doing the same, gliding inches above the swells, wingtips almost touching the blue-green water reflecting those huge, feathered bodies.

Were this any other place than where a shipwreck deposited me, I might grow accustomed to the endless stretches of sand, the trees that resemble hunched over old men and women gossiping within the market at Palos de la Frontera, and the fist-sized birds that scurry back and forth within the surf on backward-kneed legs, in search of whatever tiny creatures their quill-like beaks can discover.

Ah, to eat a meal three times a day and not a mouthful of salted beef, come dawn and dusk.

Hunger has left a grumbling void within my stomach, and I imagine my fellows and myself wading into the surf to capture a fish or two from the schools we have seen beneath flocks of gulls. However, the fish were beyond the waves, too far to risk drowning. Still, we must find a way to feed ourselves, or we are not long for this world. Thankfully, rain keeps the buckets at the corners of the sail half-full, so we are not likely to shrivel and die from thirst any time soon.

I cannot help but wonder about the native tribe to the west, across that great expanse of gray water. Since this is my first voyage, I have never seen a native, although the crew has mentioned them, saying they wear skins and, depending on their homeland, sometimes pierce their ears and noses with carved sticks or bones. The description worries me, for if they do such things for their appearance, what harm might they do to us for their pleasure? The crew also mentioned how tribes living within the same lands pursue war with each other, like with the cannibals, including enslaving their own fellows. Given these proclamations, I can only hope the tribe to our west never discovers us.

And too, I wonder about our horses to the south and the north, including how they managed to survive when my brother, Cantante, with his rippling hind quarters, sleek form, and arched neck like a dolphin swimming within the bow wave of a ship, did not. Be that as it may, I can only wish him Godspeed to whatever Heaven into which horses arrive, and I fervently pray I shall join him and your mama, Luisa, when I take my final breath, whenever and wherever that shall be.

I rise and take sticks from our dwindling pile and add them to the glowing embers of the fire, for it takes more heat than this to make our beef palatable. Gradually catching flame, the sticks pop and crackle. Beside me, where Mateo has been sleeping since Barros and Sancho arrived, as if I am an omen against bad fortune, he rises to sit cross-legged. He cranes his neck as if he is trying to see if our campmates are asleep, then leans close to me. "Have you noticed those two whispering when you and I are working on something?"

"No. How often have you seen it?"

"Only once, but I did not like it."

"When did this happen?"

"Last night, after Sancho leaned into the barrel for beef and brought some out."

I turn to look Mateo in the eye. "What were we doing then?"

"Lashing the ropes holding the sail down again."

I knew what he meant, for the wind often loosens those ropes. "Did you hear what they were saying? If not, how could it worry—"

Mateo grabs my arm. "It is how they put their heads together, like spies. Then they scowled at the beef and made faces like they were tired of it."

I smile to ease the worries of my friend. "You have been listening to too many cannibal stories. Perhaps they only wish for horsemeat."

Mateo pulls away as if the idea appalls him. "You joke in such a way, when you played the flute for Cantante as if he were your very best friend?"

"I did not mean to joke. My brother is long gone from me."

Mateo lowers his head. "I am sorry. When I saw those horses to the south, I had hoped he was still alive."

From across the fire, Barros snorts and rises, rubbing his eyes. "What are you two going on about over there?"

"That is what I would like to know as well," Sancho says, rolling over to pin Mateo and I with bloodshot eyes. "It is bad enough we have savages across the water. Now we have scoundrels right here among us, plotting and scheming."

Barros barks gruff laughter. "They are just boys worrying about their next meal like we are, Sancho. Do not say such things." He rises from his bed of sail, yawns and stretches. "I shall fetch our ration of beef." He rubs what is left of his belly, cocks one knee to the side, and releases a sputtering odor from his backside.

Sancho waves his hand in front of his face. "You stinking buzzard. Go somewhere else and do that."

Barros chuckles. "How we eat enough to relieve ourselves regularly, I shall never know. And what those leaves do to my pretty backside is a travesty of unimaginable proportions."

"Then make sure you carry your pretty backside far enough within the brush so I do not have to smell what you leave there."

Despite the worries of Mateo, he grins at our campmates. "So you smile now," Sancho says. "You two are scheming to eat Barros and I when the beef is gone. Admit it and be done with it."

Mateo rises, "I shall go for more wood," and leaves.

I rise too, but before I get to the door made of sail, Sancho jumps up to block my way. "Barros and I plan to catch a horse for food. We know you had some sick affection for that nag of yours, so shall there be a problem with us eating horse?"

I take a step back. "I said nothing on the ship. Why should I say something now?"

His black eyes focus down and then up. "Where did you get that knife within your belt?"

"Barros gave it to me before the ship went down."

"I think you should give it to me. I might need it in the future."

His hand darts toward my belt and I slap it away. "You shall not have it without a fight, which you shall lose. I am younger and more muscled than your skinny self." I whip the knife from my belt and point it at him. "Perhaps I shall feast on your tough old hide before I am dead. What say you about that?"

Stepping back, Sancho reveals yellowed teeth with a grin. "Ah, so you have a backbone after all. You shall need it eventually, I wager."

The door of sailcloth rises and falls with his retreat. I stagger back against my wall, an icy chill running up my spine. I do not relish violence, Luisa, but I shall do what I must to survive and return to you.

October 2, 1521

Dear Luisa,

We spent the morning searching amongst the trees and brush for some type of edible greens or roots, but everything we sampled turned our lips inside out with bitterness. We found a few acorn hulls within the sand beneath the trees. That was all, for birds must have feasted upon them to the point of leaving none behind. Neither Barros nor Sancho mentioned catching a horse, so I let that possibility go. Mateo kept quiet while we searched. Within those few moments when we found ourselves alone, I was tempted to convey my altercation with Sancho but I did not, fearing it would only worry him even more.

Looking back at why I drew my knife, I realize part of me took a certain perverse joy with the possibility of driving it up to the hilt within the chest of Sancho, to see his smirk transform into dread as his blood wept from his heart to my hand. I suppose it is another sign that men who think they would never turn to violence often do exactly that.

Now, as the sun glares from the midday sky, we remove our sail bedding from around our shoulders. Tied at our necks, it performs reasonably well as cloaks, either to shed rain or to keep us warm. However, what we shall wear to keep from freezing to death within the dead of winter, I do not know.

I sip rainwater from one of the buckets and collapse inside the shelter out of the sun, which, even for October, sparkles our foreheads with sweat. Mateo does the same moments later, rests for a time, and rises on elbow. "They are talking again, out by the edge of the trees."

"Let them talk. They cannot harm us with words."

"Have you thought about how, if some of us were to die, those left would have more food and water and cover when we sleep? I think that is what they conspire about."

I sit up. "Mateo, it is never good for a person to let their imagination get the better of them."

Outside, footsteps shuffle sand. The sail door is flung open by Barros. He comes in, Sancho follows, and they both sit across from the barely smoldering fire. Barros extends his hand toward me. "Sancho needs that knife I loaned you."

Sitting up straighter, I fill my chest to appear larger, like a cat about to battle another cat. "He shall not have it. You gave it to me, friend to friend."

"Sancho is my friend as well."

I get up and go outside, tie the sail up and toe a line within the sand. "If he wants it, he can cross that line and fight for it."

Sancho spits into the fire, which sizzles and smokes. "Big words from a boy with a knife."

Heat consumes my face. I place my hand to the hilt of my knife. "Cannibal or not, old man, were I starving I would cut out your heart and feast upon it beating while you watch."

Barros chuckles once, twice, and throws his head back to roar laughter. Wiping tears, he shakes his head. "My, what a rooster our predicament has created within you. I do not know what idea has penetrated your feathered head, my young friend, but Sancho only wants your knife while we go south to hunt a horse." He chuckles again. "If you are capable of eating the heart of our poor old cook as it beats, you should have no problem eating horse, yes?"

"I cannot."

"But you would kill and eat Sancho …"

"I was … I was angry. People say things when they are angry."

"Then you shall loan him your knife, yes?"

"Only if he gives it back when he returns."

Barros goes inside the shelter. Muffled words pass between him and Sancho. Barros comes outside and pats my shoulder. "There now, there now, we have an agreement."

Sancho comes outside also. "I do not like hard feelings any better than you, Carlo, but I admire your backbone." He raises his hand, palm up. "May I please borrow your knife so I may have something to quickly dispatch one of your friends with?"

I slap it into his palm. "See that you *do* dispatch one quickly, if you get the chance."

He salutes. "Yes, sir, Captain, sir. As you wish."

"Very good," Barros says, hiking his breeches. "Now, Sancho, let us see if we shall have grilled horsemeat for our supper."

The two leave for the path leading to the beach. Inside the shelter, I sit by Mateo again. "If you want to go, I understand. For some people, eating horse is better than starving."

His jaw works side to side, as if he is chewing his cud like a cow. "I do not care to eat horse either. My fondest memories are of a pony I had as a child."

Finally, I think, talk of home and something other than starving. "I live—well, lived—in Palos de la Frontera, not far from the Rio Tinto river. Do you know it?"

"I traveled through there to get to the port when I signed on as apprentice with the captain." Mateo lies back on his elbows and stares upward. "My mama and papa lived outside of Mondonnedo, on a small farm. We tended an olive orchard in trade for living there. The master of the farm was a kind man who had lost his wife some years past. They never had children, and he took to me as if I were his son."

I assume this is the man who gave Mateo the pony. "My papa owns a vineyard. I loved working there."

Mateo glances my way. "As much as you loved your Cantante?"

I start to laugh but think better of it, for only you, Luisa, and your mama, are deeper within my heart than Cantate, which, of course, includes my own mama and papa and sister. "No," I say to Mateo. "I loved Cantante better."

"I loved my mama and papa that much," Mateo says, a wistful look within his eyes. "But papa died when his leg became putrefied from falling on a scythe. He was taking it to cut grass from around the olive trees one spring."

"That must be why you were so careful about my wound."

"I was terribly lonely until I found you. I may have done myself harm had I been forced to live alone for who knows how long." Mateo pauses. "Our benefactor, who owned the farm, died of a fever not long after papa died. A cruel man bought it and forced mama to marry him. He beat me without reason, and mama would not speak against him for fear of us being put out. Then, after one very bad beating, she told me her uncle, the captain, may have pity on me and take me on as apprentice. I did not want to leave her, but it was either that or be killed. That scoundrel, her husband, never beat Mama, so I did as she begged and journeyed to the port at Palos de la Frontera, on the Rio Tinto, and I was fortunate enough to find her uncle."

Although the story from my savior saddens me, it makes me wonder about the tales of Barros and Sancho, and whether or not they are filled with similar woe. More than likely, I wager, they are the scoundrels within their stories.

Mateo and I grow quiet. A soft breeze with a hint of cold chills me through the spaces within the wall at my back. Over our heads, the sail ripples, and a sudden gust makes it pop loudly. The breeze returns, and the scene dredges a memory from my mind of a time when my fortune was similar to the fortune related by Mateo, with how he found a savior in the captain. I slide around to be comfortable, and so I can face my friend while I tell my story.

"Believe it or not," I say, "I once would not have minded eating horse meat."

"Not you, Carlo," Mateo says, his eyes widening.

"Yes, indeed, but that was before I grew to love Cantante like a brother." Anticipating my tale, Mateo sets his elbows upon his thighs, laces his fingers together, and rests his chin upon his clasped hands.

"I was a lad of thirteen," I continue, "headstrong and proud. My papa wanted to expand his vineyard, but he needed more vines to do so. Being the haughty boy I was, I suggested I take Cantante to the large vineyard of a friend, who we knew to be selling cuttings, and purchase what we needed."

"Ah," Mateo says, grinning. "I sense a life-changing story for the haughty boy."

"You are correct," I say, returning the grin. "Papa gave me a skin of money and bid me on my way. The road was well traveled by good people, so I had no worries of bandits. However, a late spring snowstorm struck, and I still had many miles to go."

Mateo sits up. "And a beautiful woman came along and rescued you and Cantante. Then she took you to her home and ravished you, and you were no longer a virgin. That would change *my* life for certain."

"While that may be a more interesting story, it did not happen that way. The snow blanketed the sky. Wind gusted the hardest I had ever seen, so I was forced to lead Cantante off the road and into an evergreen thicket. It was warm the morning I left my home, so I wore nothing but a thin cloak. However, the storm set my teeth to chattering to the point of forcing me to huddle beneath the pitiful cover of the evergreens."

Mateo shoves my knee. "*Then* the beautiful woman arrived and took you away."

After a soft chuckle, I say, "While I am fond of beautiful women, my story does not end in such a way. As I said, I was huddled beneath the evergreens. And then, like the faithful friend I now know Cantante to be, he actually crouched low and worked his way to my side and lay down."

Mateo tilts his head sideways. "He was cold. You should not have left him out in the snow."

"I thought the same at first, but he bit my cloak and pulled me to his side. All I could think was how he wanted to save my life by keeping me warm and snug next to him. I do not think there is anything he would not do for me."

Mateo slowly nods. "I agree, for I am sure he would trade his life for yours if need be."

A jolt of sadness halts any possible reply. Although I do not doubt the sentiment of my friend, my brother shall never have the chance to meet such a challenge.

"What happened next?" Mateo asks.

I grin broadly. "I woke up the next morning to a scantily dressed woman who took my breath away with her beauty. Are you satisfied now?"

"Only if she ravished you," Mateo says. "I suppose I shall never be ravished now." He sighs, long and forlorn. "Why did you leave such a fine home and family, Carlo? If I had such as those, I would never, ever leave as long as I lived."

Immediately regretting my story, for I had not foreseen how it would lead to Mateo asking about my past, I decide to change the subject. "Do you see how your worries about Barros and Sancho were unfounded?"

"What do you mean?"

"When you saw them talking, they were talking about going to catch a horse, not eating you."

"You did not act so forgiving when you challenged Sancho. Would you have really cut out his heart and ate it?"

"Not at all. Anger makes a man say things he would never consider otherwise."

"Well, you certainly acted like you would." Mateo takes a stick from our pile and pokes the embers until they flame.

The wind gusts again, sending another chill to my back. The sail pops once, twice, and a third time, before the gust falters into a steady breeze rustling the brush outside.

Mateo rises. "We need more sticks for the fire. Thankfully, those trees shed them often from this constant wind." As he goes to the door, voices come from the direction of the path leading to the beach. I rise as well and join Mateo, dreading Barros and Sancho returning with a horse haunch each upon their shoulders.

The voices come and go with the wind, but grow clearer when I catch glimpses of their sail-cloth cloaks within the trees and brush. "… your fault, Barros. Even half-starved you are too slow to catch a turtle, much less a horse."

"It is not my fault you are so weak, with your narrow arse, that you only scratched that horse with your knife instead of stabbing it."

They burst from the brush to enter our clearing. Sancho drops the knife at my feet. "There you go, worthless as it was."

I stoop for the knife and stand to slip it into my belt. "How many horses did you see, Barros?"

"Only two this time. Sancho ruined their fun when he rushed them, and they bolted."

"What do you mean by 'fun?'" Mateo says.

"What do you think Barros means?" Sancho says. "Are you such a little boy, you do not know what fun is amongst men and horses and all manner of living things?"

"I mean that lucky devil of a stallion was mounting one of his mares," Barros says. "Which means we shall have newborn foals to hunt in about eleven months or so. Perhaps even I can catch one while it still wobbles around like a drunkard, before it gets accustomed to walking and running."

Mateo starts away, and Sancho says, "Where are you off to?"

"To gather sticks for the fire."

Sancho goes to my chest, located on the outer wall opposite where I make my bed of sail cloth, and kicks it. "I see you scratching within that journal of yours. It is a waste of time and we should burn this chest. To hell with those quills and bottles of ink. It is not as if we can eat them or they shall warm us. Throw them out, I say, and use that chest for firewood."

Barros chuckles gruffly. "Keep it up, Sancho. I wager our young Carlo shall have your heart on a spit if you do."

Mateo faces Sancho, heat flaring within his cheeks. "And I shall hold this narrow-arsed excuse of a cook down and throttle his scream while Carlo does it."

Sancho eyes us in turn, finishing with me. "What thanks I get for returning your precious knife. I even sharpened it on a sea shell. Make sure you keep it so, for I do not care to feel any pain when you decide to cut my heart out."

This proclamation ends our stalemate. We retire inside the shelter, although Mateo does leave for sticks and soon returns with an armful.

Unlike our summers together, Luisa, when my papa and I watched the grapes form green clusters within the vineyard, and little work could be done except to wait, the afternoon does not lazily pass. Instead, the sun seems to hurry from the sky, blown downward by the wind now gusting and flapping the sail over our heads.

When our puny rations of salted beef are eaten, which magnifies our thirst and leaves us craving more water than sips from the skins or buckets, we sit and stare at the fire, seemingly entranced by the glow and shimmer of the embers.

Sancho pries a splinter from a stick and picks his teeth, sucking loudly after each unsuccessful attempt. Barros sits cross-legged, dark eyes reflecting the embers. Mateo completes the trilogy of us savages by sighing heavily every so often. I cannot tell why our sullen moods grip us, but I have a hint. Since that is the case, it is better to get it out in the open and be done with it. "When shall we discuss the natives? It is about time, yes?"

"Discuss what?" Barros says. "As long as they do not see our fire, we should be safe enough."

Sancho flicks the splinter into the embers, where his spittle hisses and dies. "Yes, we *should* be safe. What if we are not?"

"Why think that?" Mateo says.

"I think that because natives make slender watercraft by hollowing out tree trunks with axes made of stone. I have no doubt we are only several paddle strokes away from having our heads taken in the middle of one dark night."

"Why think that when we have nothing they want?" I say.

Mateo glances at me. "I would like to know what they eat and where they get water. We have failed to find a source for either."

"You two little children make me ill," Sancho says. "During my travels, I have learned how natives grow crops and hunt."

Mateo sits up straighter and cranes his neck forward. "How do they hunt? If they can, we can."

"They make bows and arrows."

"Huh," Barros says. "Those crooked limbs on those crooked trees are good for nothing but making a back scratcher."

"But what crops do they grow?" Mateo insists.

Sancho spits into the embers, sending up a tiny plume of steam and a hiss. "I do not know. That is only what I have heard."

The conversation unravels into the night. Barros lies down and faces the fire, to wistfully gaze into the embers once again. "This was to be my last voyage to the islands where our brothers seek gold and treasure from the natives there."

"You say *seek?"* Mateo says, his tone scornful. "Try slaughter instead."

"That is the way of the world, my young apprentice. Where ever I have traveled, regardless of the people or the place, it is a rare thing to not have someone willing to take something by force, theft, or as you say, slaughter. If the circumstances were exchanged, do you not think they would sail to our homeland and do the same to us?"

"That does not make it honorable."

Knowing we need a change of subject before anger breeds a fight, I join the discussion. "Barros, what were your plans after your last voyage?"

"I was going home to my wife and children and grandchildren in Leon. I left her there with a thriving business, making dresses and suits for the high and mighty. It is my wish to return there and take up the stitch again."

"Bless my skinny bones," Sancho says. "Here I am, having known you for at least ten years, and I never knew you liked playing with dresses."

"Ah, I did not tell you all my secrets, Sancho. As far as playing with dresses, the intriguing part is fitting them to those fancy women while they wear nothing but their undergarments."

"Bah, your wife would not let you do such a thing."

"What my wife does not know when she goes home to cook our supper does not harm her one bit. How I would love to be home again, passing my skills on to my grandchildren." Barros pauses, then eyes Sancho. "You chastise me for not sharing my secrets. What say you about yours? All these years I have known you, you have hardly said a word about home, wherever it may be." Sancho takes another stick from the pile, pries a splinter from it, and commences to pick his teeth again. "Huh," Barros grunts. "You must have the cleanest teeth in all the world by now. Come, tell us about your life before we met."

The toothpick leaves a yellowed tooth. "I am not in the mood."

"Why not, old friend? We four shipmates are merely passing the time while we slowly starve to death."

"Can we not talk about food or home?" Mateo lowers his head, and I wonder, after his interest in hunting a moment ago, why he has changed so suddenly.

"Come, come," Barros says, shoving the knobby knee of Sancho. "You have put our young apprentice in a foul mood with your own foul mood."

Sancho slaps the hand away. "What would you have me say—some tale of woe so you little boys shall weep into your hands? That I lived within a hovel outside of Corunna? That all four of my children died in childbirth? That I, like some fool, blamed my wife and beat her to the point of crippling her, and I left to purge myself of sin upon the sea? Is that a sad enough tale for you, Barros? Shall you weep all the night long over it?"

Barros aims a wary eye toward Sancho. "Would not it have been better to stay and care for her?"

"Perhaps I beat her to death instead of crippling her. Perhaps I buried her in the middle of the night and told my neighbors how she left me for another man, and how her screams were us arguing about it.

A broad grin splits the face of Barros. "Goodness gracious me. I wager you could write as sad and mournful a tale as our friend Carlo scratches within his journal."

Sancho points the splinter at Barros. "How do you know his tale is sad?"

"If you have not noticed, not only are we shipwrecked upon this wretched island, we have no food, only the water we get when it rains, and winter is on the way. How could whatever he scratches be anything other than sad?"

"Cannot we pass the time some other way than talking about our lack of food and water?" Mateo says, his disdain for the subject even more apparent.

"What is your life story, then?" Sancho says. "Why leave home little more than a child and apprentice with the captain? Surely there are other pursuits for a young man than living upon the sea."

Mateo raises his head, melancholy within his downturned eyes. "I would just as soon pursuit death than to be upon this island with the likes of you for the rest of my life."

"See?" Barros says to Sancho. "Your foul mood has now made our young apprentice consider taking his own life. What say you for yourself?"

Sancho points the splinter at me, and I dread the question perched upon his cracked lips. "Tell us, Carlo, how such as you, with a fine stallion that must have cost more money than most of us see in half a year, came to be a passenger upon a ship when passengers are not allowed."

"Adventure. Gold. Different lands to see and different people to meet," I say, hoping my lie is taken for truth.

Baring his blackened teeth in a wicked grin, Sancho shakes his head. "Well, I suppose you have gotten enough adventure to last you all of your young, *short* life."

This expected comment leaves silence within our midst.

Like earlier, another cold gust of wind blows through the wall at my back, chilling me like earlier as well. This time the wind does not abate, but gusts hard enough to make the sail over our heads shudder and pop. With our luck, we shall have a storm during the night.

I look upward, where the rope that supports our roof is tied to two tree limbs, which shudder like grasping fingers reaching for a victim. Sail cloth rustles across from me as Barros bolts upright.

"What is wrong with you?" Sancho says. "Did a pain hit your gut to warn you to go outside? If so, make certain to go downwin—"

"Be quiet with your ragged self," Barros says. "An idea just popped into my skull."

Mateo, who now lies wrapped within his sail while facing the wall, barely turns his head toward Barros. "Whatever it is," he mumbles, "I wish it would tell you to shut your mouth so I can sleep."

Barros ignores the comment. "You fellows have seen those big blue crabs within the calm waters to our east, yes?"

"Of course," I say, aggravated because we all have tried catching them, only to see them scurry away when we our feet near them.

"What if we unravel a rope to make lengths of string and tie some of the spoiled beef to it? Then we could throw it into the shallows and ease those crabs toward us until we can catch them."

"That is a better idea than running after those crabs on the beach," Sancho says, "only to have them dive into their holes.

"I told you we should try digging them up," Mateo grumbles.

"Mateo," I say, "as you know, we tried that very thing until we grew too tired to dig another handful of sand. It is as if those shelled and clawed demons tunneled all the way to hell itself." I pause as one of the nails within my wall catches my eye, then face Barros. "What if we made string and bent some of our smaller nails into fishhooks and—"

"And baited them with beef?" Barros interrupts. "An excellent idea to catch the fish within those same waters."

Observing us, the slitted eyes of Sancho widen. "Two acceptable ideas to keep us from starving to death. I have another one, inspired by my hate of salt fish after my barrel ride amongst them. Who here has not eaten smoked fish at one of our local markets?"

Barros scowls. "What idiots we are, for I am certain we all have at one time or another. What do you propose, Sancho?"

Sancho spreads his hands as wide as possible. "I propose we make a small frame of this size tall and high. I say that size for a small fire with plenty of smoke. If those fish we saw within the surf come close enough for us to catch, we can slice them thin and smoke them. They shall taste much better and preserve much better also."

I admire this plan, but I have a worry. "What about the natives seeing the smoke?"

"Must I do all the thinking for us," Sancho says bitterly. "We smoke them only at night."

"What about—"

Sancho holds up a hand to silence me. "I know, I know, what if the savages smell the smoke and come searching for the source. Do you not realize they shall think the smell is from their own fires? They burn most of the night, so their smoke shall mask our smoke."

"Another excellent idea," Barros says. "Now, let us get some rest for our walk to the south for that spoiled beef, and for gathering sticks to make a smoking mechanism for any hapless fish who may fling themselves into our hands."

Wrapping myself within my piece of sail to ward off the cold air against my back, Luisa, I can only hope our plans succeed tomorrow, for unless I continue to survive, however that may be, I shall never see your face again, and that, my daughter, is an impossibility for which I shall not stand.

October 3, 1521

Dear Luisa,

I awake within the darkness to the wind hissing sand against the wall beside me. Over our heads, the sail pops and shudders almost constantly. Toward the beach, waves crash and roar over and over again, and rain pelts the sail as if a giant hand tosses stones onto it.

The embers glow within the circle of rocks that Mateo set there recently, with suggestions of dark crimson peeking through gray ash. Shivering, I wrap my piece of sail tighter around myself and edge closer to what had been a cheery little fire before we all went to sleep.

Coming out of the northeast, the wind gains speed, alternately moaning, whistling, and screeching through the trees, like a banshee seeking to exhale our shelter into the large body of water between us and the natives.

Barros rolls over, evidenced by his black eyes reflecting hints of red from the dying fire. "What a fury of a storm," he mumbles. "I pray it shall not last long."

Except for the continued sound of the sail popping and the rain clattering upon it, the sand hissing against the wall by my side and the wind wailing a funeral dirge, the surf pounding the beach and the snoring of our companions, Silence lowers her exhausted head within our shelter.

She sleeps for several moments, until I hear Mateo weeping softly. I do not know if I should question him, for our stories of home have revealed how we each have a cross to bear, and it seems we are not so close as to bear them together yet, if ever.

"Carlo," he whispers. Our heads are somewhat close, so I whisper back, saying yes, and he adds, "When I said that about being a virgin, I did not mean to sound as if that is all I think women are for. I sincerely hoped to marry for love one day, and to possibly get my mama away from that cruel man she married."

"I understand, Mateo. You do not seem the type to use a woman badly."

"Regardless, with our present situation, it seems I shall never have a chance to love." Mateo sniffles. "It saddens me to the depths of my soul."

"We can only do the best we can. None of us wants to be here."

Silence lowers her head again, and all I can wonder is if rescue shall ever come to this slender strand of sand, trees, and dense brush, where no hope whatsoever abides.

I must have slept, Luisa, for when I awoke, gray daylight colors the sail above me. I sit up to see Mateo still asleep, wrapped within his sail. Sancho gnaws beef, and Barros scratches his own crotch as if all the fleas in hell are burrowing there.

The wind steadily howls, drowning out all but the barest hint of whistles within the trees and brush, and I imagine some great sea monster offshore huffing and puffing with every ounce of strength to separate this island from the earth. It is then that a realization of the most important magnitude strikes, and I run outside and into the path, to stop where it concludes at the beach, where I gape like a man about to meet his end.

The tide is abnormally high. As far as I can see, even to the horizon white with mist from the gale driving the sea toward me, waves hump and roll like a mass of blue whales intent on dashing themselves against the island. Throwing themselves with triumphant roar upon the beach, they flow inward in great heaving masses of foam and water, even unto the dune upon which I stand.

One by one my companions join me, no doubt wondering about my mad rush from the shelter.

"You must have had the same thought I had when you ran out here," Barros says.

Beside me, Sancho eyes him. "All of us are intelligent enough to know what this means."

"What does it mean?" Mateo says. "It is only a storm."

Sancho snorts derision. "I withdraw my comment about your intelligence, you young fool."

"Mateo," I say, placing my hand upon his shoulder. "The spoiled beef we had planned to use for fish and crab bait is washed away."

"But that is far to the south," he says, his tone pleading, and I point.

"See how the waves come to the base of the dune? It does the same as far as we can see to the south."

We stand there, dumbfounded at our continuing lack of fortune. A squall of torrential rain drives us back inside our shelter, where we drop cross-legged to gnaw our portions of beef in silence, brooding with half-lidded eyes and sulking expressions for the remainder of the day.

October 6, 1521

Dear Luisa,

For five days we endured the storm out of the northeast. To our profound loss, which heightened our sense of urgency at locating some type of food, we finished the last of the beef on the third evening, retired to our beds early, and attempted to ignore the wind howling, the rain pattering, and the shuddering and popping of the sail over our heads.

Thankfully, on that fifth day, morning broke with no rain and a settling wind, the waves and high tide well below the dunes, and, perhaps, although I have yet to sense it, a renewed belief in locating a morsel of something to eat upon this sandy hell of ours.

Having relieved myself of what little food my gut has processed, I return to the shelter, notch my wall with my knife to mark another day, and poor the overflowing buckets into our skins.

Inside, the fire smolders as my companions lie still and quiet, all positivity at the brightening weather leeched from their souls. I leave the skins in a corner and turn around to address them. "The heavens have provided us with plenty of fresh water. Is that not something to celebrate?"

"Kiss my narrow arse," Sancho replies.

"It certainly is narrower," Barros says. "As are all of our arses."

"I agree with Sancho." Mateo rolls over to glare at me. "You can kiss my arse as well."

Sancho cackles laughter. "That is the way of it, Mateo. Tell him what he can do with his useless words."

I look to Barros for support, but only find resignation within his eyes. "I think I shall swim home to my wife," he says. "No doubt I shall drown, but it is better to die in the attempt than to sit here waiting for starvation and death like a coward."

"The same for me," Sancho says, "but I shall swim over to the savages and let them find me bloated and rotting when my corpse rises. That shall put a chill into them."

"A sharp knife for my throat," Mateo blurts out, adding nothing further.

"Come now," I say, "surely we can do better than to murder ourselves when we have not tried everything yet."

"Like what?" Barros says.

"Like a snare for the rabbit that made you and Sancho dive into the brush like rabbits yourselves. Would you not like to feast upon it to take revenge?"

"No one here knows how to make a snare," Sancho grumbles.

"What about the deer?" I say. "We have not tried tracking them to where they sleep."

"Sit down and be quiet," Mateo says. "You know like all of us, those deer are too fast to catch."

I look around at my fellows, all to a one ready to die. "I cannot believe you fine Spaniard men would give up so easily."

"Spain be damned," Mateo says. "If not for their lust for gold, we would not be suffering like this."

Taken aback by the sudden attitude of Mateo, especially since he had confided in me about wanting to marry and get his mama away her cruel husband, I stalk from the shelter, intent on walking the beach.

Head down, I kick sand along the way. How can I survive and return to you, Luisa, all by myself? I have never been one to be alone, and the thought fills me with fear. After your mama died, had it not been for you and my own mama and papa, along with the mama and papa of your mama, I am certain I would have gone insane. Perhaps, as I walk along the beach, I shall find some bite of food, such as a dead fish or crab, to shake my fellows from their melancholy laments and promises to take their own lives. After all, the roaring waves lasting five days should have beaten some creature to death and deposited it upon the sand.

At the dune, I shade my eyes from the rising sun pooling crimson upon the sea, look left and right, and lower my hand. Except for scattered shells and seaweed, and a flock of those plump, backward-kneed birds racing both to and from the foam left by the surf, the beach is as clean as if my own mama had swept it with a broom.

Defeated yet again, I start down the dune regardless and stop. What was that dark mass beneath the surface of the water, just beyond the breaking waves? I shade my eyes again to see a huge school of baitfish. If only they would swim close enough to toss them upon the sand, we could have succulent, hand-sized morsels of fish roasted over the fire.

I continue watching, continue hoping, continue praying, and a thrill harpoons up my spine as a large fin slices through the baitfish, then another and another, leaving trails of white within their slashing wakes. The baitfish dart before them, some clearing the water in fear. Nearer they come. Nearer the blue fish come. A wave rises. Before it breaks, I see several elongated bodies of those large fish within the burgeoning crest of water.

What am I doing? They are almost to the beach! Running and yelling for my companions, I climb the dune, ignore the vines and tree limbs within the path, and throw the sail aside to see three sets of dark eyes peering up at me as if I were a madman.

"What are you going on about?" Mateo says.

"Fi—" I can hardly speak from my run. Pointing behind me, I gulp air. "Those blue fish are back, and they are—"

"They never come close enough to catch," Sancho says.

"They are close enough now, I tell you! Stop your talk of dying and come catch those fish!" Barros and Sancho bolt up and outside. Mateo rises also, but at a slower pace.

On the beach, heart drumming within my chest, I run to the surf. The baitfish are being slashed to pieces by the blue fish. Many are longer than my arm, with triangular shaped teeth taking huge bites from the baitfish. Blood stains the once white foam crimson as I wave my companions forward. "Come on, you sour old tom cats, but be careful of those teeth!"

We all wade into the freezing water, to attempt to slap the darting, wriggling blue fish to the sand. Fins brush my ankles, and I manage to hoist a gleaming body out of the surf. "Got one!" I say, joyous at my success.

"I have one as well!" Barros loudly proclaims to my right. "Yes, those teeth are monstrous sharp! These small fish are being torn apart!"

To my right, Sancho hoists a massive blue body by the tail. "Enough fish for a feast! Catch more, for we never know when they shall retur—"

"*Aaahhhh!* Help me! I am being eaten alive!" I look farther down from Barros, where Mateo falls into a thrashing mass of fins, foam, and blood, all from several blue fish attacking him.

Barros and I splash toward him. We each take an arm and drag him to the sand. Sancho runs over, and we drop to our knees to survey the bleeding wounds.

"Ahh! It hurts!" Mateo issues forth a gurgling scream.

"It is the salt water in the bites," Barros says.

Mateo thrashes like one of the blue fish nearby, and it is then that I see why his screams gurgle, for one of the fish has taken a huge, gaping bite from his neck, and blood is pumping forth, reddening the sand.

His thrashing slows. His chest rises and falls slower, slower still. His eyes widen. "Carlo," he hisses.

Taking his hand, I lean close. "What is it, my friend?"

"If—" Blood gushes from his mouth. He coughs it up and clears his throat. If you return home, find … find …"

"Your mama?" I am certain Mateo is trying to say her name, but all I can do is wait.

He nods once, his eyes flutter and close, and his chest stills.

Speechless at such a senseless tragedy, I attempt to stand but my knees give way. I fall to my backside upon the sand.

"My God," Barros says. "I never thought the youngest of us would perish first."

"It is my fault," I moan, near to tears. "If I had not seen those fish …"

"You cannot blame yourself," Sancho says, kneeling by me to place a hand upon my shoulder. "It was a feeding frenzy. Once wild things get the taste of blood, they tear into whatever is close by."

"Sancho is correct," Barros says. "We all were splashing like those baitfish. Just bad luck they got our young apprentice here."

We three grow silent. Along the beach, four fish lie, mouths gaping for an underwater breath. Gulls cry and dive, snatching dead baitfish from the surf, which is now as silent as Mateo, his murderers having fled.

Sancho stands. "This is a hard business, but it must be said."

I look up at him, hardly believing what I think he is about to say, for he has hinted at it often enough since we arrived here. Still, I chance I am wrong. "You mean a burial, yes?"

Sancho gestures to the four fish. "They shall not last us long, and we do not know when they shall come this close again."

"Surely you do not mean it," Barros says. "This boy was our companion, our friend."

"And he shall serve us as I would have served him, were he to need my flesh. You might recall when I mentioned smoking any fish we caught if they came close enough. Now they have, so I shall build a smoker for them like I told you about."

The bushy brows of Barros form a knot over his black eyes. "And you mean to butcher and smoke bloody pieces of this boy as if he were nothing but a fish?"

"To survive, that is what we must do. Consider this ... he was talking of cutting his own throat, and a creature of the wild has done it for him. Wherever that fish journeys, the heart of Mateo journeys."

Although the words of Sancho, unexpected and poignant, calm my thudding heart to a degree, I shake my head. "I cannot do that."

Sancho darts his eyes my way. "Even to save your own life?"

"Yes, even for that."

He faces Barros. "And you, my old friend, what say you? There may be no other way to return home to your wife and your stitches."

"Do what you must, Sancho, for I shall not say another word on the subject except I shall not partake of the body of this boy."

Barros picks two fish up by their tails and trudges toward our path.

Sancho faces me. His dark eyes, normally narrowed and keen, soften. "You are well-spoken, and you know your letters when you write within your journal. Were you educated under the monks at the La Rabida monastery? Barros said you told him about it."

"What of it?"

"When I was a boy, a local monk told me about the Christ and the Last Supper."

"The Christ sharing His body was symbolic, Sancho. Also, it was pieces from a loaf of bread, not pieces of His own flesh."

"That is true, but the meaning is the same."

I wait for Sancho, who has astonished me with his knowledge, to speak. A slight smile rises upon his thin lips, and he spreads his hands wide, as if to encompass a circle of air before him.

"Despite those teachings at the monastery, I see you do not understand the meaning. The symbolism is how the Christ gave his body to separate us from spiritual death, and I see our poor dead friend as our savior to separate us from physical death."

"No matter, Sancho, I shall not dishonor Mateo in such a way."

"Come, help me carry him back to the shelter."

"I shall help you do nothing, damn you."

"May I borrow your knife to—"

I whip the knife from my belt and point it at Sancho. "You may have it, but only if I bury it within your foul heart."

"Believe it or not, Carlo, many is the time I have wanted to do that very thing."

A gust of wind scatters sand upon the closed eyes of Mateo. Nearby, gulls squabble and cry as they fight over scraps of baitfish.

Do I judge Sancho too harshly, Luisa? More than anything I want to return home, to have you forgive me for leaving you and all whom I love. Sancho, with his wiser than expected words, looks to the future, while I, in my guilt, look to a past that may well kill me one day. I cannot forget it, however, so all I can do is live with it until you unburden me of it.

A gull waddles toward us, likely to peck at the eyes of the man who once saved me from the same fate, which, I now believe, is a greater sin than allowing Sancho to use my knife. I toss it to his feet.

"Use it and be quick about it, I shall not touch him. Do your business here, where the high tide can cleanse his blood from the sand, for if I ever see it again, I shall have nightmares the rest of my short life."

Sancho nods. I take the other two fish back to the shelter, in hopes Barros and I can deal with them in silence as we remember our young friend, Mateo.

October 6, 1521

Dear Luisa,

Sancho did as I asked, not only building the smoker he had mentioned, but building another one far away, so Barros and I would not be forced to watch him eat.

That night, Barros and I lit a pile of sticks, waited until they formed smoldering embers, and hung thin strips of fish upon the framework of sticks Sancho had made. Next, we spread a section of sailcloth over a larger framework of sticks, which encompassed the smaller frame to keep the cloth above the fish. Done with our labors, we sat nearby as the smoke gathered, to seep out from beneath the sail. We exchanged no words the entire time, but only shared the knife from the belt of Barros, and short, sharp gestures of instruction. I supposed he knew I had loaned my knife to Sancho, for he did not ask me about the lack of it within my belt.

After a time, the wind, in the usual way except for storms, calms somewhat. Shivering from a chill descending with the night, I fetch our cloaks made of sailcloth and we don them, still silently, still remorseful, still contemplating, no doubt, the demise of our young friend.

A hint of firelight escapes from beneath the sail covering the strips of fish, barely enough to reflect within the dark eyes across from me. A rustling within the brush marks the passing of a rabbit or a deer. The surf pounds the beach again and again, and I fervently prey that it carries the blood and gore of Mateo out to sea, where he may live on within whatever scuttling, swimming or squirming creature may partake of him.

I settle back upon my elbows to study the endless stars winking within the black storm of night and wonder, Luisa, which one might be the hearth where your mama resides within Heaven, and when I might join her one fine day?

Love, I think suddenly, is like those magical stars when they streak from above to burst with flame within the night sky, similar to how we each seek someone within our lives with whom we shall burst with flame, not only with physical desire, but with the desire to become one in as many ways as possible.

You, my daughter, never had the chance to see your mama and I together, but I tell you now, we were like those bursting stars, flaring with a love unending, until she burned out much too soon.

She was a tiny whisp of a girl when we met at fourteen in the market at Palos de la Frontera. I wore the simple clothes of a farmer: a blouse somewhat more dingy than white, with permanent purple stains upon the sleeves from picking grapes, and coarse wool breeches my mama had woven. Your mama wore her hair in two long braids to her shoulders, a white blouse with puffed sleeves, and over it, a sky-blue dress of common cut and cloth. Although she was plain in a way, what caught my eye were the freckles across her nose, only a bit darker than her tanned skin.

To get her attention while she examined tomatoes, being the boy that I was, I pulled her left braid and darted to the right, to pick up a tomato as well. After looking around with a puzzled expression, she faced me. "Did you pull my hair?"

"Me?" I said, wearing an equally puzzled expression. "Why would I pull the hair of some strange girl squeezing tomatoes and returning them to the cart all mushy for the next unsuspecting customer?"

"I am *not* squeezing them, I am looking for only the best ones for my mama, for only the best ones shall do for *my* family." She turned her patrician nose up at me. "I suppose you work in a vineyard as a farm hand. Do *you* even know your letters?"

"Do *you* even know how to spell tomato?"

She picked up another tomato. "I certainly do, but I shall not waste my time doing so for a mere farm hand."

I put my tomato back. "Do you believe in angels?"

She glanced at me. "I suppose you think I am so beautiful as to call me an angel."

"Not at all, not at all. I am a demon come to steal your maidenhood one fine moonlit night."

Her eyes brightened. "After we are married, of course."

I smile at this most precious of memories, Luisa. You see, I am sure, how your papa was a roguish boy, filled with teasing ways in his younger days, and how your mama returned as well as I gave her. When you choose a young man, remember how humor is the olive oil to the bread of a fine marriage—always a meal met with tender smiles and gentle arguments, which are finished with compromise and kisses instead of anger and narrowed eyes.

From out of the brush, Sancho enters the dimly lit area in which Barros and I sit. He drops my knife at my feet, including a large shell. "I told you once to keep your knife sharp to lessen the pain. Since you forgot, I brought a shell for honing the blade." He lifts the cover over the fish, takes a piece and sits to sniff it.

"You have your own damn meat," Barros says.

Ignoring him, Sancho eats.

"Is it safe still red like that?" I ask.

Sancho swallows. "I am willing to take a chance."

I take the knife from the sand. No blood stains it, so I return it to my belt and toss the shell near my chest beside our shelter. Whatever Sancho may be, he is correct about keeping a blade sharp. If ever I find myself alone here, with no prospect of rescue, I may be inclined to follow the lead of Mateo and cut my own throat to end my pain, both from being alone and from being away from home and hearth and family.

Sancho finishes the fish and goes to the nearest tree, where he breaks several tips from several branches. He then adds them to the embers, creating more smoke. "The fish taste better if your fire smokes well."

Barros takes a handful of sand and sifts it slowly into his other hand. "I would rather it taste like nothing. It shall soon be gone and we shall starve."

I miss the humor of my friend. "Come now, Barros, why so glum? Surely the fish shall return."

He rises, sips water from one of the buckets beneath the corner of a sail, and enters the shelter without a word.

Sancho goes to the bucket, sips, and returns to the fire for another piece of fish. "As much as I hate to say it, he has given up, despite this feast from the sea."

"Four fish is hardly a feast," I say.

"It is when we had none this morning and were starving." He points toward the sail covering the fish. "Go ahead. I do not know the name of this fish, but it is oily, and it shall revive you."

I do as Sancho says. Red of flesh, but not delicate in flavor, the fish has yet to taste like smoke. Like Sancho said, oil shines upon the surface of the meat. Done with that piece, I settle back to my elbows again, to consider the native tribe to the west.

Although tribes war, as Sancho has said during one of our conversations, I wonder if the nearby tribe has enemies. I also wonder about their customs, such as love and marriage. Surely they have children, so they should have some sort of family structure to help bind their community together.

I turn my attention to Sancho. "You said you have seen natives hunt and grow crops. What are they like otherwise?"

Sancho snorts laughter, lips shining with oil from the fish. "Do not tell me you hope to marry a woman from those savages to the east?"

"I only want to know their ways."

"They differ, so those here shall not have the same ways."

"Well, what do those you have seen eat from the sea? Perhaps we can use their methods of catching fish."

"I never saw them fish."

"What did they grow? Perhaps we can—"

"Enough with your 'perhaps.' The soil at the villages of the natives I saw is dark and rich. This sand here is good for nothing but growing these twisted trees and thickets filled with vines."

"We shall have to eat something when the fish runs out, and it shall run out much quicker if you keep …" I hesitate, and I wager Sancho knows why, with all my complaining about what he planned to do with Mateo."

"Go on and say it," Sancho says. "'If I keep eating your fish instead of eating Mateo.' I see your precious sensibilities about eating human flesh surrender when it comes to your own survival."

I do not reply, for his point pierces my heart, another layer of kindness peeled away to reveal the savage within myself, desperate to return home regardless of the cost.

Sancho rises and brushes sand from the piece of sail wrapped around him. "I kept the clothes of our young savior. One of us may use them when ours are near to rags, which shall not take long."

"I shall not use anything of his. The merest thread against my skin would haunt me forever."

Sancho starts toward the shelter and turns around. "Hear this and hear it well, Carlo. There shall come a day when you must climb off that high saddle of yours and grovel within the sand of this island to live. Barros and I are older than you. If we leave you here alone, your mind shall break. Do you hear me?"

I turn to face him. "I have no saddle nor horse nor friends. I am ready to be rid of you, and if Barros prefers to change from his somewhat jovial self, I am ready to be rid of him as well."

"You may say that now, young fool, but if and when it happens, you shall regret it." Sancho throws the sail back and enters the shelter, leaving me to face the smoldering embers that mirror my smoldering anger.

Yes, the savage within me is surfacing like the fin of a shark, to encircle a struggling man and flash forward when it senses weakness to remove sensibility with those serrated teeth, triangle shaped and ready to rip and tear a soul from the body.

Within the heavens, a cloud passes over the stars, and my dreams of joining your mama, Luisa, seem as far away as you are. But in a way, they seem closer as well.

All *too* close.

November 17, 1521

Dear Luisa,

Upon this narrow strip of land, winter fast approaches. Harsh gales blow every few days, hissing stinging sand against our bare feet and ankles when we uselessly search the beach for a morsel of something to eat due to our fish running out. Although Sancho went to the other smoking fire he had hid within the trees and brush, he still returned to eat a piece of fish before night fell. Neither Barros and I complained. I suppose we both thought Sancho had no appetite for Mateo, even after his sermon to me about the Christ sacrificing his body so others may live.

The days grow shorter. Great flocks of honking fowl wake us when the first hint of light bleeds from beneath the eastern horizon, staining the rolling blue-green sea with streaks of crimson. Sancho and Barros say the fowl are a type of goose. I ask if they can be caught, and the two berate me for such a question.

Our empty bellies growl and complain. Rain only comes once every few days, so we ration water with timid sips instead of the thankful swallows we enjoyed when rain came often.

As far as the horses to the north, I never mention them. However, I long to return there to catch a glimpse of sleek hide and long mane, or upright ears and flowing tail, evidence that somehow, someway, Cantante might still live.

Barros gradually resolved his ill will toward Sancho. Apparently, their years together as shipmates and friends meant more to them than I thought. I am happy about this turn of events, for it is sad enough upon this island without bitter words to make it worse.

On this, our sixty-sixth day here, we are finishing our morning walk along the beach. We consider walking the marsh on the other side of the island. Like before, when anyone mentions it out of what is likely boredom, someone vetoes the notion, saying how trudging through the dense grass and reeds would weaken us further, and we have little strength left as it is.

Walking along the path to the shelter, Barros stops to examine a limb extending from one of the humped over trees. Sancho and I stop as well, wordlessly waiting while he flexes the limb back and forth. After a moment of this, Sancho and I look at each other like men who think their companion has lost his mind.

Releasing the limb, Barros smiles brightly and claps his hands. "I, my fellow sufferers, have a plan to feast on one of those plump deer this day."

Sancho twirls a finger beside his temple. "You have something loose within your skull, old friend. Those deer are as fast as that rabbit that made fools of us."

I grin at the memory of Sancho and Barros running headlong into the brush that night, and at the memory of Mateo enjoying it as much as I. "I would like to see you try to catch one," I say. "I am long overdue a hardy laugh."

Barros twists his thick, chapped lips to one side. "Jest all you like. I have an idea, and it shall not take running to accomplish it, only a bit of work with a knife and some lashing with rope."

"Do we tie you upside-down from a tree limb over one of their game trails?" Sancho says, failing to hide a teasing grin. "That way you can snatch one up as it walks by."

Barros places his hands upon his hips. "Of all our shipmates I could have been stranded with, I ended up with two fools like you." He stomps away, bare feet thudding upon the sand.

Sancho catches up to him at the shelter. "I am sorry to make fun of you. You once loved to laugh. Now you are nothing but a grouch."

About to throw the sailcloth door open and enter, Barros whirls around. "Did you not see my smile when I smiled?"

"I saw it," I say, "and I was glad for it. What is this idea you have about catching a deer?"

"You saw me bending one of those limbs, correct?"

"Yes, what of it?"

"It was long ago, before I met Sancho. One of the crew said he sailed with another ship, which went to a land where the natives lashed sharpened spikes of wood to a low limb. Then they—"

"I know," Sancho says, pointing a dirty finger into the air to mark his epiphany. "They tied the branch back and tied it to a stake within the ground. From there they tied a line across a game trail. Then, when a deer came along, the limb sprung into the deer, impaling it upon the spikes."

"Not bad," Barros says. "You are more intelligent than your ugly face suggests."

Sancho dismisses this observation with a wave of his hand. "Am I correct or not?"

"You are correct." Barros spreads his hands approximately the width of his wrist to his fingertips. "Carlo, sharpen your knife and make several stakes to lash to the limb. Sancho, unravel one of the extra ropes to make lashing. Make enough to stretch across the game trail as well. I shall search for fresh deer tracks where we can set our trap. With good fortune, we shall break our morning fast with broiled deer meat."

"What about for our supper today?" I ask.

"The deer back home travel more during the night. I assume these shall as well."

Barros leaves for the path to the beach, and Sancho says to him, "Stay away from the forks of those game trails. We do not want to get confused about where we set the trap and have to search for it in the morning half asleep."

Sancho enters the shelter and comes back with a thick coil of rope that Mateo salvaged from the beach. He sits cross-legged and starts unraveling the strands. I get the shell Sancho gave me from beside my chest, set it upon the curved lid, and stroke my knife against it until sharp enough to shave slivers of thumbnail into the air.

Sancho looks up at me. "Never forget what I told you."

"What is that?" I secure the knife within my belt.

"Keep your knife sharp so you shall not feel any pain when you have to cut a throat."

"You mean *my* throat, not *a* throat."

"I mean what I say. If this trap fails, you may need to cut a throat to survive."

"I assume you mean I may have to cut either your throat or the throat of Barros in order to eat you."

"Assume what you shall."

"Did I not make my feelings clear about eating human flesh when Mateo died?"

"You did, but I say you shall cut a throat other than your own to survive. Now, away with you. Make those stakes like Barros commanded, for I may eat *him* if his plan fails."

Leaving Sancho, Luisa, I grit my teeth at his continued mention of eating any human flesh, much less from Mateo and now Barros. Just the mere mention of the act turns my empty stomach, rising sour bile into my throat.

By the time I have several sharpened stakes like Barros described, he has returned to the shelter. Sancho unravels the last length of rope and stands. I pile the stakes beside the shelter door while Barros swallows water from one of our buckets. I drink also, licking my cracked lips to get every drop, and return the bucket beneath the sail corner where it can catch more rain.

Barros takes several coils of the unraveled rope and sits to braid them into a single strand about half the thickness of my little finger. "This is for the rope across the path," he says. "We shall use a thick rope to stretch the limb back." He gives me some of the unraveled strands. "Braid those like I am doing. We shall use them to lash the sharpened stakes to the tree limb."

Sancho goes for water, drinks and returns. "You certainly have perked up with your grouchy self, giving orders and such."

"I am simply happy to have something to occupy my mind other than the drudgery of existing upon this island with the likes of you."

"Did you find deer tracks away from a fork like I told you? It needs to be easy to find in the morning."

"You are still more intelligent than your ugly face appears. I found a well-used game trail about a hundred steps down the beach to the south. I even marked it with a stick so I can find it again."

"Good. We would not want the next youngest of us three to go down the wrong path and impale himself upon those stakes."

"Always with doom and gloom," Barros says sullenly. "You should be happy if that happens. Then you can make another meal of tender young flesh."

I throw a braided length of rope down. "Can we talk about something else, or be quiet altogether?"

Barros shrugs his shoulders and returns to his braiding. Sancho goes for more water and returns to braiding as well.

I have not considered it, Luisa, likely because the transformation has been so slow to take place, but you may be interested in our appearance after our sixty-sixth day upon this island.

As I have mentioned, the hair of Barros is thick and curly, with gray mixed in. Now, like all of our hair, it shines with oil, for we have no soap to wash with whatsoever. Of course, Barros and Sancho have beards and moustaches, unkempt and untrimmed. Their moustaches cover their upper lips, while their beards extend from our chins, to about the half the length of a finger. As I said earlier, my beard and moustache are not so heavy, although it is more now than usual since I cannot shave.

For our clothes, our blouses are stained beneath our arms from toil leading to sweat in the heat when we first arrived here, and threads hang from seams like cobwebs hang from rafters within the barn at home. For our breeches, they are stained as well, from all manner of toil, sweat, and sand. Unfortunately, due to our lack of paper to clean ourselves with when we go into the trees and brush to relieve ourselves, our backsides likely smell like sewers, except we are so conformed to the stench, none of us ever mentions it. Please, Luisa, never wipe with leaves when a cloth is at hand, for it is not a pleasant sensation. Alas, the legs of our breeches are tattered, and our travails along the path, during which limbs and brush snag the cloth, have left us bedraggled, with threads extending from the seams like with our blouses. Alas again, for our poor feet are encrusted with sand, including callouses so thick, one might think we are akin to horses with their hooves. If I manage to return home, I may end up striking this portion from my journal, lest it wrinkle your nose and give you nightmares after you read it.

Finally, when Barros announces we have braided enough rope for his deer trap, he and Sancho wait while I gather the sharpened stakes, and we take the path to the beach.

At the bottom of the dune, he turns south. After a time of trudging through the welcome warmth of sun upon the sand, for a cold wind has sprung up, he climbs the dune and enters a game path to stop and face us. "This path forks farther into the thicket. I saw more tracks upon the right fork, so we shall set our trap there." He moves ahead and stops at the fork. "I wish the paths were not so narrow, for one might become confused and take the wrong way. Also, the deer tracks indicate they are moving away from us, and the limb with the stakes shall swing back toward anyone walking toward it."

Sancho tilts his head toward me. "You are hoping Carlo shall be impaled for our supper, I wager."

Barros and I ignore Sancho, for an uncharacteristic hint of a smile appears upon his face, which indicates he is teasing me.

Further along, the game trail narrows. We dodge and duck beneath tree limbs and wince when thorns scrape our blouses and breeches. Barros stops to point at a limb as thick as his arm. "Let us lash your stakes to that limb, Carlo."

We do as he suggests, and I note how, were I to trip the rope, the stakes, about the width of my hand apart, would bury themselves into my upper thighs.

"Very good," Barros says, lashing the last stake. "Let us finish our task and return to our home away from home and wait for our meal to arrive."

At the shelter, we sip water and watch the sun set to the west. I almost gasp at the similarity to the same scene at home, when God places ribbons of clouds along the horizon and paints them shades of yellow, orange and eventually, dark crimson at the last, when night settles over the land.

A chill descends upon our rise, made even colder by the almost constant wind, so I gather sticks for the fire. Wrapping myself within my pieces of sail for sleep, I hope we have deer meat at sunrise, for one of us shall surely die from starvation soon if we do not eat.

November 18, 1521

Dear Luisa,

For some odd reason, I rarely dream now, but this night I do. It is the evening of your birth, although you are not born yet. I wrote before how your mama was a tiny whisp of a girl when we met, and she hardly grew an inch or gained a pound as long as she lived. This, and her somewhat narrow hips, made for a difficult labor, and it was all I could do to not run from our home to escape her screams.

I startle myself awake. A hint of red shades the sky through the cracks within the wall beside me, suggesting dawn. I close my eyes once more.

After a time, I dream again, hearing the screams of your mama again, and I realize I am not asleep.

"What is that noise?" Sancho says, rolling over to look at me.

I wait, listen, and see Barros is not here. "Sancho," I say, "how long has Barros been up?"

"I did not know he was gone. Perhaps he is getting sticks for the fire."

"I gathered sticks last night."

"Go back to sleep and let me do the same. He shall return any—"

"Hush," I say, as a keen wailing, hardly there at all, comes at the edge of my hearing. Sancho must hear it as well, for he snaps his eyes open.

We both jump up and go outside, and the wail grows louder. After a quick glance at each other, we bolt toward the beach, run into the game trail, and find Barros moaning in pain from the sharpened spikes impaling his upper thighs. He manages a weak smile. "It is about time you two got here. My throat is raw from screaming for help."

Two spikes pierce each thigh, straddling the bone, thank goodness. Blood oozes from the wounds, both from where the spikes enter and exit.

Sancho hops over the limb and takes the face of his friend within his hands. "Barros, you know what we must do."

Another weak smile. "Why do you think I have been screaming, you fool. Yes, I know you must pull me from those spikes. It is not like my efforts have achieved anything."

I know enough about wounds to say what I must say. "Barros, if those spikes have pierced the main blood supply within your legs, you know you shall bleed to death in no time."

"I do not think there is enough blood for that. What worries me more is the chance of the wounds putrefying."

"Mateo stitched my leg while I was passed out and I was grateful. I didn't mention this to him, but he must not have known to leave wounds such as these open to allow drainage."

"Tell me—" Barrows winces. "Tell me something I do not know."

"You are younger and stronger," Sancho says to me. "Wrap your arms beneath his while I pull the branch." I do as Sancho says, and he grips the branch.

"Not yet," Barros says. "Find a stick and place it between my teeth. Otherwise I shall scream loud enough to have those savages paddle their vessels over and attack us."

I break a stick from the limb upon which the stakes are tied, and upon which Barros is impaled. Wincing again, for his every movement must aggravate his wounds, he snatches it from me and shoves it between his teeth. The balls of muscle at his jaws tighten, he nods, and I go behind him to wrap my arms around his heaving chest.

Sancho takes hold of the limb. "I am sorry, old friend, but I must do this in one fell swoop. The wooly head of Barros nods, Sancho jerks the limb, and the ribs of Barros flex beneath my fingers as I keep him from falling. Moaning softly, he sags over, having fainted, and becomes dead weight within my grasp.

Sancho takes a limp arm and wraps it around his neck. "Let us lie him down so I can see his wounds."

"Damn fool," I mutter, easing Barros to the sand. "What was he thinking, coming out here in the dark?"

"He is a large man, with a large appetite for both food and for life." Sancho rips the breeches apart and touches the outer edges of a hole within one leg, which still oozes blood. "He is also a lucky man. Only a wee bit left or right to his main vessel, and he would have bled to death before he woke us with his screams."

The closed eyes flutter open, and Barros manages a weak chuckle. "Luck my narrow arse. Luck would have been to break a limb here as a sign instead of at the fork to this path."

"Would you have seen it in the dark?" I ask.

"Dawn was just breaking, so I could see well enough."

"And you walked right into your own trap," Sancho says sourly.

"You and your complaining," Barros says. "If I had truly been lucky, a beautiful native woman would have rescued me."

"To eat you," Sancho says.

"Ah, but perhaps not. Many we have seen in our travels were quite friendly, bare-breasted with black hair to their waists and dark skin. Just thinking about them stirs my loins."

"Your wife would kill you."

"As I have said, what she does not know shall not harm her."

I stand. "Your words shall live in infamy, I am certain. Men from now to eternity shall mutter them amongst friends and acquaintances when they speak of their dalliances with prostitutes and mistresses."

"Enough," Sancho barks. "We must get this old fool back to the shelter and clean his wounds so I can assess them properly."

With an arm each wrapped around our necks, we hoist Barros upward, to mostly drag him through the path, along the beach, and to the shelter. Along the way, he demands for one of us to reset the trap, and Sancho scoffs at the idea, saying no deer shall use that game trail as long as the scent of blood assails their nostrils, adding that he would rather starve to death than touch those wicked stakes ever again. Within my mind I agree, for seeing those four stakes impaling the legs of our friend has left me with no taste to relive that scene, even if for broiled deer meat.

Within the shelter, Sancho rips the breeches open further and studies the wounds, eases Barros over to study the wounds upon the back of his legs and looks up at me. "How do you feel about using our water to wash these holes?"

"No," Barros grunts, trying to sit up. "I shall not hear of it."

"We must," Sancho says, gently pushing him down.

"What about salt water?" I say. "I washed my wound within the surf."

"Your wound was stitched closed. These punctures are open. We can't chance anything within them other than fresh water."

"No." Barros tries to rise again, and Sancho pushes him down.

"You have no say in the matter, you old fool." Carlo, fetch one of the buckets and tear one of the sails we are not using from the bed of Mateo. I shall use it to wash these wounds."

I do so, and Barros lies quietly while Sancho tends to the four holes still oozing blood. He stands, bloody pieces of sail within his hands. "Come with me while I take these outside. We could both use a drink of water."

"Barros could use some water."

"Not now."

I look from Sancho to Barros, whose closed eyes and steady rise and fall of his chest indicates sleep.

Outside, Sancho drops the rags by my chest, saying we can wash and use them again. Then he takes me by an arm and leads me to the dense brush, where he and Barros burrowed like moles that night after that rabbit. "I am glad you agreed about not setting the trap again, Carlo, despite our hunger."

"I agreed at the time, but what are we to do? Now that I think about it, it is worth trying again."

"I shall not," Sancho says, eyes narrowing, nostrils flaring. "Although I saw the necessity of eating human flesh, there are things I would rather not see."

"Such as what? I can hardly imagine a worse sight than Barros impaled upon those stakes."

"We were lucky because he was too hoarse to scream when we arrived. I do not relish the thought of seeing a deer impaled and bleating, as if it is trying to wrench itself away from death like a woman dying in childbirth."

At those words, I gasp and step away, knees nearly collapsing.

Sancho comes near. "Your expression of anguish tells me you agree."

"Yes … well … I suppose. Still, what are we to do for food?"

Dark eyes dart downward, then back to me. "If Barros dies …"

"You would treat your friend so harshly?"

"Were our situations reversed, I would insist he use me in the same manner." Sancho pauses to place a hand upon my shoulder. "As I would insist you use me as well."

"I felt much affection for Mateo. Not only did he save my life by stitching my leg, he was a fine young man."

"Like you have said, he must not have known wounds such as those should remain open to allow drainage. God surely has a plan for you."

I shrug the hand from my shoulder. "Plan or not, I shall never eat one of His children."

"Never say what you shall or shall not do, Carlo. The hand of death may lead a person to regret those words."

At this, Sancho returns to the shelter, leaving me with my whirling thoughts similar to the storm that engulfed our ship so long ago, a maelstrom-mix of memory and the present, both seething within my mind.

November 20, 1521

Dear Luisa,

The day after Barros was impaled by his own trap, God blessed us by filling our buckets with rain. We drank and drink until our stomachs distended, making us appear as if we were three women with overdue births. The next morning, I found a large fish alive within the surf. An injury to one side indicated an attack by some predator, possibly a shark, and we feasted with abandon last night, foregoing our normal method of drying fish for cooking it over hot coals until the meat flaked off the bone.

And then it seems, God abandoned Barros.

I woke this morning to Sancho at his side, palm upon the forehead of Barros while he still slept. Sancho heard me stir and looked my way to shake his head. "He is burning up."

"Have you looked at his wounds?"

"I would rather he sleep as long as possible. Wet a piece of sail for his forehead while I sit with him. I shall look at his wounds when he wakes, but I think I know what I shall find."

This somber mood sets the tone for the day, with Sancho remaining at the side of Barros, up and down every so often to refresh the folded pieces of sail with water.

I can only take so much of this death watch, so I tell Sancho I shall walk for a time upon the beach.

The morning has dawned calm, with only a cold breeze entering the openings within my cloak of sail to make me shiver now and then. The waves, unlike their normal pounding upon the sand, whisper with a gentle wash, where those plump, backward-kneed birds plunge their beaks to find whatever minuscule creature they feed upon. At seeing a gray fin arise from the silken surface of the sea, I shade my eyes, and several dolphins rise, their arched backs gleaming.

Such life upon this island, life we cannot use for food, yet I believe we miss opportunity after opportunity amongst the trees, brush, and marsh. No doubt the natives across the large expanse of water to our west could gather food here as if from a local market.

My feet sink into the cold, wet sand, leaving tracks behind me, and I wonder how many people have walked here before, or shall walk here in the future, such as the Spanish.

Like Mateo, my own papa and I have a poor opinion of how our countrymen are bound to spread themselves upon the earth in their search for gold and silver. We share the same opinion for how the Portuguese are purchasing slaves from the Africans. That, including why the Africans enslave their own brethren to begin with, now selling many of them to those dastardly Portuguese, puzzles us to no end.

Leaving such a forlorn thought behind, I stop at a section of the surf, where the water rushes back into the sea. Here, tiny Vs mark something beneath the wet sand, so I plunge my hands down and bring up several creatures. Their barrel shaped bodies are made of gray shell. At what I presume to be their head, two feathery antennae protrude. I turn one over to see six pairs of legs, almost like tiny paddles, scurrying within the air. Deciding on an experiment, I ease one back to the wet sand, and it immediately burrows down like an excited mole. Nodding, I say, "Sir Whatever You Are, I dub thee a mole crab. Thank the heavens you have no claws to pinch with like your sideways scuttling cousins, for if I ever manage to catch one, that is surely what it shall do."

I release the remainder within my hand, for I see no use for food within these scurrying bits of shells upon six speedy legs, and return to my walk.

As my feet plop to the wet sand, Luisa, and as the cold surf chills my toes, I allow my mind to drift back to better times, so I shall tell you more about the courtship of your mama and myself.

You may recall our meeting at the market within Palos de la Frontera, where we teased with both pleasure and zeal. Alas, we did not meet again for another year. Yes, it is difficult to believe, as much as Papa and I went to market, and many times, Mama and Beatriz as well, but the world shall turn as it deems fit, not as I would deem fit.

The following summer, when the vines within the vineyard grew along the trellises like sea-green waves, including the hint of tiny grape clusters that glistened white like cresting foam, and when Papa, Mama, Beatriz and I could rest from our constant labors at tending the farm, we attended a festival on the other side of Palos de la Frontera, held by a wealthy grower of olive trees, whom we had never met.

At fifteen, even though I had not forgotten that whisp of a teasing girl I had met at the market, my mind was on the possibility of making the acquaintance of a young girl, or a young woman rather, with whom I could fall in love and marry. With this purpose at hand, I dressed in clean breeches, an unstained blouse of white linen, a belt and boots of black leather, and brushed my hair and tied it into a copy of the tail of Cantante, halfway down my back.

When I entered the kitchen, Beatriz, twelve at the time, wearing braids, a plain farm girl dress in white, and new black shoes bought especially for the occasion, set her sights upon me, wide-eyed. "Look at Carlo," she said to Mama, who was still braiding her hair. "He looks like one of those pretty boys at Palos de la Frontera, who looks down their noses at us."

Mama yanked the braid. "Enough. If I have told you once, I have told you a thousand times a thousand, the only people you must concern yourself with are family and friends."

In a chair by the fireplace, Papa chuckled. "Listen to your mama, Beatriz. I would not have married her unless she were an intelligent woman."

"How do you know Carlo wants an intelligent woman? He likely wants one with pouty lips for sloppy kisses."

"I would not mind that at all," I say, grinning at Beatriz. "Nor would you mind kissing a boy like that when your time comes."

"Both of you are wrong," Mama said. "Marriage is about what happens when you tire of kissing."

Beatriz covered a snicker, and Mama glared at her. "What are you laughing about? I did not say anything funny."

Beatriz uncovered her mouth. "I know what happens when you tire of kissing. The goats do that to have baby goats."

"Be that as it may," Papa said, "your mama is correct. A good marriage is more about the times between such things as kissing and doing what the goats do. It is about sharing the bad times with the good. Most of all, it is about enjoying the company of your husband or wife with smiles and laughter."

These words from my wise papa reminded me of the girl at the market and her teasing ways. I was certain we would smile and laugh if we were to become close.

Beatriz waved her hand in front of my eyes. "Why the faraway look, Carlo? Are you thinking of a girl for kissing already?"

I shoved the hand away. "Perhaps you prefer a goat, Beatriz. Then you can have *very* sloppy kisses."

Beatriz answered by sticking out her tongue at me and nothing more. Then we all piled into the wagon for the ride to the festival. You may wonder if Cantante pulled the wagon, Luisa, but we had a mule for that and I am glad of it. I always thought of Cantante as a brother, and I would never ask my brother to pull a wagon.

Still walking along the beach, I look behind me to find a gull screeching much louder than usual, and I see Sancho running toward me. We meet halfway, and I wait for him to catch his wheezing breath. "Carlo." He takes a deep breath and stands straighter, chest heaving in and out.

"What is it, Sancho? Barros is not—"

"I do not understand, but his fever is better."

"Did you see about his wounds?"

"They drain pus but do not seem putrid."

"That is a good sign, is it not?"

"One can never tell with these things. He asked me to fetch you. Let us hurry back."

At the shelter, we catch our breath before we go inside. When we do, Barros is sitting up, sipping water from a bucket. "Ah," he says, putting the bucket down. "My two brothers have returned."

Sancho and I exchange quick glances, for Barros has never referred to us as "brother." Perhaps he has brothers we do not know about, and he is remembering them.

"Why the glum looks?" Barros says. "Rest by the fire and let me tell you a story while I enjoy this fine wine you have provided."

Sancho and I sit across from the smoldering embers. I get up to wrap the sail around the shoulder of Barros, for it has slipped off. Pulling away, I quickly place the back of my hand to his forehead, which is as hot as the embers of our fire. I sit and wait for Barros to drink again. When he does, I lean close to the ear of Sancho. "He is feverish again and it is affecting his mind. What shall we do?"

Sancho lowers his head for a moment, then raises it to look into my eyes. "We do nothing. He is comfortable and at peace. If he dies this way, so be it."

I nod in agreement, for I can think of no better gift than the gift of peace at the passing of a person.

Barros slurps loudly, lowers the bucket to the sand beside him, and raises his eyes to us. "Oh, I am sorry. I have drunk all the wine."

Our friend has obviously forgotten his story, so I do not remind him. "How do you feel, Barros? It is a warm day, is it not?"

"Exceedingly so. It reminds me of our Spanish summers."

"Would you like to sit away from the fire?" Sancho says. "I can help you if—"

Barros waves the unfinished offer away. "No, no, I shall kick these covers off and lie here. I shall be fine … I shall be fine."

He kicks the covers off, and it is then that I see the pus, thick and yellow, oozing from the holes within his thighs, visible through the rips Sancho has made within his breeches. I also catch a whiff of the rotten odor of decaying flesh. Leaning near Sancho again, I cup my hand around my mouth. "Perhaps his wounds were putrid deep inside, and it is weeping out only now."

He nods grimly, and we both turn our faces toward Barros, whose chest rises and falls with sleep.

Sancho rises to tie the sail back at the door. "To let the air in. I shall not have him suffer any more than possible." A cool breeze enters our home, carrying the aroma of salt, and Sancho sits again.

Silence lies her head amongst us during our death watch. For a time, Barros sleeps well. Then he trembles, jostles his head side to side, and still asleep, murmurs softly, "If only to be at home … if only to be at home." A soft sigh follows, with perhaps the hint of a smile, as if he actually sees his home at Leon again, along with his wife and grandchildren, and possibly those fancy women while he fits them for their even fancier dresses.

I risk a glimpse at Sancho. Tears stream down his cheeks and into his beard. Seeing me watching him, he shoves the moisture away with the back of his hand. "What are you looking at?"

"Nothing, Sancho." I turn away to hide my own filling eyes. "Not a thing."

My dear Luisa, it is at a time like this, when grief nips at the heart with fangs of dread, I would like to return to my memories of the festival, for I shall surely weep terribly if I do not.

When Papa steered the mule toward the other wagons and carriages, my heart jumped within my chest. There your mama stood, a woman within a circle of girls, outshining them all within a dress so blue, I could have been peering into the waves of the sea. The sleeves, wider at her wrists, were embroidered with lace, while flowers of yellow, gold, and red, along with stems and leaves of green, decorated the hem. The low-cut neckline revealed her modest bosom, fuller than a year ago, and the taper at her narrow waist gave the appearance of wider hips, just enough to wonder how she might appear naked within the moonlight.

But that was not all.

Her braids were transformed into a luminous cloud of black, falling past her shoulders in cresting waves, drawing me to her, wanting—no, desiring—to the absolute negligence of all of those around us, to take those silken strands within my hands and bury my face into them, breathing in her very essence to the depths of my soul.

Oblivious to my gaze, Mama, Papa, and Beatriz hurried away, to our host I suppose, for my eyes failed to follow them.

Leaving the circle of girls, your mama, Luisa, opened a fan and waived it before her face. Before I knew it, she was within speaking distance of me, dark eyes grinning, and all I could do was to wait for her words.

"You dress up nicely," she said. "Not too terribly bad for a farm boy." She offered her hand, which allowed me to overcome my lack of decorum. Still, I ignored her slender fingers.

"These old things?" I said, waving my hand before my blouse. "I simply threw these on at the last moment. You, my dear child, are merely drawn to my manly physique."

"Well, I do like your hair. Is it tied with a scrap of bridle from your mule? It certainly resembles his tail, full of burrs and briars."

"My hair no more resembles the tail of a mule than your bosom resembles the udders of a cow." I step close and lean to her ear. "Unless you happen to moo. Shall you moo for me, young maiden, when I spank your bottom for being so bold and insulting?"

She swatted my arm with the fan. "Get away with your stinking self. You smell like what you mule leaves within a stall."

At this, Luisa, my face grew warm, for I believe cleanliness is akin to Godliness. I even keep my teeth clean on this island now by scrubbing them with a chewed stick instead of a toothpick.

Your mama fanned my face. "Oh, do not be angry, farm boy. I did not mean to make your sweet cheeks so pink."

As I opened my mouth for a retort, a young dandy of a fellow, wearing pantaloons and smelling of hair tonic, strutted up like a rooster and bowed to your mama. "I have come to remind you of our dance, Ju—"

I leaned close to the ear of your mama again, Luisa. "I wager you offered him more than that." Then I left to find a glass of wine amongst the refreshments at the table of our host.

I would continue, but Sancho waves me toward him and Barros. "He is awake and wants to tell us something."

I kneel by Barros. Sweat beads his brow. His forehead is splotched with more white than pink, as if the blood is not flowing throughout his fevered body. Sunken within his skull, his eyes roll beneath the lids, like a man either within a dream or a nightmare, or one making an important decision. A tongue licks chapped lips, cracked at the corners, and his eyes open to slits. "Brothers," he manages, his voice a hoarse whisper. We lean close and implore him to rest, but he shakes his head once, twice, and a third time. "Death is but a door to another land, but more than anything I want to return home."

I understand this more than he can express. "We all do, Barros."

Sancho leans closer. "Of course, old friend. Lie back and rest."

"The—" Barros coughs weakly. Like a furnace within the underworld, his breath reeks of decay. "I suppose my legs are not fit for eating. Whatever of me is, I bid you use me as you used Mateo. This is my final wish, and it must be so."

Sancho takes his hand. "It shall be as you say, Barros, my friend. It shall be as you say."

Beneath the paper-thin lids, the slitted eyes, dark as storm clouds, roll my way. "And you, Carlo … I know the death of our savior Mateo left a hole within your young heart. Shall you honor my final request?"

Taking his other hand, I nod. "Yes, my friend. I shall do as you ask."

A brief smile passes upon his lips. "Cantante is the finest Spanish stallion my old eyes have ever beheld."

The word "is" makes me swallow my welling grief, for Cantante is—and forever shall be—"was."

"Do not be so forlorn," Barros says. "For like when I told you I suspected land was near, I also suspect your fine black stallion is near. Do not—"

A spasm grips Barros. He shudders and collapses fully, chest rising slower ... slower ... and slower still ... until it rises no more.

Wailing bitterly, Sancho clutches the hand of his friend to his chest and rocks back and forth. Tears wet the stained blouse, creating dark circles like thunderclouds. Violent hitches spasm within his throat, as if he is a young child crying to the point of hiccupping.

I cannot stand the sight of such intense anguish, so I go outside to escape it, closing the sail to muffle those terrible wails, high pitched and tight within the throat of the only man now upon this island except for myself.

Over the sea, storm clouds gather, almost as black and menacing as the storm that sank our ship. Lightning flashes and a bolt sizzles into the gray water. Thunder immediately crashes. The cool breeze gusts, sending stinging sand against my ankles.

What manner of storm is this, to cataract out of the blue afternoon to this island when it is nearly winter? Once I saw this same scene at Palos de la Frontera. Old men and women crossed their chests and shuffled into stonework houses. Vendors pushed their carts along the cobbles, ignoring potatoes, carrots, onions, and other vegetables spilling out beneath the clattering wheels. Mamas pulled sons and daughters beneath striped awnings. Papas wrapped their arms around them, peering up into the impossibility of such a thing.

I feel I am within the storm of my life. I have left so much to gain so little, and only death may bring me my wife, who is the most earnest desire of my heart.

No, Luisa, I shall not abandon you by seeking death. Regardless of the challenge, I shall do my best to stay alive and return home.

A feather-soft finger caresses my cheek. *Ah, Carlo, my beloved, you are so firm in your convictions. Some things, however, such as love, are worth waiting for.*

The voice, medium toned and true, is unmistakable. I whirl around, expecting what, I do not know, but I search regardless. Is it really you, my love? Have you come to take me away to be with you in Heaven?

You are not listening, Carlo. As you told me that night at the festival, listen with your heart. If you do, you shall find purpose beyond measure … beyond measure … beyond …

The ghost voice fades, and I shake my head. I must be—have to be—going insane.

The sail opens. Wiping his eyes with tattered sleeves, Sancho comes out. I have no idea if he has decided to honor the wish of Barros, that we should use his body for food, but I shall not do so. Still, the subject must be broached, for I have no wish to be here for what shall happen beforehand. Time, though, is called for, and I shall allow Sancho time to speak about that particular subject before I do.

"I am sorry for the loss of your friend," I say to him. "How he died after only three days shocked me. I would think it would take longer for his wounds to—"

Eyes bloodshot, nose running, Sancho whirls toward me. "Shocked, you say? Have you looked at yourself lately? Your bones are so visible, you resemble a beggar lying dead within the gutter of a city. We are on the verge of death every moment of every day. We do not eat enough. When we do it is all meat. A body needs more than that to survive properly."

I suppose his statement comes from the knowledge of being a cook. He is correct, however, for Mama never failed to have at least two vegetables with our meal each evening.

"You are correct, Sancho. However, I do not know what we can do about it except wait for rescue."

Sancho spits upon the sand, faces me. Twisted with contempt, his face mirrors his gesture. "I have not said anything about this so as to not upset anyone. I think I know where we are, or at least the general area where we are." He rubs a toe across the wet spot upon the sand. "We have no more chance of rescue than my spit turning into a snowflake."

"I do not believe it. We cannot be much farther north than our original course. Surely a ship shall—"

"Do you not recall how we were within that storm for two days?"

"I do, but—"

"I floated within that damnable barrel of fish for most of another day. I do not know the name of that type of storm, but I have heard of them. Not only have they destroyed ships, they can blow them hundreds of miles off course."

"You ..." My knees buckle at the weight of this news. I sit upon the sand before I fall to it. "You think we are hundreds of miles north of our original course? And you think you know where we are? How do you know of this place?"

Sancho sits cross-legged. "Have you heard of Pedro de Quexoia?"

"No, should I?"

"He was the first Spaniard to come this far north."

"When was this?"

"1520."

I sit up straight, eager at the news. "Why, that was only last year. Surely another ship shall—"

"Be quiet and listen. I spoke with one of his crew at a tavern in Spain. He said the place was so desolate—his words, not those of Quexoia—no colony could survive. That, Carlo, means no ship shall ever come this way again."

"But how do you know it is this place?"

Sancho spreads his hands. "He described it exactly like this … a wasteland of sand and brush and crooked trees, where the only prayer one might have is to die by misfortune, rather than to die slowly by starvation." He points at my face. "Which, as I have been telling you, is what we are doing."

You still are not listening, Carlo. Remember that night at the festival, for your purpose awaits you.

Luisa, the words of your mama can only mean that Sancho is wrong, and my purpose is to return home to you again one day. I shall not argue with him further. It would do no good, and it would also create hard feelings. We have gone from four to two, and we must work together to survive. Seeing the knife of Barros within the belt of Sancho, I stand, for it is time to discover his intentions toward the body of his friend.

I gesture toward him. "I see you have his knife within your belt."

"What of it? He does not need it anymore."

"Shall you do as he requested? I shall not, but since you used Mateo in such a way …"

Sancho leaps from the sand and rushes toward me, driving his hands into my chest and shoving me down to stand over me. "You think you know everything," he says, spittle hanging from his trembling lips." He grabs my collar. "But you do not know me."

As I attempt to wrench his hands from my collar, he drags me into the path to the beach, made all the easier by my pitifully thin condition.

"Stop struggling," he growls. "You need a lesson in assuming things about people. We are all each other has now, and there can be no more lies between us."

The dense brush rushes by. Sand gathers at my belt and works into my breeches, gritty against my buttocks. I am as helpless against this wiry old man as if he were my very own papa, dragging me outside to switch my backside for performing some mischief as a boy.

The crash of the surf nears. Before we reach the beach, Sancho turns into a narrow path, where I had seen him use to attend the fire to smoke the flesh of Mateo.

His steps pound the sand. His breaths rush forth like the wind. He stops, lets me go, and points. "There, what do you think of your damned assumptions now?"

I get up to look the way he points. Similar to the fire we used to smoke our fish, with a frame of sticks covered by a section of sail, the same type of contraption sits, blackened embers beneath it. "What of it?" I say, putting steel in my voice.

He grabs me by the arm, pulls me along, and throws me beneath one of those bent and twisted trees, where I fall face down to see a cross made of sticks lashed together with rope. I rise and face him. "You buried the offal of Mateo. Should I find a shell and offer it to you as reward for doing the Christian thing?"

"Young fool, why do you think I left here and returned to the shelter to partake of a few bites of those fish we caught?"

"I supposed you could not stomach more than a mouthful of human flesh, so you—"

Sancho nods. "Do you now see the error in your assumption?"

Confusion muddles my brain, until a hint of clarity appears. "You … you didn't …"

"No, Carlo, I could not eat the flesh of our friend no more than I can eat the flesh of Barros."

I stand, touch the tip of the cross, and face Sancho. "Then why did you justify it with your talk of the Christ feeding the disciples with his body?"

"It takes more than a physical struggle to survive upon this island. Is that not clear by now?"

"Undoubtedly, but you already knew we had no chance of rescue."

Hanging his head, Sancho shakes it wearily before facing me again. "One never loses hope. I do not know what fate awaits us, but I hope at least one of us lives to embrace happiness once again, even if through tragedy."

These words, similar to the words of your mama, Luisa, comfort me. I nod solemnly and pat the shoulder of my friend. "You are correct, Sancho. Now, let us prepare Barros for burial beside Mateo."

As we return to the shelter, I realize how another hope clings to my soul, which is for neither Sancho nor myself to ever be forced to add a third grave to our small cemetery.

Especially my own.

December 20, 1521

Dear Luisa,

Another month has passed, another month of scavenging for the scraps of dead and decaying things along the beach while hoping they are not too rotten to smell and not too spoiled too taste, which they always are. Even the gulls ignore the detritus of the sea, so Sancho and I know better than to use such stuff as bait for the crabs within the calm waters behind us.

Clouds rarely darken the sky. When they do, they leave nothing more than a smattering of rain within our buckets, reducing us to a single swallow of water three times a day. We even scrounge upon our hands and knees beneath the strange, twisted oaks in search of any acorns the birds may have missed. Surprisingly, unlike most acorns around the farm at home, the ones we find are sweet. Although I do not know if birds can taste, it is no wonder they have eaten the majority of these. Still, the few acorns we find would not feed a mouse, much less a man.

One morning, Sancho reported the tracks of a sea turtle to the south and talked on and on about the delicious flavor of turtle meat, making me salivate. He also mentioned the flavor of their eggs hard boiled, but says it is not the season for them as they lay them in the summer. Although I hope of rescue well before then, despite his revelation that it is impossible, the idea of boiled sea turtle eggs remains within my mind, as well as turtle meat. Sancho, however, says they rarely come ashore for anything other than laying eggs. Regardless, if we see one, we shall be upon it like a pair of ravenous hounds.

The idea of the warmth of summer does not last long, for it is now cold enough for the occasional frost, and many is the morning when it sparkles upon the trees and brush as I search for sticks with which to stoke the fire.

Aside from the sweetness of the acorns within these oaks, another interesting fact is how they have not lost their leaves yet, nor have they changed their colors, remaining the same shade of green. This is a wonder to me, for despite the rarity of the frosts, the icy wind blows with steady commitment, freezing my backside through the openings within my wall to the point of forcing me to turn over several times a night in order to keep both my front and back from freezing. Sancho, the lucky devil, receives no wind off the sea, for he sleeps upon the other side of the shelter. I asked him about changing places one morning as I awoke with chattering teeth, after a particularly icy wind made me wonder if my backside were frozen, but he simply smiled and told me his mama did not give birth to any fools. I did not think about it at the time, but I did not care to sleep close to him regardless, for his guts rumbled within the night like a man about to pass gas, which he does almost as often as Barros.

This morning is like any other. After I finish my writing, sip my water, and go into the bushes to relieve myself—Lord knows how I drink enough to manage it—I don my piece of sail for a cloak and walk the beach, more in wonder of what I now have grown accustomed to as natural beauty instead of natural dread.

As always, the gulls swoop and clamor, the crabs scuttle and scurry for their holes, and the backward-kneed birds plunge their beaks into the sheen of wet sand like plump woodpeckers, seeking whatever minuscule creature upon which they feed. I stop for moment, amazed at how a chevron of pelicans can glide so close to the waves without touching the surface, or even above the crests frothed with white and the troughs hued emerald green.

Yes, I say to myself, whatever tragedies Sancho and I have experienced, and are experiencing, God has surely touched this place with the tip of His artistic finger.

Whenever Sancho and I talk, I sense a change within him as well. Possibly it is acceptance at our fate, although he never admits it. However, Luisa, you must not worry, for I accept nothing but my return to you, whenever and however that might occur.

When I near the dune and the path to the shelter, Sancho is already there, hand at his brow while he observes the sea. His cloak of sail flaps about him. His straggly hair flutters around his head like black cobwebs. The legs of his breeches are now tattered between knee and calf as mine are. If not for our skeletal frames, with barely enough flesh to make us appear human, we might pass for those backward-kneed birds, their legs as thin as two wheat straws.

At the base of the dune, I look up at him. For whatever reason, he smiles broadly, blackened teeth glinting within the morning sun. "Why the smile, Sancho? Did a lovely maiden come to you within your dreams last night to keep you warm?"

"Cannot a man smile at a beautiful morning such as this, Carlo?"

I trudge up the dune, bare feet slipping within the gritty sand warmed by the sun. Sancho takes my hand and pulls me up beside him. "If a maiden within my dreams brought me a platter of roast pork surrounded by all manner of vegetables, I would smile all the larger."

Tempted to question his good humor, I do not, and he shoves my shoulder good-naturedly. "Why the sour countenance? Did you not enjoy your stroll?"

"For a cook upon a ship, you speak with an education, using such words as 'countenance.' How much of your life have you withheld from me?"

"Enough to keep it intriguing. As far as my smile, I have an idea to catch those pesky crabs within those calm waters that separate our island from the native lands.

I return the shove. "Must I beg for the remainder of your epiphany?"

Those dark eyes widen, and he smiles again. "'Epiphany?' My, what a word. The monks at the La Rabida monastery taught you well. Come to the shelter. I shall tell you about my, as you say, 'epiphany.'"

As we walk along the path, Sancho whistles like a man who has had more of an epiphany than about catching crabs. Not only has his entire demeanor changed, he actually strolls in enjoyment, reaching out to touch those crooked tree limbs as if they are the hands of a long-lost love.

At our small clearing I stop, and he holds the sail to the shelter open. "There are no epiphanies out here, Carlo. Come, sit and help me begin construction on mine."

He ties the sail back, for light I suppose, and drops cross-legged to his sleeping place. I do the same and watch him expectantly. Grinning like a cat who has caught a dozen mice, he takes a stick from our stores near the smoldering embers, prods them into flames, and rubs his hands together near them. I do the same, for the cold air has chilled me.

Finished with his hands, Sancho takes one of our ropes and throws it at me. "Unravel that while we talk. It is part of my epiphany." He takes another rope, starts teasing the strands apart, and I do the same.

His whistling certainly surprised me, but now he hums like a woman at her knitting. I huff a huge breath to convey my impatience, and he answers with a cackling laugh.

"Old rooster," I say, "whatever has you crowing must be very entertaining indeed, for I have never seen you act in such a way."

"It is amazing, Carlo, how life has dealt us both tragedy and epiphany. Were I not upon this fine island, happiness would not have found me here."

"Have you found a chest full of wine from the ship? If so, please share a bottle so my happiness matches yours."

"No wine, my friend, but clarity of thought has brought me this happiness." Sancho arrives at a knot within the rope, which he picks at with his fingernails. "I assume your mama and papa raised you well, yes?"

"Wonderfully well."

"Mine did not. Well, my papa did not. He had gratitude for nothing except strong drink and complaining about anyone who had more wealth than him. He could not see he had less wealth because he only worked enough to purchase a bottle every night."

I nod in agreement. I knew such men, and their lives were filled with discontentment.

"My mama did her best with what she had," Sancho continues. "Thank Heaven I was the only child, for Papa did not earn enough to keep Mama and myself fed. This reduced her to begging within the streets, which I understood." The shoulders of Sancho tighten in a spasm, then relax. "Until she became a harlot."

He places the rope aside and leans back on his elbows. "I am ashamed to admit it, but when Papa found out, my anger matched his, and when he beat her for it, it was as if every fist he threw were my own."

"I am sorry for your troubles," I say, "but perhaps you now understand how much she loved you."

"I have for a time, but not until I left my own home to sail upon the sea, for ..."

His words trail off, as if he were going to speak about either beating his wife into a cripple or killing her, if either of those stories is true. I lower my eyes, continuing with the rope. If he decides to speak about his past, it is his decision, and I shall not press him.

"Carlo."

I raise my head. "Yes?"

"What is the worst thing you have ever done?"

"I am nothing but a simple farm boy with fine parents, Sancho. Nothing more, nothing less."

Sancho snorts. "I know not why you and your fine horse boarded the ship—you both looked like shiny new coins next to us tarnished souls—but it must be more of a reason than adventure."

I hold in a sigh of relief at the fact that he does not know about you, Luisa, for I prefer keeping my personal issues to myself. My guess is the captain and his first officer, God rest their souls, possessed enough honor to not spread rumors.

"What is that I see within your eyes?" Sancho says. "Ah, I know. You left because of a woman, with your handsome self."

The temptation to ask about his wife flares heat within my cheeks.

"Do not worry, Carlo. I see embarrassment within your face and shall not mention it further. If there is anything I know, it is how a man must have his secrets."

He sits up to take the rope again and picks at the knot. "This rope is like us, Carlo. We are the length and the knot is a point within life where we made a terrible mistake, and where we judge ourselves for that mistake." Sancho stops picking. His eyes, dark and intense, focus upon me. "Do you remember what Mateo said about the Spanish slaughtering the natives to the south for their gold and silver?"

"I do, and I think he was correct in his assessment."

"No doubt, the people of the future shall agree and judge the Spanish harshly. However, we are products of our time." Sancho pokes his chest. "Like I was a product of my papa, which led me to do unspeakable things. Do you think it acceptable to judge me for being a product of my papa?"

"With the way he treated you and your mama, I suppose one should understand how it affected you."

"Do you think I would have done those unspeakable things had I been born to a mama and a papa such as your own?"

"I think it unlikely."

"Those people of the future should have been born in our time and lived in our steads. Then they would have become products of the present like the Spanish are products of our present." Sancho pauses. "And this is the important part … for if the situations were reversed, the Spanish would likely be as morally enlightened as those people of the future, and they would never dream of behaving as they do now."

Hearing such wise words from this most unexpected of men impresses me, and they give me an idea also. "Are you saying you forgive yourself for your past because you understand how you became a product of the cruelty of your papa?"

"I certainly do. Only this morning, however, and it gave me a new outlook on life. Still, my only regret is not asking my wife for forgiveness for …"

That same hesitation tells me Sancho has not fully forgiven himself. What it shall take for that, I do not know, for that burden rests upon many a pair of shoulders, sometimes without the bearer even knowing it.

A stick strikes my chest. Grinning at me, he lowers his hand to his rope. "Get to work on that rope for my epiphany."

I glare his way. "You never said what your epiphany is."

"It is simple, Carlo. It is a crab trap."

December 20, 1521

Dear Luisa,

Sancho insists upon unraveling most of our rope. He also insists upon braiding it like I did your hair, saying he needs as much as possible for the crab trap, but in a smaller diameter. I ask if he is making a net. Laughing, he says no. Grinning, I ask if he is making a noose to lasso the crabs with, as if they were horses, and he says no again. Finally, I ask if he is making nooses for us to hang ourselves with if rescue does not come. This time he actually guffaws and slaps his leg, saying we are so thin, a thread would perform the task admirably.

When he declares enough rope is braided, he stands to stretch his back, groaning about his age. "Now," he says, peering into my eyes. "I wonder if I might have a page from your journal, along with a quill and ink?"

"Might I inquire as to why?" I ask, looking up at him.

"I would like to draw my plan before I begin."

I go to the chest, tear a sheet of parchment free, and return with a quill and ink. "There you go."

He taps his chin for a moment, scratches his head for another, and drops the items to his sleeping place. "I have it within my mind well enough. Let us gather some sticks." At the door, he stops to face me and point at my belt. "Good, we shall need your knife. The sticks must be cut from the arms of those old men with their crooked limbs."

I follow him to one of the trees near our clearing. "My mama purchased crabs at the market and boiled them. How do we cook them without a pot?"

"I have never done it before, but simply setting them backside down within hot embers should work." Sancho draws his knife and uses it to point at a limb. "I need several like that one. See how it is about as round as your thumb?"

"How long?"

"I think as long as from your fingertips to your elbow."

"Ah," I say. "You plan to make a cage with a small opening. We use whatever might work for bait, and when the crab goes in, we pull the cage in before it can get out."

Sancho nods. "You are much more intelligent than you appear, Carlo."

I shove his shoulder. "You should smile when you say that, fellow castaway, so I know you are joking."

Sancho shoves me back. "Who says I am joking?"

Shaking my head at his unfamiliar humor, I choose a limb and take my knife from my belt. Despite the cold wind gusting into my cloak, my underarms soon grow wet with sweat, which trickles down my sides. If I were not so used to my own stench by now, I am certain I would find my sour odor appalling.

The rest of the day passes with the sounds of knives whittling wood, the scrape of metal upon shell when we sharpen them upon the sea shell Sancho gave me that time, and the sun lowering within the western horizon in a display of darkening yellow, orange, and finally, the red ball turning deep crimson, like iron within a forge before it is crafted into a horseshoe.

This thought reminds me of Cantante, and although my grief at losing him has eased, I cannot help but wonder if I shall ever see the horses to the north again, as well as those to the south. When Sancho and I walk to the south like we usually do in the mornings, I shall make an excuse and walk to the north, in hopes of getting a glimpse of them.

Our stack of limbs soon reaches almost to our knees. Sancho belts his knife and so do I, and he suggests we return to the shelter for the night.

The next morning, we take the braided rope and sit to lash the sticks together in the shape of a square, except with a crab-sized opening on one side. That task done, he ties a length of rope to the same side as the opening. "See? When enough crabs enter, we pull them in for a feast."

I belt my knife. "I have never seen enough here for a feast."

"If you had waded into the water, you would have."

"Is that your way of saying my feet smell like bait?"

"We should both wade in." A grin reveals blackened teeth. "Then our trap would fill to overflowing. I shall take the trap to the calm water while you search the beach for bait."

I dash to the beach as quickly as my weakened legs allow, with plans to surprise him by catching mole crabs for bait. When I reach the sand shimmering with salt water and foam, no Vs show themselves as the water withdraws. Determined to find the Vs within the sand, I walk north within the cold surf, concentrating on every grain of sand and every bit of shell turning over as the water swishes toward the sea. A flock of those backward-kneed birds rises up almost beneath my feet, white and brown plumage a blizzard of feathered snow, and I stop.

Concentrating so hard, I have walked very far without looking up. On the beach ahead, three mares stand side-by-side, staring at me. Nostrils flare. Heads shake. Tails whip. Hooves stamp the sand. If a stallion were with them, the lucky fellow would have a harem of these three lovely ladies with which to mate. Their sides, however, bulge normally, and even if they carried foals, it might be too soon to tell. How I wish Cantante were with them, to sire a son to continue his lineage and keep me company all the days I must live upon this island.

The way the mares observe me hints at how they may have gone wild. To test my theory, I take another step. With loud snorts of suspicion sending twin rods of haze into the frigid air, they whirl and trot away, sand flinging from hooves, manes flowing across arching necks, tails high and proud, and I am left awestruck at their beauty.

My task calls. I continue northward until I locate a gathering of telltale Vs within the wet sand, scoop two handfuls, and return to the shelter.

Sancho is nowhere to be found, not inside the shelter nor by the calm water, where the crab trap waits. I dig a hole within the sand and drop the mole crabs in to keep them from scurrying away.

"Ho, Sancho!" I call, but I receive no response. I search the sand near where we built the crab trap for his footprints leading in a different direct than toward the calm water. Narrower than mine, they give clues to his path, which goes in the direction of the graves of Mateo and Barros. Since he is in such a good humor, possibly he intends to say a prayer of good morning to them, or to wish them well in Heaven.

Like always, as the sun rises, the wind increases enough to rattle the tree limbs. Step after step I follow the narrow footprints, for the original plan of Sancho was to smoke the flesh of Mateo here, which is why he located this place quite a way from the shelter to keep either Barros and I from seeing such horrid labor.

Almost within sight of the place, I stop to cup my ear. A sound like rope creaking within the rigging of our ship drifts upon the cold air, sending a shiver up my spine. Surely he would not do that, not with his high spirits, genuine smiles, and childlike teasing. I run as fast as possible, chest heaving, heart thrumming, and stop at the edge of the small clearing.

Above the crosses, swaying from one of the ropes we braided, Sancho has hung himself.

Words fail me, Luisa. I jump to grab the limb and pull him down, daring to think I can save him. I loosen the rope from round his neck and lower him to the sand between the crosses, but his bulging eyes and still chest tell me I am too late.

It is then that I see he is naked, for I suppose all I saw before was his contorted face. I also see his clothes, neatly folded upon the sand beside the cross of Barros. On top of them rests a flint and steel, the piece of parchment and the quill and bottle of ink, and the needle and thread with which Mateo stitched my wounded leg.

My imagination fights to understand the meaning of this tragedy, until I take the parchment into my trembling fingers.

> To my fine friend Carlo,
>
> No doubt you are astonished at what I have done. Perhaps you may recall how my only regret is not begging the forgiveness of my wife. God willing, that is what I am doing now.
>
> Use my clothes as you shall, for it shall surely grow colder upon this island. Use the flint and steel of Mateo as well. We are lucky with never allowing our embers to falter, but one never knows when they might if sickness occurs.

> Also, my friend, I hope you catch many crabs. If not, please consider using my body as food, for whatever demons have chased you away from home, it is my fondest desire that you return there to face them.
>
> Thank you for the blessing of allowing me to call you friend. You are the only person within the entirety of my pitiful life to have drawn me out of my shell of silence.
>
> Godspeed, Carlo.
>
> Sancho

The parchment falls from my limp fingers.

Not only have I borne tragedy at home, I have borne never-ending tragedy since leaving there. What is my purpose? Why did I not die instead of Mateo or Barros, and now, Sancho? Papa and Father Cristobal always taught me how each person has a purpose in life, but what mine may be at this very moment, I do not know.

However, the weight of my predicament is now worsened by the fact that I am utterly and completely alone.

I close the bulging eyes.

Why do tears fail me? Why do I not weep like Sancho did when Barros perished from fever? Perhaps I am dumbfounded, like when Cantante brought himself beneath the evergreen tree during my journey and saved my life with his warmth.

Regardless of these questions careening within my mind, more follow.

If I am to survive to return home to you, Luisa, I must see if the crab trap works. Then, God help me, I must choose whether or not to honor the wish of Sancho, which is to use his body for food.

Before doing so, I straighten the body and cover it with the cloak from the thighs to the face, adding sand to the edge so the wind shall not blow it away.

At the shelter again, I place the items Sancho left within a corner and take another piece of sail in which to wrap the mole crabs. It is then, within the midst of this empty place, that I sink to my knees and weep for the lost lives of the three men whom I was blessed enough to call my friends, now gone on to Heaven, where no more tragedies shall assail them.

I somehow manage to end my tears before very long. Sancho has bid me survive, and survive I shall.

After wrapping the mole crabs within the piece of sail, I tie it closed with a length of rope, work my way through the trees and thickets to arrive at the calm water, and crush the mole crabs to release their scent before placing them within the trap.

My teeth chatter as I wade through the whisps of marsh grass wavering with the wind. The gusts seem to call my name, telling me to go hang myself as Sancho has done, to end it now instead of dragging out my suffering, to release life and return to my wife.

Shaking my head to clear the whispered mutterings away, I lower the trap into the shallow water and take several steps away to hold the braided rope and wait.

Across the calm water, I think I see a slender trail of smoke rising from the native lands, only to be taken by the wind. Who are they? Are they savages or cannibals, or are they nothing more than myself, a human upon this earth with no other desire than to live? Surely they consist of men, women, children, babies, and older people, like in other countries and lands. Surely they have courtships such as marriage. Surely they love and enjoy physical love, for this is one of the strongest bonds among men and women who share their lives.

Part of me longs to see them, if for no other reason than to have my questions answered. Another part, however, the part who much desired the touch of my wife, is curious about their women, particularly their young women of my age.

A slight pull on the rope within my hands draws me away from such thoughts, and I peer into the translucent water of olive green. A crab, blue and iridescent, with huge claws, is easing across the rope. Wait for more or pull the trap in when he enters? It is better to wait, for I need as much nourishment as possible to dig the grave of Sancho.

Another crab enters, then another and another. I snatch the trap in and hold it up to thank Sancho for his ingenuity in devising it. However, my thanks are short lived, for I recall how he had me braid more rope than I thought we needed, and how he asked me for parchment, quill, and ink. Now I see it … he had planned his death all along, and I was a willing participant. No, I am a fool. Had I known of his plans, I would have attempted to sway him. Still, Luisa, this is another nail of guilt for my coffin, of which I am beginning to believe I deserve.

Inside the shelter, I add sticks to the fire to create enough embers to prepare my succulent feast. Although Mama cooked crabs at home, it has been a while since we ate them, as she did so on a whim.

The sticks catch flame. They crackle and pop, send heat against my face, and I am reminded of the bonfire at the festival where I met your mama, Luisa.

I left off with the dandy in pantaloons, claiming her for a dance. As they twirled and clapped, I waited within the crowd. Yes, I could have asked another young lady to dance, but I am one of those men who do not care for putting myself on display like a rooster who thinks he is cock of the rock.

"You know she is too good for you, Brother. Her papa owns this farm." At my side, Beatriz nudges me with her elbow. "I saw you talking with her before."

I huff a derisive snort. "She is nothing to me."

"Tell that to someone other than your sister. Look at you, all wild-eyed with wonder. You are in love and do not even claim it."

The music ends. Beatriz leaves me to my sulk. As I stick my tongue out at her back, someone tugs my arm. I turn around to face the dandy, who puffs his chest and cheeks exactly like the cock of the rock he believes himself to be. Not waiting for an inquiry, I lean forward and sniff. "Forgive me, sir, but I thought only women wear fine perfume?"

A sneer bares his teeth. "What would you know of finery, farm boy?"

"I know I prefer dung to whatever it is you are wearing." I look him up and down. "Is not that contraption uncomfortable?"

His eyes blink. "I do not know what you mean."

"With your narrow waist and wide hips, surely you must wear a corset. Tell me, is it supported with elephant ribs instead of whalebone? After all, fine sir, it must take such strength to hold all of your belly in."

Cheeks puff out and turn scarlet. "How dare you speak to me in such a—"

In a rustle of cloth from her dress, my future wife arrives. "Why are you talking to this farm boy?" she asks the dandy.

His cheeks grow flaccid, although they remain scarlet. "I was just telling him how he has no chance with you whatsoever."

Her folded fan taps his shoulder. "And you are whom to speak for me?" She takes my arm. "Come, let us away from this pantalooned fool whose perfume makes me sneeze."

Grinning while we leave, I look over my shoulder and wink at the dandy, who, with cheeks flaming, stalks away, pantaloons flaring like his puffed cheeks.

I pat the hand upon my arm. "I see you prefer farm boys to pantalooned fools."

Dark eyes at the level of my shoulder look up at me. "Only for kissing. Other than that, I prefer men with means."

"Ah, so you are after my fortune?"

Ignoring my remark, she leads me to the perimeter of the festival, where torches affixed to posts illuminate the grounds as the twilight fades from the day. Beyond the torches, we enter thick woods. At a particularly large tree, she stops to lean against it. "Your fortune? Do you have one of consequence?"

Brushing her cheek with the back of my hand, I reply, "Only within my lips."

"What about your voice? Do you sing?"

"I play the flute, does that not count?"

"Which means your lips are well practiced from all that puckering, yes?"

I lean closer, catching a whiff of some delicate scent, sweet and free, perhaps within the soap she uses. "Would you care to find out?"

She whirls from the tree. "I would rather hear your flute while I sing, for if you listen with your heart, you shall find purpose beyond measure."

I chuckle softly. "Is your singing such that it brings about this serious nature within you?"

"Cannot I be serious?"

"It is just that I have never seen you serious."

"You do realize we hardly know each other."

"Your papa is a fine man, for he understands the land as my papa does. Would their common qualities convince him to allow me to call upon you so I may know you better?"

I coquettish smile purses her full lips. "We shall have to see, farm boy. We shall have to see."

What a night, Luisa, one I relive often. I would continue, but the embers are red and shimmering, and I am ready to try fire-roasted crab for the first time.

First, I bring in one of the water buckets. Crab is salty at home, so I must assume it is here as well. Then I insert a stick into the trap to allow a huge blue and white claw to grasp it and lower this fine specimen into the embers, backside down. I shall not describe the antics of the death throes of this crab, but simply allow me to say it is not a pleasant sight. Still, within moments after it ceased struggling, the aroma of crab, briny and delicious, rose from the shell now turning red.

Waiting for the entire shell to reach this state tries my patience, and it is all I can do to not snatch it from the embers. Meanwhile, I add the other crabs, desiring they be ready immediately after I enjoy this one.

In contemplation of the salty sweetness, I pull the crab from the embers with one claw and allow it to cool within the sand before me. Moments pass before I can touch the shell without hissing at nearly burned fingertips. Realizing I need a better grip than a few fingers, I place a fold of sail upon the crab and draw my knife to crash the hilt down upon the shell. Fragments fly, and I raise a steaming white morsel to my mouth.

Oh, my, Heaven must have such food upon tables of cloud, along with bowls of melted butter for dipping.

I swallow the morsel, start to eat another, and stop as my lips tingle. Eyeing the crab, I think how strange a sensation—then my tongue tingles as well, followed be the same sensation creeping into my throat. Water shall cure this strange occurrence, surely it shall, but it does not. Moments pass. My chest rises and falls with apprehension. Is the crab spoiled? Is it rancid? Does it harbor some parasite? What ridiculous questions brought on by panic, for none of those things would react within me so quickly. Then what could it be?

My panic grows further, with breaths deep and full filling my chest, and then I know what Sancho must have felt as the rope compressed his neck and throat, for my own throat constricts in a sudden spasm, and air wheezes from me like an old man about to take his final breath.

Instinct tells me to run, but to where? To our small cemetery to lie beside Sancho and wait for death with no grave? No, it is now *my* cemetery, for I am about to perish all alone upon this accursed island, where I cannot even eat the one thing I could catch regularly.

My throat tightens. The muscles spasm harder and harder. The wheezing grows louder. I waver back and forth until I retch over and over again, bringing up that tiny morsel of crab along with bitter bile. Darkness fills my vision as I fall to my side, and the last thing I see is the sail above, billowing with the wind.

Why did I leave you, Luisa, like the fool I am? It is a regret I shall carry to the grave, and likely much sooner than later.

December 20, 1521

Dear Luisa,

Do the dead dream? They must, for the words of Sancho drive me mad. He speaks of roast pork, fat hissing upon coals. He speaks of gnawing the flesh from the bone. He speaks of licking the rich juice from his fingers, even sucking greedily at them.

Regardless of how our ship carried no pigs, I dream of them swimming within a row to this island. As the ship sinks, one lone pig runs along the backs of his brethren. At the last pig, who struggles within the surf, the running pig leaps from his back into the water and swims ashore. Dripping wet, he peers back to the sea, grateful his fellows have sacrificed their lives for his.

I wake as if from a trance. Sitting before the fire with darkness outside, I hold a bone within my hand. Bits of pink flesh cling to the joints on each end. The cloying mineral flavor of cooked blood clings to my lips. All I can suppose is my dream was real, for where would this delicious meal have come from otherwise?

Outside, I see I have been busy during my dream, for the contraption Sancho bult to smoke meat is filled with strips of it, and embers release their fumes from beneath the sail.

I study the bone within my hand. This pig gave his life for me, so he deserves the best I can do for him.

Using a burning stick from the fire for light, I pick my way through the brush and find my cemetery. An open grave is ready, so I must have dug it for the remains of this most special of pigs. A quick glance reveals more bones already there, including entrails. Both are partially covered with sand. It is amazing the things a person can do while he dreams.

I hold the flame closer to the bones and see dark strands of oily hair, which must hint at the head of Sancho. Without knowing it, I have even partially buried my friend after his tragic decision to hang himself. I do not suppose he shall mind sharing his grave with the pig. After all, they both have saved my pitiful excuse for a life, so it is almost as if they are the same.

With a section of rope still hanging from the tree limb over the grave, I secure the burning stick to it for light and fill the hole with sand. Using another section of rope, I construct a third cross to match the other two and place it at the head of the pile of sand. Then I sink to my knees and place my hands together.

As I am about to close my eyes in prayer, I smell a hint of smoke. Behind me, another contraption for smoking meat shows the glow of embers beneath the edge of the sail. How I walked by it, I do not know. Perhaps I am smoking more flesh from the pig. This makes sense, for one contraption such as this would not hold the flesh of an entire pig. Yes, it is amazing what a man can do while he dreams.

Hands together again, I raise my eyes to the heavens, where stars form a near endless blanket of twinkling light stretching from horizon to horizon.

Do you see these stars, Luisa? Are you holding the hand of my sister, or my papa, or my mama, while one of them points them out to you, possibly saying how your papa sees the very same stars at the very same time, and how he loves you more than all the stars within the sky?

You are the angel of my night, my sweetheart, and you come to me so often that it almost brings me to tears. To hold your hands within mine would be gladness. To sit with you in my lap would be comfort. How I long to hug you close and feel the caress of your hair against my cheek and the touch of your breath when you say, "Oh, Papa, I love the stars. Do you think Mama can see me from Heaven?"

"Yes," I would say, squeezing you tight. "I have no doubt she can see you." Then I would grow silent, for tears would fill my eyes as surely as those stars would wink back at me, glittering with unintended malice.

I close my eyes.

Dear Father in Heaven,

Please tell Mateo, Barros, and Sancho how I miss them, and tell them I fare well. Also, Father, please let them know how my heart fills with gratitude from knowing them. Grant them rest from their journey and, if it be Thy will, allow them to fellowship with loved ones passed on, as I wish to do one fine day with my beloved wife.

Oh, no, a voice says, silken and sweet. *You have a purpose to fulfill yet, my love. You must be strong, however, for much pain and anguish shall come to you yet, possibly even more than you can bear. Still, my love, although you may not believe my words, they shall be worth the heartache.*

Opening my eyes, I whirl around. Nothing greets me except the wind moaning within the trees and the surf crashing upon the beach.

Yes, Luisa, I trust your mama to the depths of my soul, but I do not know how much more pain and anguish your papa can withstand.

February 1, 1522

Dear Luisa,

The new year plus a month has come and gone without celebration. I despise how I even forgot the day of birth of the Christ in December. I hope you enjoyed it, perhaps with a fine supper, hugs, sweets, and a song or three. Do tell Beatriz her squeaky voice is not as fine as she thinks it is, and if you must, cover your ears firmly. Yes, my darling, I am smiling as I say this, for her voice is as fine as she believes it to be. Still, if you like, you can tell her how her brother thinks it is squeaky, but be prepared for a frown!

God continues to send enough rain for survival, and I take only enough smoked pork to strengthen me for my day, which includes my morning walks upon the beach.

I saw the three mares to the north again. Unless I miss my guess, the sides of two are slightly swollen with foals. I long to see the stallion in hopes he might be Cantante. However, I must abandon those hopes, as to cling to them is folly beyond compare.

On another day I saw them again, except this time my heart sank with disappointment when a stallion, brown and gleaming within the sun, trotted amongst them. He was young and frisky, kicking up his hooves within the surf, but I suppose he was old enough to be a papa to those foals.

A week later, I walked to the south in hopes of seeing the other group of horses. Their hoofprints marked the sand, and I even noted a place where one wallowed on his or her back, likely to ease an itch, but I glimpsed not a single one.

The days grow cold and the nights grow colder. I now sleep with all the sails from my departed friends piled upon me while practically hugging my meager fire for warmth. Sancho, God bless him, has relinquished his bed, so I am now able to rest well away from my wall, where the wind once chilled my backside.

It is on this morning when I wake to realize my supply of smoked pork shall only last a few more days. If only a turtle would strand itself upon the beach. If only another pig would jump along the backs of his fellow pigs and swim ashore. If only— I suppose I should end my complaints. It seems I shall starve soon and there is nothing for it.

You might remind me, Luisa, to search for those sweet acorns, but I have crawled beneath every tree for a mile in both directions, and all I received for my sifting through the sand was aching fingers, raw knees, and knotted muscles within my neck. Well, I did find a fistful of acorns, but they have long run out. Oh, and I discovered another reason why so few acorns are to be found when I venture further away from my shelter, and it is because the deer tracks dot the sand, meaning they eat those tiny acorns like the birds do.

A question I asked myself after seeing the horses to the south is where do both groups find water? It must be somewhere amongst the thickets, where they and the others frequent. The first time I searched, however, thistles and thorns like to have eaten me alive. Goodness, but horse hide must be the toughest hide in the entire world to bear those prickly burdens!

These thoughts remind me of the strength and endurance of Cantante, and how he saved my life that time beneath the evergreen. If only he would gallop from the depths with a plump pig upon his back, I would have food until the spring, when I might feast upon a turtle or her eggs.

Sitting by the smoldering embers, my cloak wrapped around my shoulders, the wind gusting and flapping my roof above me, I set my journal aside and lie down.

Emptiness is a beast gnawing at my insides. Soon it shall devour even my backbone, leaving me a dying worm squirming my death throes while within my bed. I sit back up and return to my journal. While I have the strength to place quill to parchment, I shall continue with my story of the courtship of your mama and I.

After the night of the festival, it was back to farm chores for my family. All I could do was hope for a glimpse of her lovely face at the market within Palos de la Frontera the next time either Mama or Papa needed something. Still, disappointment furrowed my brow when, each afternoon, I asked if they needed me to gallop Cantante there, perhaps for some special item for supper, or some tool for the farm, for all I received for my troubles were shaking heads and "No, thank you, Son. It can wait for the week-end."

Beatriz, of course, understood the meaning of my angst, and she teased me until I threatened to tell Papa she had a secret suitor. Although I did not believe this to be the case, Luisa, it must have been, for she went silent immediately, mouth snapping shut like your teeth upon a grape.

So, with my impatience bulging at the seams of my hope, it was all I could do to not saddle Cantante and gallop him to her home and ask her papa if I could call upon her.

That night at supper, between bites of stewed goat with tomatoes, potatoes, and zucchini, I waited for an opening to ask Papa if we were going to Palos de la Frontera the next day, which was Saturday. However, Beatriz spoke a whirlwind of sentences about Mama making her a new Sunday dress because she was outgrowing her current one. I was tempted to tell her the "outgrowth," for the lack of a better word, was certainly not her bosom, but I held my tongue. Mama said the dress had a few more months in it yet, and Papa said she looked perfectly fine wearing her current dress. Crossing her arms, Beatriz sulked while I cut my eyes at her, eliciting her reaction of, "Whatever you are you looking at, you had better stop before I—"

A horse snorted outside, followed by the clatter of wagon or carriage wheels upon the cobbles and a knock upon the door.

I sneered at Beatriz. "I wonder who that might be? Anyone special to you?" Of course, I was hinting at her suitor, but I had no earthly idea who might be out and about at supper time.

After dabbing his mouth with a napkin, Papa went to the door to open it, then opened it wider. "Sir Anthony, what a surprise. Please, come in."

I have not told you yet, Luisa, but Sir Anthony is the papa of your mama, and he was the last person on earth I expected to see that evening. I was in for another shock, however, for he turned and beckoned to his carriage, where your mama was standing, apparently waiting for his signal. She came to him wearing a plain dress with a blue scarf binding her hair, tied at the back of her tanned neck. A dark smudge stained her cheek, perhaps dirt, with possibly the same under her nails. I rose and bowed. "Welcome, Sir Anthony. I see you have hired a new farm hand."

He glanced at his daughter, lips pursing to stop a full smile from revealing his humor at my statement. "You are absolutely correct, Carlo, no doubt you are." He glanced at his daughter again and came back to me. "You know, I have had a most difficult time hiring acceptable farm hands. Most of them prefer dresses and handsome young men as yourself. Do you not see my dilemma?"

Stepping to our living area, Mama gestured toward chairs. "Please come in and rest after your long carriage ride. May I offer you refreshment?"

"We have just had supper," Papa said. "Perhaps some stew?"

"No, no thank you." Sir Anthony and his daughter took seats. For some reason, unlike her usual animated self, she kept her head down.

Mama, Papa, and Beatriz took seats as well. I stood by the fireplace, where I could watch the reactions of his daughter. The situation intrigued me, and I could not wait to hear the reason behind it.

Sir Anthony cleared his throat. "My apologies for interrupting your meal. I am aware of how strange this is, but I would like to settle it once and for all."

"Papa, do not embarrass me. I told you it was only—"

"Hush now, my girl. You breached the subject in song and I intend to know the meaning of your words." Sir Anthony faced my mama and papa. "This afternoon, as my daughter was feeding the chickens near the coop, she did not know I was inside, counting missing hens, for I think we have a weasel to deal with. As usual, when she does her chores, she was singing beautifully, except the words were of longing for a specific young man." He turned his gaze upon me. "And that young man is you, Carlo."

Beatriz snickered. Papa cut a reprimanding eye toward her, then faced me. "What do you know of this, Carlo?" I deplored his tone, as if I had spoiled the virtue of every young maiden within 100 miles.

"No, no, no," Sir Anthony said. "Please understand, I am not here to suggest anything untoward about your son. I have admired your family ever since we met, including your hard labor in making your vineyard a success. Saying that, if our two families were to unite in marriage, I would welcome it completely."

Mama clucked her tongue. "But they are children."

"Most certainly," Sir Anthony said, "which is why I suggest they merely begin a courting process."

I rapped my knuckles upon the fireplace mantel. "Am I not allowed a say in this?"

Luisa, the expression of your mama amused me to no end, as she raised her eyes to me and her mouth fell open. Regaining her composure, she waggled a finger at me. "You should feel honored I even consider such a proposal."

"I? Honored? It was not *I* who led *me* into the woods at the festival."

Sit Anthony cocked his head toward his daughter. "Well, girl? What say you about this revelation? Have you sullied our good name by taking advantage of this fine young man?"

"My word," Beatriz mumbled. "I never knew our name to be so fine."

"Enough," Mama said. "Go to your room and allow the adults to speak."

Silently, Beatriz did as she was told, closing the door with a bang behind her.

"Sir Anthony," I said, "no one has been sullied. Your daughter is simply a tease. However, before we consider your proposal, I have one of my own." I hurried to my room for my flute and hurried back, standing by the fireplace as before. "If she shall honor us with the song you heard, I shall play while she sings."

His daughter crossed her arms. "I would as soon sing for one of those goats within your pasture."

"That can be arranged," her papa growled.

My own papa stood and walked around to face me and me alone. He is like me, one who enjoys a fine laugh, and I could see his cheeks puffing and his tight lips compressing as he held his humor within. His contortions finally eased, and he leaned close to my ear. "Son, do you truly care for this girl?"

I nodded. He returned to his seat, and I face the dirt-stained face of my future wife. "Shall you sing for me, or shall I fetch a goat ready for your kiss?"

She faced her papa. "Must I?"

"If you love him as your song suggested, yes, you must."

"Hum it for me, please," I said raising the flute to my lips. "For I require the melody first."

"That is my Carlo," Mama said. "Always the gentleman I taught him to be."

A Beatriz-toned snort came from her door, where she peered out. "If Carlo is a gentleman, I am a nun."

"With that snort," I say, "you are a pig." I wave her over. "Come, little pig, for you have a fine voice. Let us perform that tune you wrote about Cantante. Our guest may feel more at ease and sing for us if you do."

Always willing to sing for an audience, Beatriz pranced to my side. I played the song through and nodded for her to sing.

I once knew a pretty little foal,
He was finer than the sea.
He grew to be a stallion bold,
And chased his ladies three.

The song, Luisa, rises and falls, as if the melody is a pony prancing within a pasture. From our practices, I knew to play it through again. I did so, and Beatriz began swaying her head side to side with the rhythm before she sang.

Soon we had three pretty little foals.
Bounding 'round the field.
How they danced and how they pranced,
Until Papa left for the sea.

You may question the last line, Luisa, but it was simple coincidence, for I never intended to go to sea with Cantante. It was only Beatriz searching for rhyming words as she wrote her song. Now, had a known the terrible outcome of my journey, I would have begged her to write more uplifting lyrics.

I played the melody again and, to my surprise, your mama rose from her chair to join me, apparently now in a mood to sing.

Beatriz sang the words again, and we formed quite the trio, with their voices blending wonderfully. Beatriz pointed to the window by the front door, where the black head and white star of my brother bounced in time with the music.

Smiling at the sight, you mama slipped her hand around my waist to pull me close, and such happiness I had never known.

At the end of the song, Mama, Papa, and Sir Anthony applauded. We three bowed, and then his daughter ran to the window. "Oh, what a beautiful stallion. I had no idea horses loved music."

"He is Cantante," Beatriz said. "I wrote my song about him. He always leaps the fence and comes to listen when we play it."

Sir Anthony stood from his chair. "Daughter, you may forgo your song of love, for it is obvious to me how you feel about Carlo."

My papa laughed. "I have never seen such happiness as those two together."

"As I," Mama said. "Perhaps we should forgo the courtship and have them wed on the morrow."

"I was jesting, of course," Sir Anthony said. "I would like this girl to spend a bit more time with her mama and I before she starts a family of her own." He gestured to his daughter to come away, and she winked at me before going to his side. "So, my fine songstress," he said to her, "when shall Carlo come to call?"

I must stop writing soon, Luisa, for my hand begins to shake. I do not know what shall become of me if I do not find food besides that horrible pork, which obviously has no value whatsoever. As it is, my bones protrude at odd angles, my chin juts forward like the bow of a ship, and my ribs resemble those of a fish skeleton upon the beach.

Upon my bed of sails, I rest before pulling them over me. I should have dug a fourth grave beside my friends and then fallen in before I came to my weakened state, allowing the sand to blow over me eventually, but it is too late now.

God bless you, my daughter. If I have said it once, I have said it a thousand times a thousand … I wish with every ounce of my being that I had not abandoned you so hastily in order to cleanse my soul of grief at the death of your mama. Please forgive me with your prayers, for I doubt I shall ever see you again to ask your forgiveness in person.

If I do not live through the night, know I love you with all of my heart.

Your papa.

February 2, 1522

Dear Luisa,

I do not know what keeps me alive. Perhaps your mama is correct, and I have some other purpose in life to fulfill yet.

I crawled outside this morning for a sip of water and to fetch my flute. When I near death, if I have enough breath left within my body, I intend to play the song that Beatriz and your mama sang, called The Song of Cantante. Perhaps he shall hear the notes from Heaven and prepare to greet me.

Shivering from my short excursion, I wrap myself within the sails again. The barest hint of smoke rises from the embers. I would stoke them with the few remaining sticks, but I do not see the need, for the cold has embedded itself into my very bones. God above, where is my savior Cantante when I need his warmth to comfort me during my final hours?

I reach back in time to that snowy night when he saved me, by working his way beneath the evergreen to lie down at my side. What a friend, for he knew my needs as if they were his own. Now he is nothing but a spirit, perhaps a seahorse galloping beneath the blue-green waves. Please visit me, my brother, if nothing else, within Heaven.

I drift in and out of wake and sleep. Above me, as always, my roof of sail flaps in the wind. If I listen ever so carefully, I hear the surf. It must be calm this morning, for it is but a whisper upon the sand. Gulls scream. Birds twitter. The embers send a gray twist of smoke upward, where it swirls at the peak in the sail. A gust soon carries it away, like I soon shall be carried away, a ghost rising to the clouds.

Around midday, I wake to a louder than average dream. No, it is not a dream but rain pattering upon the sail. Water gathers at a low spot and forms droplets that fall near me. All I must do to drink is shift my head. I cannot even do that, so I close my eyes again.

I wake once more, likely my final time. The sun transforms the very air around me scarlet. Perhaps the clouds are toward the west, lending that golden ball a brush with which to paint the horizon. Still, droplets fall, yet each time they splatter upon the piece of sail beside me, they do so slower and slower, until I realize I must wet my lips with one before I play my flute, for it is time.

In tiny increments, I inch toward the diminishing droplets. Hurry, I tell myself. You must honor Cantante before it is too late.

And then I taste the last blessed drop! It is a tide of crisp freshness upon my tongue, cool and clean and reviving me.

However, I cannot raise myself to sit, so I take the flute from my side and place it to my lips. Hesitant and sour, the notes quaver, but I manage a verse. However, I must pause to gather my breath for the remainder. As I wheeze in and out, what sounds like the soft nicker of a horse comes from outside the shelter.

Perhaps I am dead and do not know it. That is the only thing that makes sense.

A huge black head with a white star shoves the sail aside and enters. Cinnamon-colored eyes blink at me. "No," I say to this apparition. "You are not Cantante, for he is within Heaven awaiting me."

The horse continues in, black and sleek. He turns his head this way and that, as if he is appraising my home. Then he comes closer to sniff my hair, nuzzle my cheek, and lie down beside me.

Risking my sanity, I wrap my arm around his neck, damp from the drizzle. Blessed warmth seeps into my body, for this ghost-horse has read my mind like Cantante did so long ago.

I rub his neck, fingers tangling within his mane. He smells of fresh air and rain and sunshine. "If only you were my brother, with whom I could die and be happy."

The black head rises, followed by a disagreeing snort. Those cinnamon-colored eyes gaze into mine. He shakes his head once, twice, thrice, and lowers it once more.

"What is it you want, my ghost brother? The only thing I need is food, and you cannot provide—"

Can it be, Luisa? Has this ghost horse come to sacrifice himself as Sancho sacrificed himself, so I may live and return home to you?

I turn away from the horse, take my knife from my belt and thumb the blade. Sancho said to keep it sharp for a painless cut and I have done so, honing it against the shell until too weak to make enough strokes. The edge sticks to my skin. If I apply the least amount of pressure, I would need stitches like those Mateo sewed into my leg.

The ghost horse softly nickers like before, and I swear I see the hint of a nod. "Is this what you want, my ghost brother? Shall I cut the throbbing vein within your neck, to drink your blood and partake of your flesh? The same soft nicker. The same affirming nod.

Yes, Carlo my love. You must live, for God has a purpose for you yet. Do as your brother wishes … and live!

The knife falls from my shaking hand. Insane, yes, I must be going insane. My wife and Cantante are long dead now.

The horse raises his head and pushes the knife toward me with his nose, peers into my eyes again and lowers his head beside me. The meaning, like when Cantante bit my cloak and pulled me to his side within the evergreen thicket, cannot be clearer.

I take the knife and hold it to the pulsing vein within his neck. What is the worst thing that can happen if I severe the vein of a ghost horse? Shall the cool air of Heaven flow over my hand?

But the warm breath of this horse bathes my cheek. I cannot—shall not—

The massive head jerks into the blade, burrowing it to the hilt.

My God, Luisa, my God in Heaven. Warm blood pulses from the wound onto my hand and I jerk it away. Is this— Could this—

Another soft nicker. Another knowing gaze from cinnamon-colored eyes.

The mineral smell of blood fills the shelter. I retch over and over again, bringing up nothing but bitter bile.

Yet another tragedy to bear … one from which I shall never recover. My brother did not drown after all. He swam ashore and lived happily, either to the north or to the south. Then he heard my flute and came to me, sensing my life in peril.

It is one of the most difficult things I shall ever do, Luisa, but I shall honor Cantante and his sacrifice, for to ignore him and the words of your mama, when she said I still have a purpose in life, would be a sin that sends me to hell itself.

April 5, 1522

Dear Luisa,

Please forgive me for not writing you sooner, but spring is arriving upon this desolate island, and I have been quite busy.

First, as you might guess, my physical state is much improved because of Cantante. Such a brother I shall never know again!

My muscles are filling out, for I fed willfully the day after he gave himself to me. More rain filled my buckets. With enough water to drink and enough rich meat to consume, including the fat for energy as Sancho had mentioned, I soon rose to walk the beach every morning.

Still, sometimes late at night, when the wind moans through the trees just so, my grief joins it, until we become a pair of wretched souls singing and weeping pitifully until daybreak.

On a happier note, as I have said, spring is certainly arriving. Since that is the case, you would look up at me with your huge, dark eyes and ask, "But Papa, what about the mares with their foals? Are they not born yet? And is one of them black like Cantante, with a star in the center of his forehead?"

"No, my darling," I would say. "Horses are not like people, who take nine months to have their babies."

Oh, but I can see your eyes scrunching as you tilt your head to one side, curious for more information about how long it takes horses to have their foals.

"Now," I would say, setting you upon the fence and pointing to a mare with swollen sides, "it takes a mama horse about twelve months to have her foal. That, my dear girl, is an entire year, so if any of the mares upon this island have had their way with one of the stallions, she shall give birth around September or October of this year. What do you say to that?"

"That is too long a time, Papa. All I want to know is if Cantante shall be the papa of at least one."

That I cannot say, for the group to the north has a young stallion tending them, and Cantante has a bit of age on him. Remember how I said my papa bought him for me when I was but a child like you?

"That long ago, Papa? Why does he not have gray hair like *your* papa?"

I pause to smile at your comment, for Cantante is a bit gray around his mouth and eyes now. Well, I suppose the proper statement is he *was* gray around his mouth and eyes, now that he is dead, and his teeth were worn also. If the horses to the south have a younger stallion, he may have fought Cantante and won. What strength he possessed to swim to this island, and then, to come to me as I played my flute.

A sudden thought bursts into my mind—I am now part of Cantante, for his flesh has become one with my flesh, so perhaps I shall live as full a life as he did.

At this I must end our talk, Luisa. Since it is spring, as I mentioned earlier, I should continue my chores. No worries, my darling, for I shall describe what I am doing for you.

My roof of sail is sagging, so I tighten the rope to make a perfect V in order to shed rain. I also check the lashings securing the walls from the horse stalls to the sections of hull, but Mateo, with his strength, has lashed them firmly.

One thing I made sure to do was to remove the bloody sand from where Cantante died, then replacing the large hole with fresh sand. After that I used a tree branch to sweep my little cemetery, where four crosses now stand instead of three. Yes, Luisa, I honored my brother with his own grave when my strength returned.

I contemplate my four friends. Barros, with his jovial self, could be carrying on his foolishness with some beautiful angel by suggesting he fit her for new wings. Sancho, God willing, has made amends with his wife, finally putting his tortured soul to rest. As far as Mateo, I can only hope he finds a family to replace his mama and the hateful man she married. Cantante, no doubt, is galloping within green fields, kicking up his heels and courting many lovely mares.

I touch each cross in turn and say prayers of gratitude. At the last place beside the grave of Cantante, where I consider placing a cross for myself if I do not live, I cannot guess at what life—or this island—holds for me.

At the shelter again, I drag bedding out and hang it upon tree limbs to air. Then I check my stores of ink and quills. I may have enough to finish my journal, whenever that may occur.

To store my food, I use the old barrel that held the salted beef. I also found another barrel from the ship that had washed over the dunes to the south, to lodge within a thicket. After dumping out sand, I rolled it here, rinsed it as well as possible with my fresh water, and set it beneath one corner of the sail to catch what I hope shall be a deluge of spring rains, spawned by thunderstorms.

I have not seen a sea turtle yet. Since they lay their eggs in the summer as Sancho has told me, it is too early for them to come ashore. I hope, however, to discover such a delicacy then, for I shall never touch another crab as long as I live.

Nature upon this island is blooming more beautifully than I could ever have imagined, although it is a bit strange as well.

Unlike in the fall at home, the leaves upon the gnarled trees here are turning brown and are falling, replaced by tiny green buds. I am happy to say, however, this phenomenon reveals the songbirds that must have been eating the acorns, for they bound about the branches either warbling or chirping, until they spy me and flutter away. Surely they nest somewhere, including the gulls and those backward-kneed birds from the beach, so I must devise a way to brave the briars and thorns within the thickets when I search for their eggs.

On occasion, chevrons of those huge black and white birds honk as they wing northward, and it is then I realize they must be some type of geese. Goodness, what a meal one of those would be, roasted and dripping sizzling fat onto the embers!

Out upon the blue-green swells of the sea, dolphins arch their backs from the water. Once I saw a whale blow a cloud of mist, followed by his tail curving upward, only to descend into the depths. Of course, the pelicans glide low above the waves, sometimes lunging into the air and diving like feathered spears in their search for fish.

All in all, except for my loneliness and my inability to return home, peace, in a way, has found me upon this island. Nature, as I have known since I was a boy, has a way of sending calm when it is most needed, and I assuredly need it.

This afternoon, having satisfied myself at the cleanliness of my shelter and the small clearing in which it sits, I make my way down the slight hill to the edge of the calm water, where I caught those ill-favored crabs.

The marsh grass, tall and slender, rustles with the breeze. The head of a small turtle, whose shell appears to be painted, eyes me, blinks, and vanishes beneath the gray water. I wade in, searching for any type of fish I might catch, but each time I see a silver sliver of one, it darts away.

Then I see one that makes me stop in wonder, for it resembles a type of flatfish that either Mama or Papa would purchase at the market within Palos de la Frontera. It is mottled brown in color, with both eyes upon the upper side of the broad body. After Papa cleaned one such fish, Mama placed it in a pan with a bit of olive oil and salt, pepper and garlic, and we enjoyed a meal fit for a royal family. If only I could find a straight limb from one of those crooked trees to make a spear, I might feast as we did also, except on this very day for supper.

As I climb up the sandy rise to my clearing, a sound I have not heard since I was at home rises and falls within the breeze. No, I think to myself, there are no young women out here with lusty laughter on this warm afternoon.

A male voice laughs also. Past a small peninsula of marsh to my right, the bow of a vessel appears. Sitting upon the edge of the vessel in back, which appears to be a hollowed-out log, a dark-skinned man, who wears nothing but some sort of tanned hide covering his buttocks and groin, paddles along slowly. At the front of the vessel, bare-breasted in the sunshine, a young woman holds a spear at the ready, aimed at the water before her. Tied at the nape of her neck, her black hair falls to her waist. She wears the same type of tanned hide as the man, but a necklace of tiny shells encircles her neck. I would not think her beautiful, not in the strict sense of the word.

No, "noble" fits her much better as she stands there, eyes focused, arm bent at the elbow, muscles taught. Still, the sight of her breasts, small and upright, stir me to shame because it has been so long since I lay with my wife.

Her head snaps toward me and I duck behind the brush, heart pounding within my temples. No, she has seen something within the water, evidenced by her lowered chin. Above the surface of the water, the spear has three spread prongs instead of one, which shall make it much easier to spear a fish.

Her concentration amazes me, for she could be a statue of bronze. Then I notice how the man watches her also, and I realize they must be husband and wife—that is, if these natives have such a thing. His gaze is filled with admiration, like the newly-wed man I was at my young age of eighteen years.

The woman looks back at him and speaks. Attempting to understand her words is futile, for they come forth so quickly, they blur within my ears. She points at the water and shakes her head, so perhaps she is disappointed that some fish escaped her spear. The man speaks as well, and I sense a question within the upward lilt of his voice and the glint of humor within his broad smile. He leans forward to rub her thigh. She smacks his hand away and points at the water, wanting nothing to do with his advances. Still, as she returns to her statuesque pose, she laughs low within her throat.

How I miss similar scenes with your mama, Luisa. These two young people, teasing each other with love and sexual attraction, make my sadness all the more poignant.

He sets the paddle within the vessel and goes to the woman. I am certain she feels the wobble of the vessel, but she must either be ignoring it or welcoming it.

The man kisses the nape of her neck and she leans back against him, resolving the riddle of whether or not she welcomes him. He takes the spear and drops it into the vessel. She turns to him and he buries his face within her breasts.

My heart pounds all the harder. Shame heats my cheeks but I cannot turn away. How I envy this couple!

Kissing the man, the woman slips her hand beneath his tanned hide. The man must sense her readiness, for he turns her around to expose her buttocks and enters her. They gasp in unison. The man grasps her hips and pulls her to him. Over and over he pounds himself against her, until arching backward and moaning a guttural cry of release.

The woman whirls around and points at the floor of the vessel. Grinning, the man lies down, a husband who knows his wife needs more of him than he needed of her.

She settles onto his hips and rocks back and forth, head back, eyes closed.

Although shame burns my face even hotter, I cannot leave as I should.

Her rocking grows fervent. Her small, tight cries fill my ears. I would give almost anything to be this man lying beneath this woman.

She grasps the sides of the vessel, which mirrors her rhythm onto the surface of the water with tiny waves. Her rocking transforms into one long shudder of release as her gasps echo over the silence of my island.

The man palms her cheek and murmurs something. She smiles, rises to take the spear, and points at the water like a woman who has had her way with him and now expects him to paddle for his supper.

He pops her backside, takes the paddle, and returns to his task. The bronze statue focuses upon the water. The head whirls to one side. The spear plunges and rises with one of those mottled brown fish I saw earlier, pierced through and through.

It is a miracle, Luisa. This lovely young native may have saved my life, as finding food is still a priority. Not to mention, however, how she and her husband may have just created life, God willing, like your mama and I created you.

August 3, 1522

Dear Luisa,

My spring and summer have gone well. Quickly rising and ending storms fill my barrel, but I must keep it covered with a piece of sail to stop mosquitos from buzzing inside. On occasion—thank God not too much on occasion—a hot wind shifts from the west, and biting flies make me slap my exposed skin to where I appear to have been in a fight, with my arms and legs splotched red. During these winds, I sometimes catch subtle suggestions of wood smoke from the native village far across the large body of calm water behind my island. It is a good thing Mateo taught me to keep a small fire, for the last thing I desire is to have a native arrive upon my doorstep to eat me for supper.

The first time I thought this, I did not hesitate, but when I next considered the young man and the young woman, including how their teasing, laughter, and caresses were so like those of myself and your mama, I also considered how they may not be cannibals at all, but people like all people, with hopes, dreams and, as I saw that day, love.

I am certain you recall my mention of sea turtles and birds, and my belief in how both nest here. Shortly after my last journal entry, using a large dead limb I found from one of those trees, I used it to beat a path into a few thickets to locate enough eggs to satisfy my appetite for two mornings. "But, Papa," you might say, looking quizzically up at me, "how did you cook them without a pot and water with which to boil them?"

I would nod and agree, my dear, for Sancho and I never spoke of that. Still, I managed the solution of placing them by the embers of my fire, resulting in the most delicious breakfasts I have enjoyed since arriving here.

As far as turtle eggs, I did the same a week later, when I arose at sunrise and hurried to the beach to see one covering her nest. Thank goodness Sancho told me about them, and how they usually came ashore at night. Thank goodness as well for his insight on turtle meat and how to cut them from their shells, for his instructions resulted in several twilight meals of roasted flesh so fine in flavor, I might have been feasting within Heaven upon a cloud.

With blessings of both ample supplies of meat and water, I am able to report how I scrubbed the turtle shell with sand and now keep it within my shelter for a basin in which to wash my face every morning with a piece of sail. Imagine that, Luisa, all the comforts of home, except of course, without my darling daughter by my side.

"But, Papa, you forgot something. How did the pretty native woman save your life?"

Ah, my darling, how intelligent you are becoming, for I meant to tell you that very thing and it completely left my mind.

You see, although I said she saved my live, it was actually her spear with three barbs that did so. I have mentioned how the limbs upon the crooked trees upon this island are not straight enough to make a spear, which should be fairly long. Also, if I have not mentioned it, the wood from these trees is extremely hard, along with how any straight limbs of any length are larger and would tire me out before I could cut it from a tree, much less trim the other end.

"Please, Papa, tell me what happened without all that."

Now, now, allow me to speak, for it is good to know about trees and such.

To get a proper spear, I took several sticks from the smoker Sancho made and lashed the ends together. I then lashed two sticks to one end, but around enough lashings to make them separate, creating three spread spearpoints. It worked so well, I have been able to spear one of those mottled brown fish whenever I crave one. Yes, I shall answer your question before you ask it. They are as delicious as the ones my mama cooked at home, which means as long as those fish are present here during the cold of winter as they are now, and I have no reason to think otherwise, they shall feed me the rest of my stay.

With much relief at this thought, including regret that I had not thought of it before Mateo, Barros, and Sancho died, I am now as comfortable a castaway upon this island as a man in my situation can be.

I close my journal, set the quill aside, and hear your demand: "Papa, you need to tell me what happened when you started your courtship with Mama."

I would, Luisa, but it was the same as most courtships. We became familiar with one another past our initial attraction by taking long walks, either beneath the olive trees on the farm of her papa, or amongst the grape vines on the farm at my home. For the most part, agreement came easy. However, when we discussed where to live after our marriage, our families disagreed more than we did, in that our mamas and papas wanted us nearby for when any grandchildren arrived. From the red faces and cutting eyes when the subject arose, one would think we were falling off the face of the earth, never to be seen again.

Pausing from my writing, I sniff the air. The wind is switching from out of the east to the west, for I catch the hint of wood smoke from the fires of the natives. Then, every sound except the roar of the surf goes quiet. Even the constant screeching of gulls fades, as well as the chirping of the birds within the trees. I shudder at these unsettling changes, feeling as if someone is lowering myself or a loved one into a grave.

I start to place quill to parchment again, but the bitter smell of wood smoke grows stronger than it ever has before. Curiosity draws me outside, where, within the sky, hazy smoke, gray and drifting from the west, continues out to sea. After hurrying to the path leading to the calm water, I gasp at the sight before me. From the native village, smoke plumes upward from several sources within the trees. When it clears the green foliage, the wind curves it across the water and blows it toward my island.

At first I do not know what is happening, but when I consider how the smoke comes from several sources not associated with the distant yellow flicker of the campfires I have seen at night, my only conclusion is someone is attacking this village, including the young man and woman I saw that day, and they are burning their homes.

This revelation brings the words of Barros painfully back to me, when he said regardless of where he had been in his travels, someone was always willing to invade and kill in order to take what they wanted.

I sit upon one of the low tree limbs and watch for any vessels escaping the village, but even if they do, they are too far away to see. They are likely dead, the poor souls. What a shame for the young man and woman, as much a shame as when I lost my very own wife.

My heart aches with regret. I return to the shelter and lie down. The biting flies soon buzz around me and I slap myself, more to feel the sting of my hand instead of the anguish of losing those I love.

The sounds of my island gradually return. Gulls scree. The surf pounds. The wind whispers through the trees. Birds warble and chirp, returning to their lives of feeding, nesting, and simply living.

The day grows hot. Sweat beads my brow. It gathers beneath my underarms and runnels in cool paths before reaching my bed beneath me. Moist air fills the shelter, bringing with it the aroma of salt from the sea. The thickness of it clogs my throat, but I do not know if it is that or if it is my sorrows welling inside me.

As you know by now, Luisa, my love for your mama knew know boundaries. However, even with my shame at watching the young couple join together in love, I miss the closeness of such things. Still, to love again, even though I joined myself to your mama for all time with my vows, would be a welcome occurrence within my life. Do you think she would mind? I hope not, for love is love, and if I return home again, I would hope to find another woman who would love me as I love your mama, and I would hope another woman would love you as much as any children we might have as well. What a blessing that might be, including the joy of a brother or sister for my darling daughter.

Above the sail over my head, the brightness of the sun moves to the west. The shadows of tree limbs reach their way across the thick fabric, as if wooden claws scrabbling for a heart to squeeze, which is my very own.

I roll over to face the wall to the west of my shelter. At the upper edge, where the sail does not quite meat the graying wood, the sky bleeds golden, to orange, to scarlet, signaling sunset. I should rise and have a bit of smoked turtle and a few sips of water, but the memory of those two young natives, including how they shall never enjoy another moment together by a fire during a meal, talking of their day, their hopes, their dreams, drags me into an abyss of intense melancholy, even to the point of my eyes aching with tears.

Luisa, the tragedy of losing your mama, which bid me retreat from Spain and you, has made me a fool. How many fond memories have I kept alive, only to fully deny them by not writing her name within my journal? Yes! A fool!

Juliana, how I miss you. Still, in the short time we were together, you brought me happiness never ending, and a daughter who brings light to my darkness. Let me write your name three time so I may remember to never withhold it from my lips again.

Juliana.

Juliana.

Juliana.

Now, my dear Luisa, please forgive your papa for keeping the name of your mama away from you while I write. I now understand fully the tragedy of leaving you, for if I could not bear to even write the name of your mama, how could I have been thinking rationally when I set sail from you that terrible day last—

My God above! I have been away from home since last July! A year—no, a full year and another month! How could I allow time to slip from my grasp in such a way, as if the days were ether and my fingers were the bone-thin appendages of a skeleton grasping at my departing sanity?

Surely I have gone—or am going—insane. If I do not catch sight of a vessel soon, one which shall give me hope of a brighter future, I may as well hang myself like Sancho did, God rest his soul.

August 4, 1522

Dear Luisa,

I wake with eyes crusted from crying during my dreams. The worst dream of all, however, is the nightmare of how I do not recall those dreams. They must have been of your precious self, Luisa, and your mama and my love, Juliana, to make me weep in such a way.

My roof of sail is still. No smoke from the native village wafts my way. Birds warble and chirp while gulls cry, both tending to their breakfasts. Shafts of hard sunlight bore through the horse stall where I slept before Sancho died, to form bars of yellow across my body.

Rising from my bed, I notice the embers do not smoke. I hold my hand above them and receive nothing but the slightest warmth. After gathering dead grass from around the roots of the nearby thicket, I form a mound of it on top of the embers and strike steel to flint. Several strikes later, the grass smokes, and I lean close to puff it into flames. More sticks from my pile shall create glowing embers with which to cook one of those mottled fish this morning.

Spear in hand, I walk down the inclined path through the thicket. At the edge of the marsh, wading out into the cool water, I scan the water for a fish, spear at the ready. A few steps away, a pair of those twin eyes upon one side of a mottled brown oval upon the sand hints at breakfast. When I near, it darts away.

I pause from my hunt and peer across the calm water. Slivers of gray smoke twist into the sky, all that remains of the native village. Something hard brushes my foot, and I look down to kick a crab away. Ever since the one almost killed me, I want nothing whatsoever to do with them.

On the hunt again, I turn right—and stop. There, within the marsh grass, not fifty steps from my path, a small vessel like the one the young natives used that day is tucked within the green blades, barely visible. I suppose the eastward wind blew it here during the night, where it lodged itself within the marsh.

Considering how it might come in handy for fishing, I wade over. When I get near enough, I see I was correct about them being made from half a huge log, the inside hollowed out. Blackened wood is visible above the far edge, so the natives must have burned some of the wood out as well as cut it out, likely with some type of handcrafted woodworking tools.

Mere steps away, I stop again. Upon the floor of the vessel, a native lies face down. The legs are bruised and bloody below the tanned hide covering the buttocks and thighs. Black hair, dark and wet with more blood, cover the bare back, where more bruises splotch the skin as if this person were pummeled with fist after fist.

Strands of hair partially cover the one cheek facing me, which is also bruised and bloody. I go to the other side of the vessel, wriggle to it through the marsh, and stop to gape when I fully see the face. This is the young native woman I saw that day with her husband, and God help her, her belly is slightly rounded with child. More tragedy to bear, for the child must have been conceived that day in April, which means the poor babe is about four months old.

I pull the vessel free of the marsh and take it to my path. This pitiful young soul deserves a decent burial, and a decent burial is what she shall receive.

With the vessel dragged onto the sand where the tide should not carry it away, I start to pick up the lifeless body but stop. She should be stiff and cool, but her skin is supple and warm. I turn her over and watch her chest, which rises and falls slowly. My God above, her life has been spared as my life has been spared, for whatever reason I do not know.

I study her face. Her cheeks are bruised and one eye is blackened, but those injuries do not explain why she does not rouse. Then I touch a huge bump above her temple, and I understand the extent of her injuries.

As I carry her to the shelter, she moans softly and I see why—her right arm hangs at an odd angle, meaning it is broken. Also, her nails are filled with what appears to be skin and blood. What a battle she must have fought against her attackers.

I gently place her upon a section of sail and fetch water to wash the dirt and blood from her body and wounds. That job done, I ease the blouse Sancho left me onto her slight frame, for her customs may not allow a stranger to see her naked from the waist up. Now, to set her broken arm.

At home, a baby goat once broke a hind leg when it leapt to and from the back of the nanny goat and fell awkwardly. Papa said he might as well cut the throat and dress the bawling goat for our supper, but Beatriz cried so pitifully, he bound the leg with sticks and rags. Within no time at all, the leg healed perfectly, but the goat knew better to jump on the nanny again. "Let that be a lesson," Papa said to Beatriz. "Beware of foolish deeds, for jumping onto a nanny is like jumping into bed with an immoral man ... one shall gain you a broken leg while the other shall gain you a broken heart and a fatherless child."

With that memory making me grin, I cut two stout sticks, several strips of sail, and set the arm and bind it. The native woman moans, but she never wakes.

I sit cross-legged opposite the fire and watch her chest rise and fall. Dark lashes and brows. A somewhat upturned nose. A few scars upon her cheeks from the pustules many people get when they are young. The neckless of small shells she wore is gone, as is her husband, I suppose.

A sudden thought draws me upright. What shall she think when she wakes to discover me at her side and herself within a strange place? My long hair resembles that of her husband, but my clothes do not. My skin, olive-toned even in winter, is darkened from the sun. Still, I have no doubt she shall be frightened of me.

She moans again. The full lips purse. The bruises around her mouth and upon her lips must pain her, especially since her lower lip is swollen and split from the fist of her attacker.

I study her more intently. The right eye, which I have said was bruised, is also swollen terribly. I doubt she shall open it anytime soon.

Another thought occurs to me, this time taking me to her side and raising the blouse to study her slightly rounded belly. It is bruised as well, and I pray she shall not lose her baby, for love and purpose shall help her heal.

I go to the sea to remove my clothes and scrub them with sand. I also scrub myself as the sand moles wriggle beneath my feet, making me grin at their tickling selves. Of course, the gulls, pelicans, and backward-kneed birds carry on with their regular duties. One of those crabs that frequent the beach even scurries from a hole and stops to appraise me with those twin eyes upon the ends of twin stalks, as if wondering why this strange person has reddened himself with handfuls of sand. The idea is simple,

Mr. Crab, for I wish to be presentable to my guest when she awakes. "See? I say, taking two handfuls of sand to my hair and scalp to wash both, "I am ever the clean gentleman, and I do not wish to offend her with my sour smell as well."

One stalk lowers and rises, then the other, both in either question or curiosity, or perhaps to tell me I have lost my mind completely.

"Oh, no, my little friend, I am quite sane. That should be obvious by now as I have not attempted to eat one of your cousins within the calm waters on the other side of this island and vomit my insides out."

By diving beneath the waves, I rinse the gritty sand from my hair and scalp and return to the beach.

"Oh, Papa! Your breeches and blouse are still wet upon the sand where you left them! Shall you return to the young native woman as naked as the day you were born?"

I smile at Luisa's words. We are a pair, she and I, for we think alike to the point of speaking alike. Still, she is correct, so I hang my clothes upon a bush at the entrance to the path and don them when they are somewhat dry.

Inside the shelter again, where I sit to appraise my patient, I notice blood dripping from the back of her left arm, just below the shoulder. I go over to inspect a rather large cut, made as if one of her attackers slashed a knife toward her as she ran away from them. My God, what this woman must have endured when her village was attacked.

Now I thank God for Mateo and Sancho, for without them, I would not have a needle and thread with which to stitch the wound closed. She stirs during my efforts as I clench my teeth in concentration, but I have seen my mama sew enough clothes to perform a reasonable effort. I clean the wound, wondering how I missed it before, and am rewarded to see no more blood dripping from the stitched cut.

After returning the thread and needle to the corner of the shelter, where I keep my knife and the shell with which I sharpen it, I scoop water from a bucket with the shell, raise the head of the woman and offer her a sip. The throat reacts with a hesitant swallow, which transforms to a single cough before she takes more water. I assume she last ate the evening before the attack, so food is not as much a concern as water. However, she shall need to eat eventually.

I return to my side of the shelter and sit again, staring at her, for it has been so long since I have seen a lovely woman such as she.

"Now, Papa, she is not as pretty as Mama, is she?"

I suppose not, Luisa, but she is not beastly in the least.

"Could you love her like you loved Mama?"

I snort laughter. "Do not be foolish, child. I could never love another as I love your mama and my love, Juliana."

"I do not think Mama would mind."

Yes, she would, for she was quite jealous whenever we went to the market after we married. If a young maiden dared glance my way, the glare of your mama would cut them as quickly as a knife.

"I doubt she thinks those thoughts in Heaven. She would want you to be happy like I do."

You are both as sweet as the roses in the bed by our front door, Luisa.

A groan comes from the native woman. She licks her lips, groans again, and wakes. Her dark eyes focus upward, likely wondering what kind of fabric hangs above her. The head tilts to the right, and I prepare for her shock at the presence of a stranger.

Instead, she winces and touches her broken arm, then runs her fingertips along the sticks and tied strips of sail, hopefully admiring my handiwork. The dark eyes look upward again. Her chests rises and falls quickly, and I sense panic at her surroundings. I rise to sit at her feet, and her gaze finally meets mine.

Fear and confusion abide within her drawn features, within her widened eyes, until tears flow down her cheeks. She holds a single trembling hand toward me like a woman reaching for her husband. Our fingertips almost brush when she jerks away to kick herself against the wall, muttering words I cannot say, much less spell.

I offer my palms to her, hoping she sees I am not an attacker. Slowly bringing a fingertip to my chest, I say my name, "Carlo."

The one dark eye not swollen shut darts within the socket.

"Friend," I say. I touch my right arm, point to hers, and add, "Better?"

No words. Not a sound except the wheeze of breath from her throat.

I fill the shell with water again and offer it to her. She refuses. I sip and lick my lips, smile and offer it to her again. This time she takes it and drinks until it is empty. I offer more, but she waves the shell away. With the shell in the bucket again, I sit and touch my chest like before. "Carlo." Then I point toward her and nod. Please understand me, I think, and tell me your name.

She touches the sticks and strips of sail again, possibly understanding how I helped her. Her hand raises, lowers, and raises again. A fingertip touches her chest. "Watseka."

As you see, Luisa, I can say and spell her name. He voice is medium toned and feminine, one I enjoy hearing. "Watseka," I say.

She nods and points toward me. "Car …"

"Carlo."

"Car-lo."

I smile to acknowledge her effort. She touches her broken arm again and faces me. "Car-lo?"

The question is obvious within the upward lilt of her voice. I nod slowly to acknowledge how I bound her arm. Realizing we need to conquer our language barrier, I touch my arm. "Arm."

She touches her arm. "Ninik."

"Ninik," I say, and the slightest of smiles hints upon her swollen lips. Time to broach a subject I dread, but I need to know more about the attack on her tribe. I move the piece of sail beneath my feet aside and attempt to draw a vessel like hers, with two people inside it. Looking up, I see she watches intently. I touch my chest— "Carlo" — and point at my eyes— "see you." She cocks her head to one side, unsure, I suppose, of my meaning. I draw two people upon the sand, except these two people are standing side by side holding hands. Then I point at her, say her name, and point at one of the people. She frowns until I point at the other drawing and clasp my hands together, making my meaning clear that this person is her husband. Her lower lip quivers. Her eyes fill. Tears roll down her cheeks and fall to the blouse Sancho gave me.

For a while she softly cries. As her sobs fade, I offer her more water, which she refuses. Time passes between us silently. I want so much to hold her, but I am an idiot for thinking it.

Perhaps food shall take her mind off her sorrows. I go to the barrel outside for some smoked fish and take it inside to offer her. A barely raised head and a quick wave of her hand signals no interest.

Tell me what to do, Luisa, for I am at a loss.

She raises her hand to the hollow of her throat, as if she is attempting to finger the necklace of tiny shells that is gone, likely broken away during her fight with an attacker. The hand falters, moves slowly between her breasts, and her fingertips find a button just above her slightly rounded belly. She works it back and forth, slips it from the slot, and slips it back. "Button," I say, pointing to one of my own.

She lowers her hand from the button to her belly, where she caresses the round shape beneath the dingy cloth of the blouse.

"Baby," I say. Placing my forearms together before my chest, I rock them back and forth. "Baby." I bring the imaginary baby to my lips and kiss her forehead. "Baby."

This time Watseka looks me square in the eye, nods, and rocks her arms as I do, wincing at the pain within the bound arm. "Papoose." Pressing her lips together as if she is making a decision, she points at the fish within my lap. I keep part for myself, give her the other part, and we eat silently.

Our meal done, we sip water from the shell. She then lies down again, exhausted, I am certain, from both her attack and our discussion.

Like hail beating the cobbles outside our home, Luisa, questions clatter within my mind about this young woman. The most important, as you may know, is if she is the purpose your mama spoke of.

I wish I could put myself within her place, see what she has seen, feel what she has felt, but I cannot until we are able to communicate as well as we are able. However, if we can reach an understanding within our limited knowledge of each other, we may learn, regardless of our differences, how our inner selves have more in common than our outer selves shall ever diminish.

A quick shake of my head reminds me how this thought is part folly, for people use differences to foment hate in order to gain influence and power, and as Father Cristobal instructed us students, they do those things also to gain riches and wealth. "After all," he liked to say, furrowing his bushy brows while jabbing a swollen-knuckled finger toward us, "the love of money is the root of all evil. Too many divide us with hate for nothing more than monetary gain, forsaking those they claim to serve. Do you not see that, my students?"

I nod to honor one of the wisest voices of my childhood. Thank God Watseka and I do not have the world and those evils to corrupt us.

In her sleep, as if to remind me of what is truly important, she moans softly.

What secrets does she hold? Are they many or few? Are they simple or complicated? Are they—

"But, Papa, you are keeping a secret, even from yoursel—"

"Hush now," I say softly. "Allow the past to remain within the past and let me concentrate on the present, as well as the perspective of my new friend."

August 5, 1522

Dear Luisa,

Watseka sleeps until the setting sun touches the horizon above the trees that once shaded her home. She lies quiet for a time, eyes blinking now and then, and I wonder if she needs to relieve herself of the water she drank. I stand and motion to her. She looks my way, and I squat and attempt to twist my expression into one I likely have when I need to go to a thicket.

A nod answers me, but when she rolls over to rise, she gasps in pain. I should have thought of how the slightest movement would hurt, for bruises cover much of her body. I go to her and offer my arm. Instead of taking it, she takes a step toward the door, gasping in pain again. Looking back at me, she tips her head, and I go to her with my arm held out.

She loops the unbroken arm into mine, and I lead her to the path that leads to a secondary path and the place I have been using. Her nose wrinkles at what can only be the sour smell of my leavings, even though I covered them with sand. The arm slips from within mine and she waves me away, not quite steady upon her feet.

I wait behind a tree, listening to her groans of pain as she likely attempts to squat. Several unrecognizable words hiss from the thicket, words with the aggravated tone I might use if I were forced to ask someone to take me somewhere to relieve myself.

"Car-lo."

I enter the thicket. She waves me over, holding out her arm. So, we have crossed one bridge of intimacy. What shall be our next?

Inside the shelter again, we eat fish and sip water. Between the two, Watseka touches the bed of sail cloth beneath her, then looks at the roof made of sail. "I touch my bed of sailcloth beneath me. "Cloth." I touch my blouse and breeches. "Cloth."

"Clo ..." Her eyes narrow.

"Cloth," I say.

"Cloth?"

Smiling broadly, I nod vigorously. "Very good."

She touches a button on the blouse I dressed her in. "But ..."

"Button."

She smiles as well, but only a hint. A sip of water wets her lips. She offers me the shell and points at it in my hand. "Nibi."

I touch the shell. "Nibi?" A quick shake of her head says she meant the water, not the shell. "Water," I say flicking a droplet toward her.

Her eyes narrow at my play— "Nibi" —and she eats another bite of fish.

Difficult and slow, our language needs an aid. Since writing upon the sand worked yesterday, it should work today.

With our meal done, I move my bed of sailcloth aside and take a stick from those I use to stoke the embers of the fire when needed. Watseka eyes me warily as I start to draw my island with two figures upon it to represent us, a far land to represent her home, and several figures to represent her people. I touch the two figures with the stick and then point at us in turn. "Watseka. Carlo."

She nods, understanding immediately. I point to her people, and her head lowers. "Watseka?" I say. She looks up and I touch the people. "Watseka people?"

She reaches over the dead embers and wipes away the figures, keeps her palm down and slices it sideways through the air between us. All I can make of this sign is her people are dead, including, as evidenced by her tears yesterday, her husband. I draw several circles with people inside them, one at my feet, another farther away, and get up to draw another by the door. My intention is to touch each circle of people and say people, but with the lilt of a question within my tone, for I would like to know if she has other people nearby in case she would like to leave.

In turn, I do so at the first and second circles, and Watseka wipes each away. When I start to touch the last circle, she presses both palms toward the door, as if she means those people are much farther away than that. She then takes the stick from me and draws four meandering lines that converge into two, with one of her vessels between the two lines. I assume the lines are rivers, which must mean these people live some distance from the coast. After returning to her seat, gritting her teeth as she does, she draws two figures upon the sand at her feet, says "Car-lo, Watseka" and jabs the stick into the sand.

Well, Luisa, it seems my guest has more people. However, they are too far away for a journey, and she has decided to stay here with me. I cannot say I blame her, with a child coming. Still, I pray the baby was not harmed by the beating. The last thing in the world I hope to experience is delivering a child, only to have her stillborn or dying soon after birth.

We spend the remainder of the morning taking short, hesitant walks, her hand clutching my arm. I hope to alleviate any stiffness within her muscles from lying down too much, or from the beating she took.

After our midday meal, while she naps, I spear more fish and smoke them and catch up on writing within my journal. When I return it to the chest, I am tempted to take my flute out and play it later for Watseka. I decide against it. Perhaps another time, after we know each other more intimately.

"What does that word mean, Papa? Do you mean friends?"

Listen to you, my mischievous one, sneaking into my thoughts.

"You did not answer me, Papa."

Yes, it could mean friends.

"I think it means more than friends." Luisa giggles. "Like kissing."

Well, perhaps you should listen to my own mama and papa for advice. Certainly not Beatriz, with her girlish ways of thinking about boys.

"We all just want you to be happy, Papa. We love you so."

Tears burst from my stinging eyes. Shaking my head in an attempt to loosen those last words of my daughter from my mind, I rise and stumble from the shelter to not wake Watseka with my weeping. I love you all, my darling. My every wish is to return home to you. More than anything. More than even life itself.

Ah, Carlo, my love, do not weep. As I have said, a purpose awaits you. Be patient, my love. Be patient and you shall see.

Nearly blinded with tears now, I run to my small cemetery, lie at the cross that awaits me beside the grave of Sancho, and fold my hands over my chest. Take me now, God. Take me and be done with it. I wish to be with my Juliana, for I see no purpose in living.

"But, Papa, you—"

"Car-lo?"

I open my eyes to see Watseka kneeling beside me, concern within her dark eyes, within the tone of her voice, within the way she leans toward me, with one hand out.

But no, her concern is not for me. Her hand is red with blood, as well as her thighs below the hide she wears. God, no, not another tragedy upon this hell of an island.

Watseka cries now, sure of what is happening. I take her hand and lead her back to the shelter, where I have her lie down. Water, I need water. I bring in a filled bucket from the barrel. Boil it like the nun did for Juliana? I have no pot. What a nightmare. I use my knife to cut sail cloth into smaller pieces while Watseka wails with a small, thin voice, eyes shut tight. She raises her head. The cords of muscle within her neck bulge. A long scream fills my home—keen enough to cut the very soul from me.

The sun climbs the sky. No gulls scree overhead. No birds warble or chirp in the trees. Death is coming and they shy away. Even the wind has stopped whispering within the thickets.

All I can do is kneel by Watseka and hold her hand, whose grip compresses the bones of my fingers until I swear I hear them crack. A gasp and another scream, both numbing my ears, comes from the black tunnel of her widened mouth. I pull my hand from her grip and open her thighs to see the top of a head the size of a large olive, which bursts from the birth canal in a gush of blood and fluid. Minuscule fingers curl into fists. Bloodstained nostrils no larger than a grape seed flare for breath. Toothpick ribs beneath parchment-thin skin attempt to expand and contract twice before making the attempt no more. Then, like a sail in a dying wind, the pitiful body collapses in death. Watseka falls back in a heap of sweat and rapid breaths.

I start to wrap the baby within a piece of sail but must stop to cut the cord tying her to her mama. As I do, the afterbirth comes out, resembling one of those huge purplish jellyfish that floats upon sea waves, trailing stinging tentacles by the dozens.

After setting it aside, I press the pieces of sail to the opening of the birth canal and gently lower the thighs until the brown legs are fully closed.

Only then does the magnitude of the death of this tiny soul engulf me. I finish wrapping her and hold her within my palm to my chest, sobbing like Sancho did for Barros by rocking back and forth while sitting upon his knees.

Ah, Luisa, it is as if you had died when you were born. Thank God that did not happen, for my heart could not have withstood losing you.

My sobs finally end, and I look to Watseka to see how she fares. Calm and quiet, cheeks wet with tears, she simply stares at me, as if she is dumbfounded at this stranger who grieves so much for a child not his own.

I place the tiny wrapped bundle within her lap. For a moment we are still, two people attempting to understand the mystery of life and death, until she raises her hand and cups my cheek with her palm. "Car-lo." My name fades within the air like a morning fog dissipating over the vineyard at home.

To offer my condolences, I kiss the cooling forehead of the baby. A sudden shudder shakes my shoulders, for I am on the verge of tears again. Watseka sits up and pulls my head to her shoulder, and it is as if the Heavens have opened to release a bolt of sunshine into my heart.

For you see, Luisa, to be loved is one thing, but to be understood is everything.

August 6, 1522

Dear Luisa,

After our meal the following morning, Watseka slowly stands. Bloody pieces of sail fall from beneath the hide covering her thighs as she leaves the shelter, I suppose, to relieve herself. I rush to the sail and pull it aside. No blood drips from her and I am glad. Still, she shuffles along upon the sand until she enters the path.

Taking this moment for myself, I write within my journal. Time drifts away, and all I know are my thoughts and the scratch of the quill upon the parchment. Three pages later, Watseka is still gone. Perhaps she needed a walk to clear her head from the grief of the previous day, although I am sure it shall take much more than that, especially since she has not signaled for any type of burial for her tiny daughter, whose bundled body lies beside the place where Watseka slept.

I place quill to parchment once more. Pages pass. The quill takes ink from a bottle. My mind lingers upon letters, words, sentences. Again I thank God for you, Luisa, in that you were born healthy and squalling instead of quiet and unable to take a single breath.

Hesitant footsteps scuff sand, growing louder as they near. Watseka moves the sail aside and comes in to sit beside me. Without a word, she takes a blackened ember from the cold fire and marks streaks across her cheeks. Then, leaning close to me, she does the same to my cheeks. Nodding in approval, she stands and offers me her hand. As I take it, I feel the grit of sand within her palm. She gestures to her daughter. I pick her up and clutch her to my chest, unsure at what we are about to do.

We enter the path, passing the thick brush. Slight scratches line the brown arms of Watseka, so it seems she has been within a thicket for something.

The surf pounds. Gulls scree. Birds sing and warble within the trees. Wind whispers instead of howls. Warmth emanates from the rising sun. Sweat slickens my underarms.

She takes the fork that leads to my small cemetery. There now, and I am amazed.

At the cross where I lay yesterday, Watseka has dug a small grave. Upon the mound of sand, woven from the green stems of tiny white flowers, lies a wreath no larger than the ring I placed upon the finger of my beloved Juliana. To one side of the mound is a palm-sized pile of some type of pod I have never seen upon this island. I have heard of people burying their dead with food for their journey to the afterlife, so perhaps this is some type of food Watseka knows of, and which I do not. Beside the pile of pods lie several young shoots that resemble some of the grasses that grow within the marsh, another type of food, I suppose. Yet again, another pile of what must be food lies to the side of that pile, which is some kind of thick stem with buds along the sides. Although I understand the serious nature of the burial, my mouth waters at the chance to taste something green and crunchy instead of firm and fishy.

Watseka takes her daughter from me and places her within the grave. Still kneeling, she adds the piles of green foods, adjusting them all around the sail-wrapped form. Satisfied, she takes the tiny wreath of flowers and encircles the even tinier head. Taking my hand, she pulls herself up, grimacing from the pain I am sure she still feels from both the attack and giving birth.

When she is steady upon her feet, I release her hand and hold up a finger. Regardless of our language difficulties, I cannot help but speak. "Watseka, I shall return in a moment."

I run to the shelter and fling my chest open, take out a handful of sea shells I have collected during some of my walks upon the beach, and run back to the grave to place them around the body. Standing, I nod at Watseka, who acknowledges my gift with the slightest of smiles from her swollen, split lips.

She raises her chin to the sky, slips her fingers into mine, and begins singing a lyric that chills me to the bone with her high, mournful notes.

Part of me wants to weep again, but another part raises my head also, desiring to honor this woman and her loss, which I feel as keenly as when Juliana left my world.

Sunlight warms my face. Wind caresses my cheeks. The hand of Watseka grows hot within mine. The singing ends. She turns to look up into my eyes, for I never noticed how tiny she is, the top of her head only rising to my chin. Although one eye socket is still blue with bruising and swollen almost shut, the other dark pupil finds my own. She raises her hand to the back of my neck and pulls me down to kiss my forehead, my nose, then my lips, and it is all I can do to not love her then and there.

A sudden gust of wind whips my hair about my face, waking me from what must have been a daydream of desire, for Watseka, still singing, continues holding my hand.

Forgive me, Juliana, if I care for this woman. You are alike in many ways, arriving within my life like when Cantante saved me from that winter storm so long ago.

Watseka stops singing and kneels to mound sand over her daughter. For a time she is silent, nothing more than a woman staring at the grave of her child, as I stared at the grave of my beloved. She turns to me, points toward the pounding surf, and leads me toward the beach, where we walk along while gazing at the shells, the sea, the gulls, the backward-kneed birds plunging their beaks into the shimmering sand scattered with flecks of foam. A chevron of pelicans rises and falls over the blue-green waves, and several of those pesky stalk-eyed crabs zigzag toward their holes upon spike-like legs forming a white blur.

Yes, the raw beauty of this place amazes me, but it does so far less than the woman who might well be my purpose in life, as Juliana has told me.

I hate to ask, Luisa, but would you mind if I stay here? I mean, of course, if Watseka and I come to love one another. After all, you said you want me to be happy.

No answer rides the wind. Nothing, not a hint. Watseka pulls me to a stop and looks up into my eyes, perhaps sensing my confusion.

I take a strip of sail from my pocket, one I sometimes tie my hair with, and go behind her to tie her hair. She must wear it like this often, for the nape of her neck is a deep, dark, mahogany brown from the sun. The collar of the blouse she wears flutters within the breeze, raising goosebumps upon her skin regardless of the increasing heat of the day. Upon her neck, fine hairs, even darker than those upon her head, flow together like storm-tossed waves beneath a blackened sky. I dare to caress the skin beneath those fine hairs with my fingertips—just a hint—just a delightful hint—before regaining my poor excuse for gentlemanly composure by taking her hand and leading her to the shelter so she can rest.

September 12, 1522

Dear Luisa,

Watseka and I are having our first argument, and it is one I would not wish upon any man.

We were eating smoked fish last night, along with some of the greens she showed me how to harvest, and she actually threw the piece of fish I had given her back at me, striking my face. This happened as I was looking down to take a second portion for myself. When I raised my head to see what could ever be the matter, she actually stuck her tongue out at me. To make matters even more profound, she added insult to injury by spitting into the fire between us and slicing her hand through the air. "No," she said, having learned some of my simpler words. "No fish, Car-lo. Watseka no fish."

Tired of smoked fish myself, I held my palms up, shrugged my shoulders, and raised my eyebrows in the eternal expression between couples married or not … *I am only a mere man, my darling. What more can I do?*

This morning, she rose with the sun and prodded me awake with her toes. "Car-lo Car-lo Car-lo."

Bleary eyed, I rolled over to face her, wondering whether or not I should have told her my name when we met. "What, beloved?" No, Luisa, she does not know what that word means, but I hoped the endearing tone I used might stop her from prodding me again.

Seeing she had my undivided attention, she raised her hands to her head as if they were ears and hopped around the shelter, looking for all the world like one of the rabbits upon this island.

I nodded vigorously, desiring roasted rabbit dripping sizzling fat onto shimmering embers myself as well.

Watseka took a length of rope from those that Sancho had me braid into a thinner rope, hung it around her neck, and snatched the single layer of sail off of me, needed on these cooler nights.

Outside, I stretched and yawned and went to the smoker to check my previous catch. As I knelt to look beneath the sail holding in the smoke and warmth, she grabbed my arm and pulled me toward the path. Along with wondering about telling her my name, I wondered if I should have bound her broken arm that is healed now, for she hooked it into mine as we walked. In a flash of white teeth she smiled, and I forgave her everything.

Well, until this very argument we are now having.

She jerks me to a stop and kneels to study the sand. Looking up at me, she places her hands to her head for ears again and then points to a few tiny indentations upon the sand, apparently rabbit tracks. Her eyes close. Her head shakes. I have experienced this frustrated expression with Juliana, so Watseka must have forgotten something. She stands to paw at my waist, from where she sometimes takes my knife, and raises a single eyebrow at me, another sign of aggravation I have experienced from Juliana.

Of course, I run to the shelter for the knife.

When I return, she spreads her hands along a length of tree limb and points to where she wants me to cut it. Nodding, I take the knife from my belt and set metal to wood. Before I can begin my assigned task, she pokes my back and moves the blade a finger width more from where I am about to cut. I stick my tongue out at her like she did me last night, which elicits the same in return, followed by another brilliant smile. Of course, all is forgiven once again.

With the stick cut to her measurement, I offer it to her, and she ties the rope to one end. That task done, she pulls me by my blouse sleeve to the rabbit tracks again, where she makes a circle with her fingers, meaning, I suppose, she wants me to form a loop with a slip knot with which to snare a rabbit by a leg.

On the farm at home, I have made my share of knots. Still, when I finish, Watseka jerks it from my grasp and pops my hand as if to discipline me like a naughty child.

This, my dear Luisa, is *not* immediately forgiven.

I jerk the rope back and pop her hand for good measure. She waggles a finger in my face. Leaning over to almost touch nose to nose, I lock gazes with her. "Watseka, no."

"Car-lo, no."

"Watseka …"

"Car-lo …"

Her pressed lips contort into a grin as do mine, and yes, Luisa, all is forgiven.

To make my long story shorter, she instructs me in the proper method of making a snare for rabbits, and we enjoy one this very night.

As we finish eating, a cool wind hisses sand against the wall at my back, for I have allowed Watseka to take my place to avoid the cold. As always, the surf crashes like muted thunder. In ones, two, and dozens, visible between the tops of our walls and the edges of the roof of sail, stars twinkle into view.

Watseka rinses her hands with water from a bucket and dries them with a piece of sail, and I do the same. After tossing the rabbit bones outside, she returns to sit beside me, something she has never done.

The wind hisses sand once more. Within a nearby tree, an owl asks who we are to invade his tranquil island. Some small animal scurries within the thicket beside us, then goes silent.

Watseka rubs her arms where goosebumps rise and adds sticks to the fire. They catch with yellow flame, highlighting her profile. Black hair shines. She tilts her head down and the dark curtain falls over her cheek. The flames rise, illuminating brown thighs and small feet, both crossed before her. She raises her head and her hair falls back, revealing a tiny scar where her attacker smashed a fist into her eye. Leaning close, I take in the scent of fresh air from her hair. My arm touches hers … she turns to smile at me. What a lovely moment, Luisa. The loveliest I have experienced in years.

Watseka wipes the sand smooth before us and takes a stick from our pile. She draws two lines and a single figure between them, then draws another line farther away, adding more figures to the other side of the line. Even farther away, she draws the same two lines representing the river, with one of her vessels within it, adding several figures there also. Pointing the stick at the lone figure within the nearest drawing, she says, "Car-lo."

I nod. "Yes, Carlo."

She points to the next closest figures, which must be her people within the village now burned. "Watseka—" She shakes her head, draws two figures holding hands, and points again. "Watseka. Uhanu."

I nod again, understanding Uhanu was her husband.

Before pointing at the farthest drawing, she adds a smaller figure beside two of the larger ones, and one of them hold hands with the smaller figure. She points to the smaller figure. "Watseka."

I nod once more, understanding how her mama and papa must live within the village beside the two rivers. Still, I would like to know more about this village. I take another stick and draw a line with half a sun above each end of the line. This simple picture, I hope, shall relay my idea of a single day. I point to the picture. "Day."

Watseka draws a line from one sun to the other and nods. "Day."

I breathe a sigh of relief for her obvious intelligence, walk two fingers from her drawing of me to her drawing of the river and the people, and raise one hand to touch the tips of my fingers and thumb of my other hand, one at a time to ask how many days the journey is.

Nodding so hard that her hair slips back and forth over her shoulders, Watseka holds up a hand and touches one finger. Shaking her head in frustration again, she takes my hands, raises them, and touches our fingers in turn. "Pejig. Nij. Niswe. New. Naanan. Nigodwaaswe. Nijwaaswe. Nishwaaswe. Shaangawse. Mitaaswe. Mitaaswe ashidj pejig. Mitaaswe ashidj nij. Mitaaswe ashidj niswe. Mitaaswe ashidj new. Mitaaswe ashidj naanan."

You may have noticed, Luisa, since you likely know your numbers by now, how Watseka has counted to fifteen. I tried my best to write her words by their sounds, so forgive me if they are difficult to read. "But, Papa," you might say, looking up at me, "how do you know she counted to fifteen?"

Well, it is simple, for after the first ten words, she added two more words before them, which should mean the number ten plus each of the first ten words.

With bright eyes, I see you smile with understanding.

I raise one of the hands of Watseka and count our fingers to fifteen. She nods and I am tempted to curse. A fifteen-day journey through dense forest would be difficult, but with the addition of her attackers lingering about, the danger is multiplied many times over. It is no wonder she preferred to stay with me instead risking such a journey. Still, if one of us were to become deathly ill for some reason, her people would likely have a healer of sorts, so the journey might be well worth the effort.

"But, Papa, you are not a native and they might kill you. And you do not know their words."

Ever the voice of reason, are you not, Luisa? Do I not resemble a native? My hair is as long as the hair of Watseka. My skin is not as brown, but it is close. Aside from that, she would speak for me to her parents and tell them how I saved her life. No, Luisa, you must not worry about such things, for I have no intention of either of us growing ill for any reason whatsoever.

"What about your clothes? They mark you as from another land, do they not?"

They do, but since they do not bother Watseka, they should not bother her people.

Watseka smooths away the drawing of her and her husband, points to the small figure representing herself, and says, "Carlo."

If I understand, she wants to know how far away my home and parents are, so I hold up my hands and spread and fold the fingers until they reach ninety days, which is a rough estimation of how long my voyage from Spain to here took.

Her eyes narrow. Her lips purse. She follows this display of possible confusion by walking her fingers from my island to where my stick-figure parents and I stand, asking if I walked here.

Between the two lines representing the two tracts of land, I draw a vessel such as hers. Jutting her chin forward, she nods in understanding. A moment passes. She tilts her head to one side. Blinking eyes signal intense concentration. After standing, she moves her hands back and forth within the air beside her, cheeks puffed as if holding her breath.

Did you guess her motions like I did, Luisa?

"I did, Papa. She wants to know if you swam here."

Yes, she does, so I wipe the vessel away and draw a broken one to replace it.

Seemingly satisfied with my explanation, Watseka sits beside me again and leans over to place her elbows upon her knees, her chin upon her clasped fingers, and stares at the fire.

Without conscious effort, my hand rises to her back between her shoulder blades, beneath silky hair that she washes weekly within the calm waters behind the island by scrubbing it gently with handfuls of sand. I rub small circles there, feeling the slight rise of the bones within her spine. As my palm and her skin grow warm together, I expect her to look back at me, but she does not. Without a sign to let me know what she thinks of my touch, I take my hand away.

Except for the pop and crackle of the fire, like so many times before, Silence lies her head within the shelter. Watseka rises to sit between my outstretched legs and leans her warmth against my chest. A breathless moment passes, maybe more, a dream rising within my mind. My hands tremble upon my thighs. She takes them and wraps my arms around her. I can feel the expansion of her chest within the circle of my arms, the pace of it rising, rising, until she places my hands to her breasts and gasps. I take one hand away and pull her hair aside to kiss the nape of her neck. "Car-lo", she murmurs. Car—."

"Noooooo!" she screams, rolling away and jumping over the fire.

All I can do is sit here, wondering what I did wrong when she obviously wanted me as much as I wanted her.

Watseka drops cross-legged to her bed, head down, and starts to weep.

Our brief enjoyment of each other has obviously upset her, and I dearly want to know why. "Watseka," I say, holding my palms up in question while attempting to tone my voice plaintively.

I expect no answer until her sobs end. When they do, she raises red eyes to me and beats a fist against her chest three times. "Uhanu, no Car-lo," she wails, face twisted into a grimace. Then she strikes the same fist against the side of her head. "Car-lo Car-lo Car-lo."

Dumbfounded, I am tempted to weep myself, for these actions mean her husband still resides within her heart, while I only reside within her head.

I lie down, pull my bedding over myself, and roll away from her. What am I to do, Luisa? All I am to Watseka is a friend—nothing more, nothing less—and that is all I shall ever be.

April 1, 1523

Dear Luisa,

I apologize for waiting so many months to write, but my heart refuses to give me the words.

The morning after Watseka told me how her husband remained within her heart, I woke to find her gone. I thought nothing of it for a while. Surely she was gathering food or walking the beach, but when she did not return after a time, I rose to look for her. About to enter the path to the beach, I saw no new footprints, so I went partway down the path leading to the calm waters. Halfway across it, paddling hard toward her former home, she was leaving me.

Although I was unsure if my attraction for her was love or lust, evidenced by my ungentlemanly actions of the previous evening, my heart beat as if it were a fist attempting to smash through the center of my chest.

Alone again. Drearily alone. Nothing and no one to keep me company, both during the long summer days and the longer winter nights to come. How I hoped she would turn the vessel and come back to me.

"She shall come back, Papa. Cannot you see within her eyes how she cares for you?"

I have never noticed. Not truly. Perhaps I saw what I hoped to see.

"I saw it as well. Be patient, Papa. Please be patient."

Bidding your voice to be quiet, Luisa, I climbed the sandy path to the shelter and returned to my bed. Perhaps sleep would transform me into death, for I surely had no reason to live.

The day passed the same as any spring day from last year, with birds warbling and chirping, gulls screeching, a pleasant breeze rippling the roof of sailcloth, a hint of salt adding flavor and aroma to the season. When the sun shone brightly through the cloth directly overhead, and when my stomach rumbled like muted thunder, I rose to sip water and have a bit of leftover rabbit still skewered to a stick leaning over the smoldering embers. Sated, I nodded off from the growing heat, ignoring the sweat forming within my armpits.

Or at least I thought I had nodded off, for I could not have, since I heard sand scuffing outside the shelter with the familiar rhythm of the familiar stride of Watseka. The sailcloth door flung back, and she entered to prop a bow and several arrows against the wall on her side of the shelter. From a tanned bag made of hide, she pulled the blouse of Sancho out and tossed it at me, nodded, and left. Moments later she returned again to set two clay pots and another, larger leather bag on her side of the shelter. She now wore a leather covering from her shoulders to her knees. The meaning could not be clearer ... she wanted nothing more to do with me in a personal way, and this included not wearing a blouse she thought was mine.

She sat and took what looked like a bone needle from the large bag. I have never considered how natives sewed but I should have, for the garment that covered her is stitched at the sides and along the sleeves. However, the thread isn't fine, so I do not know how it is made.

After threading the bone needle, she stitched a tear within her leather blouse and returned the needle and thread to the large bag. Upon her feet again, she snatched the bow and arrows and stomped outside. I was tempted to laugh, Luisa. If she wanted deer meat so badly instead of rabbit and fish, she had paddled a long way to gather her things from her former home.

"Perhaps she wanted to bury her husband, Papa. If so, perhaps that means she is trying to remove him from her heart and place you there instead."

You are too young to understand how losing a loved one can scar a person. I shall keep your mama within my heart always, so I understand how Watseka feels.

"Do you …"

Out with it, girl. Tell me what is on your mind.

"Do you … well, do you love me that much also?"

Like the stars and the sun and the moon all wrapped in one, my darling.

"But you never said goodbye."

I know, and I ask your forgiveness. I shall ask it in person when I return, all right?

"I thought you wanted to stay here with Watseka?"

I was wrong to think she could love me. I am nothing but a convenience to her.

"But—"

I slapped my palms against my temples— "ENOUGH" —and your plaintive voice faded from my mind.

The sun fell from the sky to signal the end of the day. Gulls quieted, the birds as well, and the salt breeze softened with the golden twilight. Barely whispering to me, the surf calmly spoke, and I closed my eyes to await the return of my intrepid huntress.

What a foolish notion. Watseka is a huntress who belongs to no man, especially me.

Feet scuffed sand. A grunt of effort signaled her return, possibly dragging a deer. The door opened and she motioned to me to come outside, where she opened the hind legs of a doe and nodded at me, as if she wanted me to take her place.

We gutted and skinned the deer in silence. Near the end, darkness forced me to light a stick from the embers and hold it while she quartered the deer, illuminated in flickering yellow light.

She roasted slices of loin, and we consumed them with sips of water. The meat tasted somewhat strong in flavor, but it was one of the finest things I have ever eaten. With our meal done, she motioned me outside, where I held a burning stick while she continued slicing meat.

The night blackened further. The moon climbed from the horizon and rose within the sky like the glowing half-fingernail of some great giant observing us. My eyes and the stick within my hand grew heavy. "Car-lo." Watseka pressed her lips into a thin, hard line and raised her hand for me to lift the stick so she could see.

Each time I yawned, I received the same stern expression and the same sharp reprimand of "Car-lo," until Watseka was done and the remainder of the slices were smoking upon the contraption Sancho had made.

Daylight brought a toe prodding my side. "Car-lo." Watseka gave me a pot and motioned me to follow her and gather greens.

The next day she let me sleep, but when she woke me with two of those nasty crabs from the calm water within her hands, I shook my head and rolled away. It was as if she knew how they made me ill and intended to commit my murder.

The crabs clattered as she dropped them in a pot. The toe prodded my back, and I rolled over to face her. "Carlo," she said, tilting her head toward the door. She went outside with the other clay pot in hand, and I followed her to the beach.

There she gave me the pot and walked along the surf. Moments later she leaned over to scoop a double handful of wriggling mole crabs and dumped them into the pot, followed by two more of the same. I had no idea what she intended to do with them, for the largest were not much bigger than my thumb, and the smallest were no bigger than the nail upon my little finger.

Turning back the way we came, she motioned to me with another tilt of her head. Having no further commitments, I followed along behind her, as if I were my faithful friend, Cantante, whose indomitable spirit still lives within my muscles and bones. Unfortunately, my soul was not as strong as his, for I might have told Watseka to stop treating me like a servant.

Although this is how much of our time passed through the winter, Watseka did take enough deer to fashion me a blouse and breeches made of tanned deer hide. I even found out how she made her sewing thread, which was to save the sinews from the deer and allow them to dry until she could separate the fibers. Shall the ingenuity of humankind never cease?

"But, Papa, how did she tan the hides?"

I do not blame you for asking, since we bought our leather goods at the market within Palos de la Frontera.

Watseka first scraped the flesh and hair from the hide with stone tools she brought in her large bag. If the deer was old, the hair hard to remove, she soaked the hide within a slurry of ashes from our fire mixed with water, placing both within the turtle shell I still have. Now, Luisa, the final step to make the hide soft may make you a bit squeamish, for Watseka cooked deer brains within water to make a paste and rubbed it into the hide.

"What is 'squeamish,' Papa?"

It is when you feel sick to your stomach.

"I do not feel that way at all. I am much stronger than you think. I got it from you, you know."

I am glad to hear it, young lady. Oh, I forgot. Watseka still had to work the dry hide after the treatment with brains to make it supple, and that is how it was done.

"Thank you for telling me, Papa. What else happened between you? I hope it gets better. I love you so and want you to be happy."

My darling Luisa, your words break my heart and set me to sobbing, to where I cannot write for the tears falling to my parchment.

"I am sorry, Papa, but I do love you."

Thank you. I cannot say if things between us get better or not. In fact, things got worse as time passed, which brings me to today.

After Watseka made my blouse and breeches, she even made me a pair of slippers from another tanned hide. I had hoped all this attention meant her heart was letting her husband out and taking me within, but I was wrong.

The minute I tried on my new clothes, she nodded once and has not spoken to me since. It is as if she owed me a debt for saving her life and now considered it paid in full.

This lasted from February until now, and I have been the most miserable wretch a man can be. Unless it is raining, she even refuses to eat with me and—

Forgive me, Luisa. My mind plays tricks with my memory these days, and I forgot to tell you what Watseka did with the mole crabs.

The best thing about her recipe was how those shelled creatures didn't make me sick like those other crabs. The next best thing is how she crushed them within one of her pots with a stone tool, added water, and made it boil by heating rocks within the fire and adding them to the pot. She also added some greens to the mix, creating a delicate soup that made me lick my lips in amazement.

"What about all those tiny shells, Papa?"

It was simple, my dear, for they all sank to the bottom of the pot.

Now, where am I with my story. Oh, yes, how Watseka now refuses to eat with me unless it rains.

Other than how she has not uttered a single word since the middle of February, that is all I have to tell. I have even thought about playing my flute for her, but I doubt that would help.

Think of me often, Luisa. Send up your prayers to your mama and Cantante, for I need their help now more than ever.

April 2, 1523

Dear Luisa,

Today is the same as yesterday. No toes prod my back. No demanding voice for "Car-lo" wakes me from my sleep. No chores await me after we break our fast or have our midday or late day meals. If I did not know any better, I would say I live alone upon the moon.

As night falls, I add sticks to the embers for light and fetch my flute from the chest, for I plan to break our stalemate with a heartfelt tune.

Although I sometimes hate this island and the sea, both possess a definite charm. God and Nature place their fingertips here often, weaving their Holy presence by painting so many lovely scenes of animals and birds, whales and dolphins, golden sunrises and scarlet sunsets. Even the very breath of those two eternal forces cleanses the air as twilight falls, with the softest and gentlest of breezes, as delicate as your brow when I kissed it, Luisa, moments after you were born.

Facing the setting sun, Watseka presses one hand to the coarse bark of an oak, the other to her side. She wears her hair down these days, possibly recalling the time I kissed the nape of her neck and wanting no more of that. Her calves are dark brown and muscular. One foot is tipped upon the toes, the other rests upon the sole. The sole of the tipped foot stands out a stark white against the darkness of the nearby thicket. That soft, gentle breeze flutters her hair. A sign from you, Juliana, to play my song for her?

No, not yet. I prefer to let night devour the day, the moon to rise on the cloudless horizon over the sea, the surf to sing a lullaby to both of us with that familiar whisper of wavelets upon the sand.

Like some great beast awaiting within the shadows to the west, the blackened horizon bites the last hint of light from the sky. Watseka goes into the shelter, and I follow.

Taking my customary seat, I scoot back a bit from the flames, lest I grow too warm. Watseka does the same. Without preamble, I take my flute from my pocket, raise it to my lips, and play the same song that Beatriz and I used to draw Juliana out of her refusal to sing so long ago.

Watseka, who is searching a large bag for something, faces me. No smile hints upon her lips. No interest brightens her dark eyes. She takes sinew and needle from the bag, along with one small shoe from a pair she is making for herself, and begins to sew.

"Do not give up, Papa. You caught her eye for a moment."

Hearing your words, Luisa, I continue playing while observing Watseka. The melody rises and falls, and soon her head matches it with the slightest of movements, almost like Cantante did, except his enjoyment was much more pronounced, even to the point of slinging his black mane back and forth over his sleek neck.

I close my eyes to recall the evening when your mama lowered her guard and sang with Beatriz and I. What a magical moment, Luisa, one I never tire of remembering.

"*Aiaeeee!* Car-lo!"

The shrill scream from Watseka jerks me from my past. She jabs a trembling finger toward the shelter door, where the black head of a yearling horse, including a star upon the forehead, is shoving the sail aside.

My flute falls from lifeless hands.

"Papa! It is the son of Cantante! He really is a papa after all!"

Watseka jumps up to snatch her bow and arrows from the wall behind her. I bound from my seat and grab her hands. "No, Watseka. Horse, not deer."

Illuminated by the fire, black eyes dart away and back. She attempts to pull from my grasp, but I keep holding one hand while pulling the bow from the other. Just as I believe the situation is under control, she takes a stone knife from the larger of her bags and lunges toward the horse. Left with no option, I grab her hair and set her upon the ground, where she kicks herself against the wall, eyes wide, teeth bared in fury.

I hold my palms toward her to offer peace, then pick up my flute. Only the nose of the yearling extends inside the shelter now, nostrils flaring. He must love music as much as his Papa to not bolt at the antics of Watseka and myself.

The song fills the air again. The nose enters further, until the forehead and white star nod up and down. While blowing a single note, I reach out with a tentative fingertip to stroke the velvet nose. The head snaps up but lowers again. A snort blows wetness to my hand, followed by a curious sniff. I inhale for another note, play it softly, and scratch the white star. Long lashes blink. Huge eyes close and open. I wave Watseka over but she refuses. "Come," I say. "Friend."

Perhaps it is the tone of my voice. Perhaps it is the soft breaths of the yearling. Perhaps it is only curiosity at this gentle beast who is allowing me to scratch the white star. Regardless of my surmises, Watseka rises and comes to me. After inhaling for another note, I take her hand and place the fingertips to the white star, where she scratches.

Outside, another horse nickers, then another and another. The yearling backs away, and I open the door to allow firelight to illuminate the small clearing.

It is a miracle, Luisa, for the entire herd of three mares and one stallion from the north stands there, appraising Watseka and I, including another yearling, a golden mare. She leaves the group and comes forward to join the black yearling. If I am to believe what I see, a message passes between their gazes, and she offers her velvet nose to Watseka for a rub.

Watseka, apparently taking my lead from earlier, strokes the nose, wonder within her dark eyes.

The brown stallion snorts, breaking the spell. All the horses wheel to trot into the path toward the beach. Taking the hand of Watseka, I lead her inside the shelter to her bed, and I sit upon mine. "Horse, Watseka. Good?"

"Just how many words does she know, Papa?"

In the future, young lady, any words she uses were taught by me before our misunderstanding. Now, please leave us for the night.

"Goodnight, Papa. It was wonderful seeing all the horses."

Goodnight to you as well, Luisa. It is wonderful having you with us.

"Horse?" Watseka asks, head tipped to one side.

"Horse," I say, taking a stick from the pile. After smoothing the sand at my feet, I draw two horses with stick-figure people astride them. "Carlo, Watseka," I say pointing at the two figures in turn.

Watseka shakes her head. "No, Car-lo." To illustrate further emphasis toward my ridiculous proposal of teaching her to ride a horse, she twirls a finger in a circle beside her head, and I burst out laughing.

"No, Car-lo." She points at her feet, then walks two fingers across the sand before her. "Watseka walk."

I take this as a challenge, for I intend to have Watseka and I riding two of the older horses before the end of the summer. Barros told me how they were already broken to the saddle, so it should be little problem. Still, my hope is to ride the son of Cantante when he is two years old, which shall be this fall. Perhaps the young mare shall be ready for Watseka to ride as well.

"But, Papa, they need names, do they not? And why can't you ride them now?"

So, my curious girl, you are still here. The yearlings are not strong enough. Their bones must be fully formed also."

"You can still name them."

Let me lie down and think about. Taking my cue, Watseka lies down as well. All right then, Luisa, what shall I name them?

"I am sleepy too. I shall think on it while I dream and tell you tomorrow. Goodnight, Papa. I love you."

I roll over to avoid Watseka hearing the soft sobs I choke back. Firelight flickers upon my wall. The soft spring breeze enters the openings to feather against my cheek. Tears burn my eyes as if wasps plunge their stingers into them, filling them with venom. I lost so much before leaving home, but I never expected to continue that loss during my voyage. Between the shipwreck and the deaths of Mateo and Barros, along with the deaths of Sancho, Cantante, and the daughter of Watseka, including how I thought Watseka had left me, I doubt I can bear much more loss.

"Oh, Papa! Beatriz helped me pick names for the yearlings! The son of Cantante is Canción, for it means a song. The golden female is Armonía, for it means harmony. What do you think? I like them very, very much."

I think you are a miracle, Luisa, that is what I think, for you have ended my crying and dried my tears.

"Goodnight, Papa."

Goodnight, Luisa. God bless you.

April 3, 1523

Dear Luisa,

Prodding toes awaken me. I roll over to see a bright smile from Watseka.

Strips of deer meat roast over the embers. Within the turtle shell beside the rocks encircling the fire, bird eggs boil within water heated with stones. Within one of the clay pots, steam rises with the green aroma of shoots gathered from the marsh.

"Car-lo, eat."

I rise to sit cross-legged. Watseka hands me a clay cup she must have had within one of her bags. Already holding one, she nods at me before drinking. About to sip, I feel steam warm my face while taking in an aroma similar to tea, but somewhat herbal in nature. Not only are we on speaking terms again, it seems she truly cares for my wellbeing. Thank you, Cantante, for saving my life again through your son, Canción. Otherwise, I may have eventually hung myself like Sancho did.

Between bites, Watseka glances my way. She has tied her hair back to reveal her neck, but the last thing I shall attempt is to kiss her there again. When the meal is done, I nod to her and pat my stomach. "Good, Watseka. Mmm."

Grinning demurely, she waves my comment away and rises to scour the clay pots with sand, rinsing them afterward with water. I offer to help but she waves me away for that as well, so I go inside to write. However, I only get one page done before she comes inside. "Car-lo. We walk."

As we stroll along the path, still cool from the night air, she studies the sand. I am not sure what she is looking for, so I say nothing.

"Car-lo," she says, several steps later. "Horse."

I lean over to see the tracks of the horses from last night. The sight of them apparently impressed her to the point of wanting to see where they went.

We follow the tracks to the beach, where they turn north. Ignoring the crashing surf, the screeching gulls, the single chevron of pelicans gliding low over the waves, and a flock of backward-kneed birds darting toward the surf while their beaks probe the shining sand wet with foam, Watseka focuses on nothing but the hoof prints.

I glance over my shoulder in case the horses to the south are upon the beach, but they are not. I would like to see them soon, for I have not as of yet.

Facing Watseka again, I cannot help admiring her slender form, similar to the form of my Juliana. However, her calves and arms or more muscled, and she is darker than Juliana ever was, especially where her skin is not covered by her clothing. Long silky hair, black and stick-straight, hangs to her narrow waist. As small as she is, childbirth might be difficult, but Juliana had no problem with it except the normal pains that make every woman scream as if she is about to pass from this world.

Watseka turns left and climbs a dune. I follow also, and the soles of my feet warm from the sun shining upon the sand. At the top of the dune, she plunges into a narrow path lined with briars, holding her arms inward to avoid their touch. Although I follow her example, bloodless scratches soon mark my arms. Sand flies from her feet as she quickens her pace. Our breaths huff loudly. For a person frightened witless of the horses last night, she is anything but frightened now.

We break out into a huge clearing. Watseka runs to a pool of water and kneels to dip a fingertip in to taste it. I do the same and nod at the fresh flavor, not salty in the least. Hoofprints surround the pool, so this is where the horses have been watering. No source is present, so it must be fed by a spring. On the edge of the surrounding thickets, most of the brush is browsed short, and I imagine the horses have found the greens Watseka and I eat as well. What a blessing for them. Not only can they survive here for years, they shall likely thrive also.

Apparently satisfied with her exploration, Watseka enters the path. I follow her back to the beach, where we slowly stroll south, toward the area I now call home.

What a perfect spring day. The rising sun warms my face. Mist from the surf shares the taste of salt upon my lips. The whispering wash of dying waves cools my feet. Ahead of me, Watseka leaves narrow footprints upon the sand, dainty like those of a child, until the surf washes them away as if they had never existed.

She skips to a large shell, pink and spiraled, and picks it up to caress the smooth surface with her fingertips while staring at the sea. A sudden gust of wind whips her hair about her shoulders and strikes me full in the face, blurring my vision. Ghostlike, her slight form shimmers through my tears. She turns to offer me the shell but drops it instead, a look of concern within her blinking eyes and slightly downturned mouth. "Carlo?"

For the briefest moment, she reminds me entirely too much of Juliana, and before I can control my expression, a grimace of sadness betrays me.

Watseka sits with her legs folded beneath her and pats the sand beside her, so I sit as well. With a fingertip, she draws two lines with two stick people there. "Car-lo, Watseka."

I nod.

She draws two more lines, adding curves to represent waves, I suppose, then points to the sea. After I nod again, she draws a vessel like hers, except it is broken like the one I drew when I explained how I arrived upon this island. This drawing is followed with another one further away, including two stick figures holding hands. "Car-lo oos, Car-lo djoodjoo?"

Recalling how she taught me these words for papa and mama, I nod to tell her I have a mama and papa, and they are upon this land far away, across the sea.

She looks away, biting her lower lip as if a question troubles her mind and she is afraid to ask it. "Watseka?" I ask, waving my hand toward my papa and mama in hopes she shall not be afraid.

Her finger jabs toward one figure— "Car-lo" then at the other— and she raises her palms in question. Ah, so she wants to know if I have a wife like she had a husband. I draw a cross upon the sand and lie back to fold my arms across my chest and close my eyes. She pats my chest. I open my eyes to see her pat her own chest. If I understand correctly, she wants to know if I loved my wife. In answer, I nod emphatically and hug myself. She pats her chest, says "Uhanu," and hugs herself as well.

A sigh heaves from deep within me. We are two people in love—myself with my dead wife—herself with her dead husband—and I do not know if we shall ever lighten the weight upon our hearts by releasing their ghosts. Even more so, I was a fool for allowing myself to touch her breasts and kiss the nape of her neck in our moment of passion. As upon this island, weakness kills, and my weakness resulted in our months-long loss of friendship, which could have ended both of our lives from loneliness.

A huge wave crashes ashore. White with foam, the surf rushes toward us. We get to our feet and back away, as our drawings—our very lives even—are washed from existence.

Needing something to lighten my mood, I motion to Watseka for us to continue our walk, this time to the south in hopes of seeing the second herd of horses.

She leaves the same narrow footprints upon the wet sand, sometimes darting away to study a shell. Within the rearward wash of the surf toward the sea, sand moles leave their telltale Vs. Out upon the blue-green swells, as the black fins of a group of dolphins extend to glisten within the sunlight, blowholes puff clouds of mist, which turn into splashes of color, similar to miniature rainbows.

The sight reminds me of the promise of the rainbow, one promise of hope among many that Father Cristobal taught us students at the La Rabida monastery. Time and time again, so many that I cannot number them, I have prayed for hope since leaving Palos de la Frontera and my daughter. Within the past months, those prayers have included Watseka and I, for our relationship to be one of peace and friendship. Now, despite my anger at myself for losing control that desperate night, when lust overcame logic, I consider the possibility of us becoming more than friends. However, I must remind myself of our conversation moments ago, including how our lives are still tied to our loved ones through death.

Shaking my head savagely, I curse under my breath. You are a fool, Carlo. Be glad you are alive and have someone to keep you from hanging yourself because of loneliness.

"Car-lo! Car-lo!"

Pulling myself from my anger, I turn to look where Watseka is pointing, and I hear the horses before I see them. Hooves pound sand within a thicket. Snorts blow. Voices whinny. Sleek heads and necks rise and arch above the brush like the backs of dolphins.

In a burst of browns and tans, the herd runs down a dune, sand flinging from their hooves, and stops to eye Watseka and I. A shrill whinny shrieks within the thicket, and a handsome stallion, hide like coined gold, joins the herd. After a moment he leaves them to snort defiantly at us from flared nostrils, then wheels and leads them away to the south.

Watseka grabs my arms. "Car-lo! Car-lo! Horse!"

I extend a hand as if holding a bow and pull the other one back as if drawing an arrow. Watseka pulls my arms down. "Horse, Car-lo, horse. No eat."

I drop to my hands and knees. Watseka frowns, so I pat my back, intending for her to mount me as if I were a horse. Her black brows furrow, until she breaks out in a grin and smacks my behind. Grinning also, I pat my back again, and she hops on. She weighs so little, I hardly know she is there. Still, I do my best to give her a ride, although her feet drag the sand beside me.

Ah, Luisa, I am a child again, except this time I am the horse instead of my papa. How I wish I were home to give a you a ride like this once more.

"But, Papa, you—"

Laughing like a child herself, Watseka rolls from my back and shoves me over to sit atop me. Shining dark eyes. A huge brilliant smile. The curve of breasts peeking from within her leather garment. Silky hair hanging within my face.

She pulls my nose, leaps to her feet, and runs after the horses. Smiling so hugely that my cheeks ache, I run after her.

Yes, we are friends again, but if we shall become more than friends is a question I cannot answer.

October 4, 1523

Dear Luisa,

I woke this morning to the unmistakable sound of Watseka vomiting outside. Yes, our nights since we married have been filled with love, and a child can only be the result of such love.

I run outside to hold her hair away from her mouth. The days are cooler now, this morning especially. Gooseflesh dots her back and my arms. She retches until nothing but colorless bile drips from her mouth, wipes it away and stands, chest expanding and contracting as if she were Armonía after a hard gallop. "Good morning, love," I say, smiling.

"Good—" She burps terribly. "Good mor-ning, Carlo." She places a hand over her navel. "Papa, yes?"

I take her tiny form into my arms. "Oh, yes, love. I want to be a papa more than anything in this world."

She pulls away to frown, likely at some of the words I have not taught her yet. I smile hugely while nodding vigorously. "Yes, love. Carlo papa."

I am pulled down for a sour kiss, not minding in the least, and we go inside the shelter to dress and break our fast. Well, for myself to break my fast. The mama-to-be only sips water and nibbles a type of flat bread she started making recently from the peeled, dried, and ground cores of a plant whose top resembles the tail of a cat. It is somewhat tasteless and bland, so I do not ask why she has not made it earlier. Perhaps it is good as a light meal for a woman with child, and she made it for that reason alone.

We spend the day as we have for the last two weeks, preparing for winter by smoking strips of deer and fish, tanning deer hides, and gathering those cattail plants to hang them inside the shelter to dry.

We usually finish as the sun starts descending toward the west, giving Watseka time to make winter clothes from the furs we collected at her village, myself for working already tanned deer hides until they are supple and soft. I also, of course, continue writing within my journal. When we are dead and gone, long years from now, I plan to leave it to our children to remember us by.

It is another afternoon now. A chilly wind whistles through the wall where my former bed was located. Thank goodness Watseka and I now sleep on her side of the shelter, away from hissing sand, the freezing winter nights of last year, and the grit within my hair. Still, I must sit somewhere while I work, so I use the area to the right of our bed, where I scrape a stone knife across a deer hide to remove the hair. Watseka separates a dried length of sinew into threads for sewing.

A sudden thought comes to me. I set the hide aside and, upon the sand between us, draw the village beside the two rivers, where her other people live fifteen days away. She leans over to look at it. "What, Carlo?"

I do not know the word for doctor or medicine. Holding my chest, I cough terribly, raise my fingers to my mouth as if I take a bite of something, and my coughing ends. She tilts her head to one side, puzzled at my performance. I pinch my thumb and finger together and point to them. "Medicine." I cough again, take my imaginary medicine, and again, my coughing ends.

"Ah," she says, nodding. She then says a word I can hardly pronounce, much less write, so it must be her word for medicine.

I point at myself and raise my medicine between us. "Doctor." Then I point to the drawing of the village by the rivers. "Doctor here?"

"Yes, Carlo."

I draw our island and two stick figures to represent us. "Watseka, Carlo. Yes?"

"Yes."

I place two fingers from each hand to our figures and walk them to the village by the rivers. "We go?"

Eyeing me, she wipes the sand clean of my drawings. "We stay."

I kiss her cheek and return to scraping the deer hide. At least I know we have a doctor we can visit if the need arises. Unfortunately, this doctor is a fifteen-day journey away. If either of us, or our children, are ever gravely ill, I hope the journey goes much faster than that.

Within our clearing, a horse nickers softly. We ride Canción and Armonía as often as possible, and they sometimes bed within the nearby thicket. Our talking must have attracted them.

Watseka stands and stretches, dons a light fur she has sewn into a cloak, and motions me outside.

A full moon illuminates the land similar to either morning or dusk, when the sun clears the horizon or is about to set. The breeze chills me, so I get my own cloak and return. Watseka pats the golden neck of Armonía, murmuring low and soft, even hugging her. Canción comes over, shaking his mane. I rub his neck and scratch his white star. He nickers with satisfaction.

Watseka swings her leg over the back of Armonía. "Ride, Carlo."

I fetch the bridles from the shelter, mount Canción, and our friends trot along the path and to the beach, where we stop at the edge of the surf. Watseka reaches for me. I take her hand and we sit silently, transfixed by the beauty of the moonlight shimmering a golden path toward us, from the horizon to the foam at the hooves of the horses.

I am tempted to say I have never known such happiness, but I did before Juliana died. No, not every moment held this bliss, for no couple, married or otherwise, is immune to disagreements, but we shared more bliss than I can hardly recall.

Still, when I think back on it, one of those times was when we walked hand in hand within the vineyard of my papa on a moonlit night such as this. The warmth of her fingers entwining mine. Her smile with each and every glance. Our bare feet wet with dew from the cool grass. Her dark eyes looking into mine. Moonlight shining upon her hair.

Eyes stinging momentarily, I almost weep at this memory. Watseka reminds me so much of Juliana, sometimes to where I imagine her atop me, gently sharing my rhythm, and especially when she falls to my chest, spent with love, to whisper my name within my ear as I whisper her name within hers, and *love, love, love you so very much.*

The surf whispers closer. The horses step rearward. One of those scuttling crabs scurries sideways and Canción snorts at it.

What an exquisite night. I tug my bridle to ease Canción toward Watseka for a kiss. Dark hair, eyes, lashes, all so much like Juliana. We kiss once more before returning home.

Sitting within the circle of firelight with my journal, I scratch away with another quill. Few are left within the chest, nor bottles of ink, nor pages of parchment. What shall my final entry be? Regardless, I am certain it shall be filled with happiness, for I can foresee no further tragedies for us upon this island. After all, Watseka only lost her daughter because of the man who attacked her.

A gust of wind hisses sand against the far wall, flickers the flames, clatters the limbs, shudders the sailcloth over our heads, pricks my arms with cold—like the night I would have died within the snow if not for Cantante warming me.

And the words of Father Cristobal whisper from the past … *My goodness, children, I just had a chill, as if someone has just walked across my grave.*

Watseka mumbles within her sleep. Rolling over, she sighs. So sweet. So innocent. I lower my head to pray.

God of all the earth, please keep us safe upon this island. More importantly, allow Watseka to bear our child without issue. If I were to lose them, I would certainly be forced to take my own life in order to follow them to Heaven.

Then I have a thought—if death comes, I would take a lock her hair, tie it with part of the red ribbon that holds the curl of hair from Juliana, and enclose them within my journal forever, physical reminders of the love I have been blessed with during my short life.

As if to quell my fear, the wind calms, the flames still, the limbs go quiet, the sailcloth lies smooth.

Thank you, God, thank you for all your many blessings.

I close my journal, lie down beside my wife, and hold her close.

And thank you most of all for Watseka, who bears our child to come.

"What about me and Mama, Papa? Do you not thank God for us as well?"

Of course, my darling, of course. Always and forever.

A girlish giggle. "I knew that, Papa, I was only teasing. Goodnight."

And goodnight to you, Luisa, my love. Goodnight to you.

April 17, 1523

Dear Luisa,

The last two weeks have been miserable. Storm after storm, each after a brief respite of sun, have risen from the west, sending curtains of rain, cannonades of thunder, and flashes of lightning so bright at night, they illuminated the sleeping form of Watseka across from me.

With each new swirling wall of black clouds, rain thudded against our sailcloth, once even turning into hail. Water ran in rivulets to settle at sags and drip to the sand, forcing me to tighten the ropes supporting the cloth to reduce the dripping. This caused the water to stream into the one bucket and the barrel at two of the corners of the roof outside, giving us a waterfall of sound for a lullaby with which to fall asleep by. Still, although we enjoyed our liquid lullaby, we moved our bedding to avoid being soaked during sleep or while we sat impatiently. Oh, and we also changed from our leather clothing into my old cloth clothing, for it dried quicker after trips to the thicket and chafed the skin less.

"Goodness gracious, Papa. Did you see each other naked?"

Watseka changed one morning while I visited the thicket. I changed when she did the same afterward. You see, she gave me the idea.

"You regretted not seeing her naked, did you not?"

Stop your teasing, or is Beatriz telling you to ask me that?

A girlish giggle, somewhat muffled by a hand over a mouth, sparkles around me. "I shall stop, Papa. What did you and Watseka do all this time? It sounds dreadfully boring."

Well, we gathered food and ate as usual. Other than that, I caught up with my writing, gathered sticks and brought them inside to dry, and attempted to keep my teeth clean by chewing a stick every morning until the end frayed into a brush, followed by working the woody bristles around my gums. Watseka already did so, and that was where I got that idea as well. Besides, woody bristles worked much better than the toothpicks Mateo, Barros, Sancho, and myself once used.

One night after I went to bed and rolled over to face my wall, where water dripped along the openings between the boards, I rolled back over and saw how Watseka kept her long hair so lovely. From the large bag she brought from her village, she took out a comb. I could not imagine where she got it from, until I realized it was made of bone with slits cut into it. As the embers of our fire set her features aglow, over and over she combed her hair, paying particular attention to tangles within the ends.

The scene mesmerized me, along with how her partially unbuttoned blouse revealed more of her breasts than usual. Forced to pull my gaze to her face again, I saw her eyes meet mine, followed by a slight smile from her full lips. With shame heating my cheeks, I rolled over again. Water dripping along the boards provided welcome relief from her smile, her hair, and her full lips, which I longed to kiss.

Ignoring my shame, I soon turned my head in time to see Watseka unbutton and remove her blouse. The embers shimmered with reds and golds, highlighting curves and contours, peaks and valleys, and I whipped my head toward the dripping boards again.

This happened last night. Thankfully, this morning we awake to sunshine and clear skies, for we both could use a warm day upon the beach while searching for the horses once more.

Our morning meal passes silently. Watseka even allows me to help scrub the clay pots. Without a word, I start toward the path, and she joins me.

From the pounding of the rain, the beach resembles the cobbles lining the streets at Palos de la Frontera, somewhat even in texture but not so bumpy. Watseka runs to the surf, black hair streaming behind her. I attempt to swallow the turtle-egg sized lump within my throat at the sight, for she resembles none other than my whisp of a wife, Juliana. Nearing the surf, she frightens a flock of those backward-kneed birds into flight, and they dart in unison over the waves, to land further down the beach.

"Car-lo!" she yells, waving. "Horse!"

Arriving at her side, I see the tracks come from the north and are heading south. I shade my eyes and see horse-shaped blurs trotting down the beach. Watseka shoves my shoulder, bolts toward the horses, and I run after her.

As we near the herd, a shrill whinny bursts from the thickets, and the golden stallion charges down the dune toward the brown stallion. I grab the arm of Watseka to stop her. The stallions intend to battle for the mares, and I do not want slashing hooves or kicking hind legs to harm her.

The mares and foals from both herds, including Canción and Armonía, watch the stallions. At first it is a stalemate, ears pricked forward, snorts issuing forth from flaring nostrils, front hooves pawing and throwing sand. Then they rear and strike, whirl and kick, blows thudding upon necks, shoulders, and chests.

Watseka glares at me, tears within her eyes. She has come to love the horses already, and she cannot bear to see them fight. She slaps my arm and points toward the stallions. "Car-lo, no!"

The onslaught of hooves continues, except now the stallions lunge forth to bite sleek necks and snatch away mouthfuls of mane. With each gnash of teeth, with each bloody wound upon either golden or brown hide, the stallions scream and rear and buck.

Watseka jerks from my grasp and runs toward the pair, waving her hands. A hoof barely misses her head before I can snatch her away by the arm and drag her aside while the two slash at each other. She tries to run again, but I wrap my arms around her and hold her close. "No, Watseka, no, they shall hurt you."

A hard knee doubles me over. I fall to the sand holding my gut, nearly retching at the pain centered within my groin. Having fallen facing away from the stallions, I cannot even roll over when I hear Watseka screaming, "No, horse, no!"

Two sets of hooves pound sand. Two groups of horses whinny on the move. Either one stallion is the victor, or Watseka lies dead upon the trampled sand where they fought and bled.

Warm hands grasp my arms and turn me over. Silken hair fresh with the morning falls to my cheeks. A finger waggles within my face. "No, Car-lo." She bites her arm and says "No" again. Apparently, with all the seriousness she can muster, she refused to allow the stallions to bite each other. However, she has no problem kneeing my crotch hard enough to make me almost faint.

I attempt to stand while holding my stomach at the same time. She takes my hand, pulls me to my feet, and leaves in the direction of the northern herd of horses. I shuffle along behind her until my pain eases, which is not for a good while.

When we reach the beach near our path, she brushes sand from my clothes, nods like a woman satisfied with her work for the day, and climbs the dune to offer me a hand.

At the shelter again, I lie down. Watseka brings water in one of the pottery cups, kneels beside me, and lifts my head to help me sip. She fills another cup and sits across from me to drink.

The pain still throbs within my groin. Were I ever to consider having more children, I doubt I ever shall.

Watseka sets the cup beside her, wrinkles her nose, and stands with one of the pieces of sailcloth she uses while bathing within the calm water behind the island. I sniff my own sour underarm and agree. We have not bathed in two weeks, and I cannot even stand myself. As she leaves, I am tempted to follow for a glimpse of her naked body, but the ache within my groin and the shame within my heart do not allow it. Instead, I crawl to my chest for the journal, ink, and a quill, and record the day until now.

What more can I write to you, Luisa? I am somewhat at a loss for words at the moment, or either my pain is making me lightheaded.

I dip the quill in ink and set it to the parchment.

The wedding of your mama and I was a grand affair. Her mama and papa hired musicians, had mounds of steaming food placed upon huge tables within the yard, and invited practically everyone within Palos de la Frontera. Illuminated by flaming torches upon posts scattered about the area, everyone danced, paused between songs for wine, and danced again. Before very long, several men wobbled upon unsteady legs, and their wives helped them into wagons or carriages and drove them home.

"But, Papa, that was after. What about before, and what about the wedding dress?"

Of course, my darling, of course. My apologies for not starting with the dress.

"Oh, yes, Papa, but please tell me about her hair first. Were there flowers within it? And bows? And—"

Yes, Luisa, all woven into her waves as lovely as can be, with a lace veil down her back.

"What color was it?"

Well, her mama wore both the veil and the dress when she was married and gave it to your mama. It was made of shimmering silk with lace and beads sewn on. It also had a tiny waist that matched the waist of your mama perfectly. From there it flared outward, accentuating her slender hips, with the hem hiding her dainty feet. Might I say, she was the fairest bride Spain has ever seen, or shall ever see.

"I am certain she was, Papa. What happened next?"

As I was saying, many men grew wobbly, and their wives drove them home. Even Sir Anthony became somewhat intoxicated from the two bottles of wine my papa gave him for the occasion, and his wife had to help him inside. By that time it was late, and my mama and papa and Beatriz had left, so your mama and I piled into our carriage and galloped Cantante down the road.

Another unmuffled giggle. "You can stop there, Papa. I do not need to know what happened after that."

I set my quill aside. A fine idea, Luisa, a fine idea indeed. Oh, I hear Watseka humming a tune as she comes up the path. Perhaps I shall bathe also, before my sour self runs her away.

I gather my leather clothing, a piece of sailcloth to dry myself with, and pass Watseka as she strides toward the shelter.

At the edge of the water, I look for those pesky crabs. The last thing I want is to step on one, for just the thought reminds me of their poisonous flesh. Well, poisonous to me but not to Watseka.

As the sun is directly overhead, the water warms me. I remove my clothes, scrub them with sand, and place them over marsh grass to drip. Walking back out into deeper water, I hear something rustling within the thicket near the bank and whirl around. Perhaps a horse is nearby, or a deer, or a— I frown when black hair reflects sunlight. Then I wave a giggling Watseka away.

Instead of leaving immediately, she takes all my clothing and laughs hysterically while running up the rise to the shelter. All I can do is shake my head—until I look down to wonder if she were laughing at my—

Grinning myself, I continue bathing. At least she has a sense of humor.

Bath done, I trudge up the sandy rise to find both my leather and original clothing hanging from a tree limb. Covered properly again, I go inside the shelter, where Watseka is threading tiny shells onto a length of sinew. She must have brought the shells from her village, for I have not seen them before. Snickers chortle within her throat. She puts the shells and sinew down and offers me a tiny triangle of sailcloth. I take it and shrug my shoulders in question. She points at my groin and rolls onto her back to laugh like a screeching gull, apparently thinking all I need to cover myself is this tiny piece of cloth.

Perhaps her sense of humor is a bit much. However, her teasing and laughter and pranks can only mean she has grown extremely comfortable with me, and that is a good sign indeed.

Our evening meal consists of those crunchy greens, some turtle eggs we saved by burying within the shade, and some smoked deer, all washed down with crisp rainwater. As darkness falls, Watseka adds sticks to the embers for light and continues working with the shells and sinew.

Several yawns later, she takes her comb from the large bag and runs it through her hair, grimacing at a tangle. Without the least bit of hesitation, she hops over the fire, sits cross-legged before me, and hands me the comb.

A tingle of anticipation jolts my spine. I can almost feel her warmth, can almost smell the fresh air within her hair. To unsnarl the tangles, I comb the ends of her hair first. Tangles gone, I work my way up, and the comb snags on the leather collar of her blouse. She looks back at me with the slightest of smiles, unties several laces, and lets the collar open enough to bare her shoulders, glowing a rich brown within the firelight. I attempt to finish her hair, but my hand trembles so, I am afraid I shall scratch her neck with the teeth of the bone comb.

A soft sigh swells her sides. She leans back, not quite to my chest. How a wish she would take my hands and place them to her breasts, but I rise and drop the comb into her lap before such a thing happens. The last thing I want is to allow lust to make a fool of me again. I require the strength of love instead of the weakness of man before we lie together, regardless of what Watseka might think.

Silently, she goes to her bed. Silently, I go to mine.

Outside, the wind rustles the limbs. The glowing embers pulse with heat as I did a moment ago. A stick pops and falls, sending up a brief shower of sparks.

Perhaps teaching Watseka to ride a horse shall take my mind off of my physical attraction to her. However, we must earn their trust first, and I have no idea what we can do to make that happen.

April 18, 1523

Dear Luisa,

During our morning meal, I notice Watseka has picked more greens than we can eat, filling the two clay jars. I hold one up and shrug my shoulders to ask why, but she ignores me. Afterward, she goes outside and comes back to hand me my flute. When I raise it to my lips, she shakes her head. "No, Carlo. Horse."

What a fool I am for not remembering this. Since Canción enjoyed my flute playing like Cantante did, the music may draw him to us again, including the rest of the northern herd. I point to the leftover jar of greens. "Horse?"

Nodding, Watseka taps her temple with a fingertip, as if she is intelligent for thinking of using the greens to draw the horses as well as the flute.

"Yes," I say. "Watseka is very smart."

She questions my words with crinkled eyes. I tap my temple and nod. Raising her eyebrows, she nods again.

Very little wind blows this morning, hardly more than a breeze. Instead of pounding the beach, the surf whispers against the sand as Watseka and I walk north in search of the herd of horses. She sees them first, brown blurs upon the beach, and walks faster. I grab her arm to stop her, draw a length of rope upon the sand, and grasp at it as if I have a rope and put it over my head. I mean to make a bridle, but I do not have a nose like a horse with which to show her my idea. She nods, however, so I give her the flute and run back to the shelter for the rope Sancho and I braided.

On the way back to Watseka, I cut the rope and knot it into two bridles with reigns. Not only shall we be able to control two horses due to their familiarity with bridles, we can guide them as well.

At the place where I left Watseka, her narrow footprints continue. I quicken my step, for she is far ahead and nearing the horses. Before long I hear notes coming from the flute. It is all I can do not laugh out loud, for she is holding the flute to her lips with one hand while offering green shoots to the horses with the other.

When I reach this spectacle, I do chuckle at the horses, who simply stare with huge, dark eyes, manes and tails feathering gently within the breeze. Watseka tosses me the flute. The notes almost play themselves, repeating the song that drew them that night. From within the herd, the son of Cantante takes a few tentative steps forward. "Hello there, Canción," I say pausing my playing. He stops and jerks his head upright, dissatisfied with the sudden lack of music.

Watseka waves the shoots and says, "Canción, Canción, Canción," singing his name like you would, Luisa. To tempt my laughter even more, she takes a bite of one of the shoots to show Canción what they are for. Chewing, she looks back at me as I chuckle, then frowns and puckers her lips to blow, which releases bits of chewed shoot. Despite my laughter, I try to play, but all I can manage is a single note that sounds like Barros releasing a foul odor from his backside. Watseka snorts laughter and waves away my foolishness.

Despite our humor, laughter, and silly noises, Armonía, the golden yearling, leaves the herd and joins Canción. I play again, this time a decent tune. Step by step, Canción and Armonía come, ears twisting this way and that. Step by step the other horses come, tails switching behind them. Both yearlings are so entranced, they walk right by Watseka and continue to me. Thank goodness, two mares stop to take bites of the green shoots from her, and she beams a huge smile. I continue playing while going to Watseka. She offers the shoots to the yearlings following me, and they snatch them greedily from her hand.

I stop playing to see if the herd stays. They do, still eating. I risk rubbing the neck of one of the mares. Except for a ripple of her hide and mane, nothing else happens. I motion Watseka to the mare, where she rubs the sleek neck as well, murmuring words I do not know. Between the food and the music, our goal is met, for both mares allow us to rub their necks. I even manage to slip the bridles over their noses and place the reins across their backs.

Watseka touches one of the ropes, eyebrows arched in question, and I realize I have not explained how we shall guide the horses with the bridles. To do so, I take the reins within my hands and gently tug, which results in the mare turning her head slightly left and right. The dark brows of Watseka lower with understanding.

The mares munch contently from our hands. I rub the sleek neck of one while Watseka does the same to the other. We croon to them softly, scratch foreheads, tousle manes. They nicker and close their eyes, enjoying the attention.

Beside Watseka, I kneel to tap her foot and lace my fingers together. Like a horse about to be shoed, she lifts her foot. Taking it into my hands, I lift her gently onto the back of the mare, whose eyes widen. She takes a few steps backward, snorting at the unfamiliar weight upon her back. I take the bridle in hand and walk slowly along the beach. The other mare follows, along with Canción, Armonía, and the remaining horses. The brown stallion hangs back, snorting and twisting his ears at the spectacle of a young Spaniard gentleman taking his wives. Watseka, who left the empty clay pot upon the sand when she mounted the mare, holds the reins. Satisfied with how the mare strolls along contentedly, I take my flute from my belt and play again.

Canción and Armonía stop, ears twisting, nostrils flaring. In a flurry of gleaming hooves, arching necks, flying tails and manes, they prance along beside us. Behind me, hooves pound sand, until the stallion streaks by at a full gallop. I mount the other mare and steer her to join Watseka, whose bright smile fills my heart.

"Oh, Papa, how I wish I were there to ride either Canción or Armonía. Your beach and the horses must be Heaven itself."

They are, my darling, and so is Watseka.

"I am glad for you. You needed someone to keep you from being alone. Still, it makes me sad with how she lost her husband and baby and her people."

It makes me sad as well, Luisa. Hopefully, those times are gone.

"Do you think you and Watseka might become more than friends?"

I cannot deny that hope. Friendship is better than nothing, so I shall not press the issue.

"I think it shall happen, for Watseka is part of the purpose for which you still live."

She is, is she? I hold in a grin. Perhaps you can tell me more about that.

"It is something you should learn on your own."

Very well. I do not mind an intrigue of your making, especially since it is similar to your mama's intrigue.

The rising sun warms the hide of my mare. She and the rest of the herd turn toward the surf, and I return my flute to my belt. Their hooves splash white foam and scatter a flock of those backward-kneed birds into the air. Canción and Armonía, including two foals from this year, with long spindly legs and bristly manes, dash into the waves, kicking up their hooves while whinnying excitedly. Watseka leans over to hug the neck of her mare, in love with horses already.

We give our mares their heads, and they wade into the surf up to their bellies. Except for the foals, the rest of the herd follows, even the stallion. The calm wind creates hardly any waves, and soon the entire herd swims along, snorting. I did not plan on getting our leather clothing wet, so I slide from the back of the mare, remove both bridles from them, and wave to Watseka, who follows me. My feet barely touch the sand as I tiptoe back to the beach. Watseka, however, swims along on her back, feet kicking swirls within the calm water.

Upon the beach again, I squeeze water from my blouse. A wad of wet leather splats into my face, and I look up to see Watseka running toward the surf, naked. Not watching her is impossible. Thankfully, the blue-green water enfolds her. To avoid the lovely sight, I look down while squeezing water from her clothing.

"Car-lo!" she yells, waving me in. I do not, for I fear I shall lose control like I did that night. She yells again. I shake my head and hold up her clothes to let her know she can wear them again, being only wet instead of dripping. She swims to the beach, takes the clothes, and strides back to her clay pot, which is a gray dot to the north. I dare not follow, dare not give in to my lust over her lovely form, dare not—

I whirl away and hurry back to the shelter. A change of clothes is in order, as well as giving myself the time necessary to allow my lust to calm from insistent to something less so. Still, I am thankful for how we can now ride the mares. Come tomorrow, I would like to explore further north and south, if for no other reason than to get a lay of the land, including how large this island is.

At the shelter, I drape my clothes across a limb to dry, although I shall wash the sand from them later. Dressed within my old clothing, I look up as Watseka comes through the door, either water or sweat glistening upon her naked body. The sight of her so close turns me away. Clothing rustles, so she is likely getting dressed as well. Her hand grasps my arm and turns me around. She rises on tiptoe to kiss my cheek, possibly thanking me for our ride. Nodding, I smile, more so because she is dressed instead of naked. We stand there silently. Like at other times, she has not fully buttoned the blouse, and the curve of her slight bosom rises and falls enticingly. Juliana, my love, I sincerely hope you can forgive my carnal thoughts, for it seems I have absolutely no control over them whatsoever. Well, that is not true. At least I possessed enough control to get away from Watseka instead of swimming with her naked like she wanted me to.

Still watching me, Watseka slips her arms around my waist and hugs me. The slight weight of her head upon my chest is the same as yours, Juliana, when we danced after our wedding. I welcome her warmth. I welcome her hands pressed into the small of my back. I welcome her briny aroma, as if she were a goddess arisen from the sea.

She releases me, tousles my hair, and goes outside, presumably to start on our midday meal. After returning my flute to the chest and hanging the bridles upon a tree limb to dry, I retrieve some turtle eggs from their hole within the cool sand beneath the shade of one of the trees, pour water into our pottery cups, and go inside, where Watseka is placing pieces of one of those wonderful mottled brown fish upon the rocks near the fire to warm them.

Like so many times before, Silence lowers her head inside my home, now the home of this lovely young woman as well. I admire her strength, her courage, her humor, even to the point of excess. Am I completely happy? No, but I am as happy as a man in my situation can be, and I believe Watseka feels the same way. Otherwise, she would have left me long ago to join her people to the west, who live near the rivers she drew for me.

The afternoon passes lazily. Watseka works on her neckless of shells while I sharpen my knife. She looks up at the scrape of metal against shell and takes her stone knife from her large rawhide bag, studies it and offers it to me. I offer her my knife, and she nods at the edge. Her knife is as sharp as mine. I never knew someone who made knives and hide scrapers from flakes of stone, and the results are amazing. We trade knives again and return to our work.

"Papa, can I ask you something?"

Of course, Luisa. You can ask me anything.

"Are you and Watseka going to marry?"

I hold in a chuckle. Because we seem married now?

"Perhaps a little. Is she very much like Mama? If so, I think you need each other like you and Mama needed each other."

We shall, see Luisa, we shall see.

August 1, 1523

Dear Luisa,

I am certain you would like to know if Watseka and I have moved any closer to matrimony during the last four months, but the answer is no, not at all. In fact, she has not done the least little thing to make me think we are growing closer, such as having me comb her hair, sneaking to watch me bathe, or swimming naked within the sea.

Part of that is because since my last journal entry, we have been riding the mares often, including hunting, gathering greens, and spearing fish. It may sound boring, but boring is within the mind. Believe me, if I could change everything that sent me here, I would.

Be that as it may, let me tell you about a few of our adventures.

First, several days after our initial ride, I attempted to gallop my mare by snapping the reins hard and heeling her flanks even harder. I suppose she was sensitive there, for when I heeled her, she grunted and wheeled, kicked and bucked, and I went flying over her head to thud within the sand upon my back. Watseka slid from her mare while I wheezed, having had my breath knocked out, and ran over to see about me. Fortunately for her—and myself—I caught my breath just as she arrived, because I thought I was about to perish and she did too, evidenced by tears filling her eyes. She helped me up and brushed sand from my back, covered her mouth and burst out laughing. Needless to say, I shuffled back to the shelter, my horse riding over for the day.

The next day, however, virtually the same thing happened to Watseka, except she landed upon her bottom, jumped to her feet, and gave the mare what I supposed was a tongue-lashing with native curse words, waggling her finger at the mare the entire time. It was my turn to laugh as she limped back to the shelter, cursing me as well.

A few days later, after we forwent riding to enable our aches and pains to subside, we rose at dawn, ate quickly, and rode the mares north until midday, with Canción and Armonía at our sides.

If this is an island, it must be a huge one, for we never reached the northern shore. Other than that it was all the same, filled with thickets, trees that resembled crooked old men and crooked old women, and sand and surf as far as the eye could see.

We did the same thing the next day, but toward the south, starting out after midday because Watseka and I had to smoke a deer she took that morning as it mistakenly strolled into our clearing. For whatever reason, neither Canción nor Armonía came with us. Perhaps they needed a day off from their first adventure, or perhaps they decided to stay within the cool shade like Watseka and I should have.

Like some great eye beaming down, the sun felt as if it were cooking us—myself because of the sweat soaking my underarms, Watseka because of how it soaked her back beneath her blouse as she rode ahead of me.

We did see the southern horse herd standing within the surf, but they tossed their heads and trotted off when we neared them. Frowning at them, Watseka flipped a derisive hand and continued past their tracks upon the sand.

The day grew hotter. Heat wavered above the sand in the distance. We rode the mares to the shade of one of those crooked trees and dismounted to drink water from one of my skins, lying back afterward to allow the breeze to dry the sweat from our bodies and clothing. Before we knew it, twilight was settling around us, with a full moon birthing itself from the horizon across the sea.

Oh, Luisa, in case you were wondering, the northern herd did not follow us either day. After our initial time with them, when we fed them and I played the flute, they treat us like neighbors. Thank goodness for that, with how the southern herd runs each time we near them. Ah, well, horses are like people I suppose. Some get along with everyone while some do not.

As the twilight deepened, the gulls flew over our heads toward the west, where I supposed they roost somewhere. Several flocks of the backward-kneed birds wheeled over the waves on their way south, to wherever they roost as well. One lone pelican glided out to sea, dove for a fish, and floated upon the silver water while gulping it down.

Although the sun was lowering behind us, heat still gripped the island as did a wetness within the air. If I did not know any better, I would say someone was holding a kettle beneath the island to steam us for a meal.

Watseka rose, stretched, and walked to the surf. Upon reaching the water, she removed her clothes and ran in for a swim. The sight of her drew me like one of those magical stones that draws steel, but the need to acquire some relief from the heat drew me more, and I was soon beside her, naked as well.

She ignored me for a moment, but her humor would not allow me any peace. Swimming upon her back, she kicked water in my face. I splashed her in return, and she dove to escape me. Something grabbed my ankle, and just as I thought it was one of those pesky crabs, she surfaced before me to wrap her arms around my neck and throw her head back in laughter.

It would be an understatement in the extreme to say I did not enjoy her smooth skin against me, the round firmness of her breasts, the contours of both thigh and calf, the yellow from the dying sun coloring her lips golden.

In a swirl of foam she released me, swam to the beach, and dressed. I did the same, and soon we were riding home as God painted the western horizon with a fiery sunset—yellow to orange, to a deep molten scarlet, like a horseshoe glowing within a forge.

At the path to the shelter, we removed the bridles and sent the mares northward with a pat upon their behinds. As we watched their hooves kick up sand, tails raised high, manes flying about while their necks arched up and down, I slipped my arm around the shoulders of Watseka. I had not planned it whatsoever, but it seemed as natural as breathing.

She patted my hand and faced me. "Carlo hungry?"

Although she had learned some of my words during the summer, she surprised me by saying my name so smoothly. I answered by taking her hand and leading her to the shelter.

When we arrived, I raised the sailcloth over the smoking deer meat for a piece of loin to cook over the embers within the shelter. Watseka took the water bucket inside. We already had some greens leftover from this morning to eat with the deer, and this is where we are now, our meal done, myself writing the events of the past months within my journal.

Sitting cross-legged upon her bed, Watseka works on a third shell necklace. She must love them to make so many, or either she does so to have something to do.

"Carlo?"

I stop writing. "Yes?"

"I …" She blinks several times, likely because she does not have the words for what she desires to say. She steps around the fire to sit beside me, draws four crosses upon the sand, and raises her palms upward with her familiar way of asking me a question. No guess is needed for this query, for she must want to know who lies beneath the four crosses, like her infant daughter lies beneath the one.

To explain all the attributes of my friends would be impossible, so I simply touch the crosses in turn, starting with the one on the right. "Mateo. Barros. Sancho. Cantante."

Watseka ponders the names for a moment before drawing her vessel, but broken in two. No guess is needed here either, for the drawing is the same as the one I made to show her how my ship sank. I touch the broken vessel. "Mateo, Barros, Sancho, Cantante, my friends." If you are wondering why I act as if Cantante were human, Luisa, it would be difficult to explain why a horse is buried there. Besides, as I have said so often, I feel as though we were brothers.

"Friends?" Watseka asks, squinting at this new word. I draw a line to represent her village, including several stick figures within it, and touch each in turn. "Watseka. Watseka friends."

"Ah," she says softly while nodding. She points at the crosses. "You sad?"

"Yes." I bump her shoulder with mine. "Happy now."

She takes my hand, kisses my palm, and goes back to her bed.

After putting away my journal, ink, and quill, I lie down and listen to the breeze rustling the branches outside, the pop and crackle of the fire, and the beat of my own lonely heart. The scent of the sea enters the openings within my wall, briny with ancient aromas of salt, surf, and sand. A gust hisses sand against the wood, flutters my hair against my face, and dies a sudden death.

How many long nights must I remain here? When Sancho said no ships would ever come this way, I may have believed him within my head, but my heart now prefers to think otherwise. Yes, I have a life here of sorts with Watseka … we have everything we need and more. However, I desire the warmth of family and the tender touch and welcoming embrace of my darling daughter once again. Still, when must I relinquish this dream? And what shall it take for me to do so?

I roll over to face Watseka. She lies with her head upon her folded arm, her hair in braids, which I have never seen. Her lips purse and I think of her kiss upon my cheek. Beneath closed lids, her eyes dart, and I cannot help but wonder if she dreams of me.

An owl asks *who-who-who* do I love? I am not certain about one person in particular, Mr. Owl, although I do know I love Juliana, Luisa, and my family.

After that, we shall see.

August 2, 1523

Dear Luisa,

After our morning meal, Watseka secures her stone knife within her belt. "Knife, Carlo," she says, without any hint of humor in her expression, so I secure my knife within my belt also. She takes her bow and quiver of arrows from where they both lean against the wall on her side of the shelter, which makes no sense because of the deer from yesterday. Regardless, I follow her outside to see if she intends to hunt.

Instead of taking the path to the thicket, she takes the path to the calm water, where we bathe and keep her vessel. At the marsh, she waves me over to help her pull the vessel into the water. I hold it steady as she climbs inside and picks up a paddle, then climb inside myself. Turning to look at me over her shoulder, she points toward the place that once was her home, across the far expanse of water, and I now know she plans to go there for some inexplicable reason.

Our paddles dip into the waves, which crest with the freshening wind. The twin braids down the back of Watseka lie still, when unbraided they would have blown into her face. If I did not know better, I would say she planned this journey last night. Lucky for me, I tied my hair back when I woke this morning, or it would be blowing everywhere.

The wind increases. Spray from the crests wets my lips with the flavor of salt. The arm muscles of Watseka tighten with each stroke, yet she drives the paddle into the water like a woman on a mission, and our speed increases until we leave a wake behind us. Whatever she has on her mind, it must be of great importance, for when we go out within the vessel to spear those mottled brown fish, we move about easily, as if we were paddling more for pleasure than for purpose.

My shoulders tighten. My lower back as well. My arms are leaden weights attempting to drag my hands to my sides. Sweat beads upon my forehead in cool droplets before running into my eyes to sting them. I pause only to wipe them away, and then only when my vision blurs.

Undaunted, Watseka continues to paddle, arms corded like twisted rawhide.

What was formerly her woodland home gradually comes into focus. Unlike the crooked old men and women trees upon my island, her trees stand tall and proud. Broad leaves reflect the sunlight, the wind whipping their limbs. Several trees with needled limbs stand even taller and straighter than the others, yet their tops sway back and forth, bending instead of breaking. I cannot imagine the scene of battle upon which I am about to step, but Watseka is like those trees, and I doubt anything shall ever break her.

We arrive upon land, where tall grass has been turned brown by the summer heat. After pulling the vessel ashore, our footfalls crunch as we walk. Watseka takes an arrow from the quiver across her back, sets it into the bow, and motions me to stop. I take one more step, however, to arrive at her side, and she whips around to glare at me. "No, Carlo," she hisses through clenched teeth. She takes my knife from my belt and shoves it into my hand, which, along with how she holds the bow at the ready, tells me we may be in danger.

Although it has been a year since the native village was attacked, I catch a whiff of ashes. Ahead, blackened rectangles made of overlapping bark, most burned to the ground, signal our arrival. Bones gleam where the sunlight shines through the trees, the remains of bodies, scattered by animals, I suppose.

Watseka stops. Her head turns slowly, pausing as she likely focuses on anything that may hint to the possibility of danger. She does this twice more before her shoulders relax, then returns the arrow to the quiver and continues toward the center of the village.

Here and there, partially covered with dead leaves, gleaming white skulls from both children and adults lie alone. Some adult skulls, however, lie side by side with either one or two smaller skulls, as if a mother had held her children close as the death blow fell, a knife slashed, or an arrow or spear pierced. How Watseka survived this carnage, I do not know, but I am happy she did.

At a partially burned structure, she goes inside, and I follow. A skeleton lies here also, the skull crashed by a massive blow. From a corner of the home, she takes a bow and a quiver filled with arrows and gives them to me. At another corner, she takes two large rawhide bags, adds several stones like those her knife is made of to one, then adds two clay pots and two clay cups like those from which we drink. She goes to these things with the assurance of a wife within her own home, and I cannot help but wonder if the skeleton belongs to her husband.

A stack of furs lies within another corner. She gathers those and sets them outside the door. A spear like the one I watched her use that day last year leans against a wall. She takes that outside also. Sighing heavily, she turns to survey her home once more, then goes to the corner where the furs were and kneels to gather a baby-sized outfit of tanned clothing, similar to the deer hide clothing she made for me.

I cannot say how long she knelt there, for I could not stop watching her. The sun and moon may have passed above us for an eternity, but I would not have noticed.

Soft sobs escape her as her head bows and she clutches the clothing to her breast—the clothing for her daughter, whose tiny body now lies beneath the fifth cross within my cemetery. I set the bow and quiver and bag outside and return to wrap my arms around her shaking shoulders. Weeping great sobs now, she turns within my arms and holds me tightly, and I cannot help sharing her grief with my own tears.

My God, Luisa, I cry as if I had lost you when you were born. I could not have borne such a thing. I could not have borne it at all. I would have gone insane with grief.

Our tears gradually subside. Watseka raises her head from my shoulder, wipes her tears with the outfit of her child, then wipes mine. She takes my hand, leads me outside, and places the clothing within the first rawhide bag.

Inside again, she gathers the bones into the second bag and takes it outside, to lower it reverently beside the other bag. For a moment she stands there, eyes scanning the burnt homes, the gleaming bones, the finality of death from her attackers. She starts to pick the bag up, but rage twists her face into a mask of hate. To the right of the door lies another skull, as well as a stone club. She snatches the club from the earth and screams with what I would call a cry of vengeance, then pounds the skull into bits and pieces and continues pounding them until they are beaten into the dark earth. Sweat drips from her face. Her rawhide clothing is blackened with the wetness of it. The wooden handle of the club slips from her fingers, yet she remains upon her knees, breath wheezing within her throat as her sides rise and fall.

I can only guess what has happened here. I saw the smoke in the morning, so the attackers must have slipped into the village as the people were waking. Perhaps Watseka was still asleep, and her husband heard the commotion and ran to the door to be killed, falling back inside. Perhaps she fought with the murderer, slashing him fatally with her stone knife while he beat her, broke her arm, and cut her other arm, then knocking her out with a blow to her head before he fell. Perhaps she woke and stumbled to her vessel. Perhaps she paddled away, or perhaps that wind from the west blew her vessel to my island. Regardless of my theories, none of them matter. All that matters now is Watseka.

"Watseka," I say, offering her my hand. "Let us leave this place."

Ignoring my hand, she stands to walk along until she goes inside another home, where she waves me over. Inside, two skeletons lie within a bed of furs. Watseka folds the furs over them, drags them outside, and continues to the edge of the village.

I can only speculate again, but I believe these skeletons belong to the papa and mama of her husband, since her own mama and papa live within the village near the two rivers.

She stops near several mounds of earth covered with leaves, what must be a cemetery for her people, and kneels to begin digging within the dirt with her hands. As the aroma of earth permeates the air, I go to a tree and break two limbs from it. Since we are only burying bones, it shall not take long to dig graves, but we can use all the help we can get.

Uncovering stones and moving them aside, I question myself about the bones of her husband, for if she shall bury his mama and papa here, why not him? I do not attempt to ask, however. Trust must be earned, and Watseka has earned mine. Even if she wishes to bury the remains of her husband within my cemetery in order to watch over him all the days of her life, loving only him until we both die from either age or illness, if that is her wish, it shall be mine as well.

August 3, 1523

Dear Luisa,

The wind howled terribly during our return to the island. Our arms cramped. Our backs ached. Spray soaked us through. We arrived several miles south of the path, left the vessel there, and slogged along the sandy beach to carry what we could to the shelter. Thankfully, the wind died at dusk, so we went back to paddle the vessel to the path and bring the remaining items inside. By the time our day was over, we were too exhausted to eat and too wet from salt spray and sweat to sleep within our clothes, which were also filthy from digging the graves. All we could manage was a fire to change into our clean clothing by and to fall into our beds to sleep.

I wake to a stomach rumbling with a demand for food and the aroma of deer meat sizzling upon a stick over the embers of our fire. Watseka sits across from me, working on her third necklace of shells. The bow and quiver leans beside the other one. The bag of stones sits beside the two she brought when she paddled to her village the first time. The furs are folded and stacked within a corner. The bag holding the bones of her husband are near the door, with the rounded dome of the skull barely showing. The baby-sized leather outfit meant for her daughter is folded neatly, and it lies upon the furs.

We break our fast in silence. Watseka finishes the necklace by tying it with a knot. She then hangs it from a rusty nail protruding from near the top of her wall, where the others hang. After a glance at the bag holding the bones of her husband, she takes a large, flat stone from the other bag, including three others, and sits with them before her.

I had not noticed how the large stone and one of the smaller ones were rounded and smooth, as if they had come from a river. She places a rough white stone upon the larger one, takes the other rounded one within her right hand, and hammers it down on the rough white one. A flake cleaves off. She picks it up, tests the edge with her thumb, and sets it aside. So, this is how her people make stone knives and tools—interesting. She cleaves three more pieces of stone into sharp flakes and puts everything away, loops the three necklaces around her neck, picks up the bones of her husband, and says my name, meaning, I suppose, I should come with her.

Outside, she points to one of our clay pots. I take it and follow her to the tree where we keep our turtle eggs, when we have any, buried within the sand. She sets the bag aside, digs three eggs up, and puts them within my pot.

I sense a plan taking shape, one which I considered while we were at her village. Leaving her husband beneath the tree, she motions me to follow her into the path leading to her vessel.

"I am here, Papa. What do you think her plan is?"

We shall see, Luisa, we shall sea.

"What happened to her mama and papa and her people was very sad. I do not understand such things at all."

Beside Watseka, as our feet plod upon the warming sand, I consider this statement from my daughter before I answer.

I do not understand it either, Luisa. Perhaps their attackers needed food.

"Could they not hunt and fish and gather greens for themselves?"

Some people prefer to take instead of work. I do not like it, but it is a fact of life.

"But— Oh, I see you and Watseka are almost at the marsh. I shall be quiet and see what she does."

Watseka wades into the marsh, pulls several young stems from the water, and breaks them off into my pot. She does this until it is half full, and I follow her back up the sandy path to the shelter. Here she takes her husband into her arms and leads me into the path toward the beach, then takes the fork to my cemetery.

"I see now, Papa. She is going to bury her husband like you said she might."

I am afraid so, Luisa. I am afraid so.

"Why are you sad? Oh, I forgot what you said about her bringing him here to mourn him for the rest of her life, and to love only him until she dies. I should not have asked, for that makes me sad as well."

Do not dwell upon it, my darling. She must have loved him very much in life to love him this much in death.

"Oh, Papa," Luisa wails, "I cannot help but cry. I shall return when you are happy again."

To the depths of my soul, I do not know if I shall ever be happy as I desire, but I shall do the best I can. Regardless, my heart grows numb with the prospect of living out my days unloved and practically alone, even with Watseka sharing my life.

At the cemetery, she sets the bag down, kneels, and starts to scoop sand aside in handfuls. She goes rigid, stands and runs into the path. If my guess about the burial is correct, she is returning for the three stone knives she made earlier.

Soon her feet pound upon the path. Soon I see her black hair, now unbraided, flowing about her shoulders. Soon I hear her hard breaths bourgeoning from her heaving chest.

She stops at my side, places the three stone knives into the pot within my hand, and drops to her knees to continue digging. I set the pot beside her husband to help, and before long, the shallow grave within the white sand is ready.

Watseka removes the bones one at a time from the bag and places them into the grave, as close to the form of a person as possible. After a few adjustments of the skull and ribs, she takes one of the necklaces from her neck and loops it around the skull. Knowing what she is doing now, I set the clay pot beside her, and she adds the greens to the grave, along with the stone knives. I expect her to cover the bones, but she remains kneeling.

Upon the tree limb above the grave of Sancho, a length of rope still hangs, enough to make a cross. I cut two sticks, lash them together, and place the cross at the head of the freshly dug grave. Watseka does not acknowledge my contribution—neither word, nor nod, nor glance passes between us. I step back from her and wait, for that is all I can do.

A sudden gust of wind rattles the tree limbs. To the west, a flash of lightning brightens the horizon. Several of my heartbeats pass before the thunder reaches us, rolling … rolling … rolling.

Black clouds gather to shade the calm water, turning it steel gray. Huge raindrops splatter to the leaves, pause with another gust of wind and stop completely, but that is not the end.

Extending from the roiling black clouds, a dark curtain of windblown rain obscures the land across the calm water, a line of squalls similar to those at sea. Lightning cataracts down, thunder blasts, the ground vibrates. I run to the shelter, but when I arrive, Watseka has not followed me like I thought she would.

To run out into the lightning may well end my life, but I cannot leave her. I run back, soaking wet now. She still kneels, motionless. Water runs from her hair and down her back in rivulets and nearly covers the bones of her husband. Wishing I did not have to yell over the clatter of the rain and the crashing of the thunder, I touch her shoulder. "Watseka! We must go!"

As before, she does not acknowledge me. Despite her obvious love for her husband, I cannot allow her to die within the storm. I grab her shoulders to pull her to her feet, but she whirls to scratch at my face. Not only am I at risk of being struck by lightning, I am at risk of losing my eyes. Still, if I am to die, I would rather die with the ability to see this grief-stricken woman kneeling beside the grave of her husband.

Lightning. Thunder. Rain. The pounding surf. I kneel beside her and lower my head to allow the rain to cleanse me of what I now know is my love for her—a love which shall never, ever, be returned.

August 6, 1523

Dear Luisa,

The storm finally abated, leaving us unscathed. For the remainder of that day and the following night, we attended the grave. I gave in to exhaustion by falling upon my side and sleeping, but Watseka never wavered. I gave in to the need to relieve myself by stepping into the thicket, but Watseka never wavered. I went to the shelter for water, brought the bucket back and offered it to her, but Watseka never wavered, even refusing to drink.

However, this morning, as dawn breaks with a crimson sunrise to the east, Watseka falls over, either asleep or unconscious. I hold her within my lap and trickle water into her mouth. The cords within her throat tighten as she swallows, swallows again, swallows once more, and her eyes flutter open. "Uha … Uhanu?" The hint of a soft smile. The warmth of her lips to mine. The easy rise and fall of her breast as she drifts off to sleep within my arms.

I carry her to the shelter, place her within her bed, and prepare a light meal of fish and those crunchy greens for when she awakes, likely to wonder if I have covered her husband with sand.

To have been him for only one kiss tears at my heart. What a love they must have shared, the same as the love that Juliana and I once shared.

After a few bites of the meal, I retrieve my journal to record recent events. Done with those, I ink the quill and set it to parchment, for I should continue to write about the best time of my life, which are those days before Juliana died.

We made our new home within a cottage roughly halfway between our former homes, with the idea of making it easier to visit both places. This way I would have a reasonable ride to the vineyards of my papa to work, and Juliana could either come with me within our second-hand carriage, or she could easily visit her own mama and papa as well. We filled the cottage with furniture from our former rooms, including wedding gifts of kitchen items. The fireplace did not draw well, the single bedroom was drafty, and a persistent mouse refused to leave despite my attempts to roust it from a hole beside the fireplace. Regardless, we were as happy as two newlyweds could be.

Within six months, of course, Juliana was with child, and I, the papa-to-be, beamed with delight. Unfortunately, she spent many a morning retching so terribly, I had to stay home from work to tend her. Well, I say I "had" to stay, although she bade me to go, but I could not bear to leave her in such a pitiful condition.

Be that as it may, two months later, her thin frame from lack of food began to plump, including her belly, for she ate nearly everything I set before her. A month later she was cooking feasts of lamb, fish, pork, and anything else she could find at the market within Palos de le Frontera. Furthermore, we spent the early evenings making plan after plan for our child, naming her Luisa for a girl and Luis for a boy. After those quiet talks, more often than not, we joined with great passion, then fell asleep holding each other.

Both our mamas and papas visited often. The ladies chatted away, asking how Juliana felt, if she experienced any pains, if she experienced any bleeding. Of course, they only spoke of these things out of earshot of our papas, for their cheeks would have turned scarlet from embarrassment. I only heard these conversations once, when Juliana admitted to some cramping at four months. The ladies clucked their tongues and said she was likely experiencing cramps from overexertion, which made me vow then and there to forgo our nightly bouts of passion. However, Juliana would not hear of it, taking the initiative to pretend—her words, not mine—I was Cantante. To say I was disappointed would be a lie, for the sight of her closed eyes, her growing breasts, and her gentle motion above me, all with her eyes closed while biting her lower lip in concentration, sent spasms of completion through me all too soon. Did that matter to Juliana? Not at all, for she continued until her needs were met as well, signaled by an arching back and small gasps of release.

I set my journal and quill aside, for it is another morning. Watseka, waking now, has slept the entire day and night through, no doubt exhausted from her ordeal at the grave of her husband.

I go to her side with water, but she waves it away and hurries outside, likely to relieve herself. She returns to eat and drink. Afterward I stand. "Watseka, come."

We take the path to the cemetery. At the grave of her husband, where the rain has drained into the sand, she drops to her knees to cover him. Unsure if I should help, I remain standing. With all of her preparations—the shell necklace, the stone knives, the greens—I feel this is something she would rather do herself, not to mention how she scratched my face when I attempted to take her inside out of the storm.

Sand soon mounds beneath her hands. She touches the cross I placed there, fingers the lashings. A deep sigh swells her sides. The morning breeze flutters her hair. She stands and faces me, raises one hand and holds her thumb and finger apart a small space, and taps them to her chest. "Uhanu."

I narrow my eyes in question. Is she trying to tell me she still loves her husband, but possibly not as much because she realizes she must move on?

She tilts her head. "Carlo? You see?"

"No, Watseka. No."

She balls her fingers into a fist and gently taps my chest. "Watseka?"

Is she asking if I love her? I suppose so, for this is what she did when she told me how Uhanu still filled her heart. Still, I cannot admit my love, for if she denies me again, I shall weep enough tears to fill the sea.

She steps close, raises her hand to my face, touches the scratches she left with her fingernails. Her eyes glisten with tears. She pulls me down to kiss where she is still touching. Her lips warm me, her tender expression of concern as well. She takes a step away and pounds her fist to her chest. "Carlo Carlo Carlo!"

Am I to understand she now loves me as she loved Uhanu before? Dare I wish such a miracle? Dare I dream of such a purp—

Ah, my love, you finally see part of your purpose within life, of which I told you about. Take Watseka within your embrace. Let her hear the thunder within your heart. Let her feel the warmth residing within your soul. You are capable of so much love, and it is time to release it once again.

I take the face of Watseka within my trembling hands. Kiss her forehead. Kiss the tip of her nose. I allow my lips to hover before hers. I wish her to kiss me, for only then shall I know her true feelings.

We stand there for a time. The sun-kissed sand warms our feet. The wind tousles hair about our faces. The gulls call their shrill cries. The surf pounds the beach.

Our lips finally join, tenderly at first ... so tenderly. Then, with unsated hunger, a devouring lust engulfs us. Tongues touch. Bodies press. Hands roam curves and contours and tug at clothing.

I pull away, gasping, and pound my chest with my fist. "Watseka Watseka Watseka!"

What a smile she beams, lovely as the dawn. She takes one of the two shell necklaces from her neck, places it over my head, and gestures toward the grave. "Watseka Uhanu." Then she places her hand to my chest. "Watseka Carlo."

What can I do except believe her placing the necklace around my neck means we are now married? An astonishing thought bursts into my mind. Since she made those three necklaces well before now, and since she took us to gather the bones of her husband, has she been planning our matrimony all that time?

She smiles again, likely at my amazed expression. I nod vigorously, grinning like a boy after his first kiss, and place my hand between her breasts. "Carlo loves Watseka."

"Lo ...?"

"Love." To underscore the meaning of the word, I dot her forehead, nose, and lips with kisses, ending with a kiss like before, probing and ardent.

She shoves me away, grinning slyly, dark eyes luminous, and takes my hand to lead me to the shelter. When I start to undress, she wrinkles her nose. "No, Carlo." After gathering pieces of recently washed sailcloth, she shoves them into my chest, jabs a finger toward the door, and I leave to bathe within the calm water, following her humorous orders.

While I scrub within the summer-warm water with sand, a naked Watseka waves from the rise at the top of the path. I return the wave, scrub as quickly as I can, my hair too, making sure to fully rinse the sand from it, and dash back to the shelter naked. As I enter, Watseka leaves, snatching the pieces of sail from me.

I go to a corner, brush sand from my feet, and return to my bed, where I lie down to wait.

What a journey my life has been. I have loved and been loved, lost my love and now have earned another. I have a daughter waiting for me in Spain, whom I shall likely never see again. Still, I do not doubt her desire for my happiness, nor the desire of Juliana within Heaven. Is it possible for a man to receive such blessings? It must be, for I am such a man, blessed beyond compare.

Watseka returns with my dirty clothes and throws them to a corner. Water drips from her hair hanging down her back and shoulders. The ends reach her bottom. Strands of it partially cover her breasts. She takes a piece of sailcloth from our stores and folds it into a large triangle. Grinning deviously, she points to below my waist while swinging the cloth back and forth and I must agree, for no small triangle of cloth can cover me now.

She returns the cloth, starts toward me and stops. Her mouth hangs open, as if an idea has occurred to her. Her feet patter as she goes outside. My chest creaks open on rusted hinges, slams shut, and Watseka returns to give me my flute. I toss the flute aside. "No, my dear, I do not think so."

Her lips purse into a pout. "No, Carlo," she says, pointing to the flute. Hands raised to her lips, she blows, so I sit up to take the flute and play. She closes her eyes and sways her head to the rhythm, followed by her hips and legs. Before I know it, she dances a circle around the smoking embers, hair flying, feet kicking sand.

I sputter several times, for it is difficult to play while my mouth attempts to grin involuntarily. Sweat beads upon her brow and breasts. I play faster, her feet kick higher. The beads of sweat join to runnel down her smooth stomach and into her navel—and beyond.

I jump to my feet and throw the flute down, intending to take her within my arms and to my bed. Before I can, a horse snorts. Watseka runs outside and I follow, where Canción and Armonía nicker softly. I huff an exasperated breath. These two are like children interrupting their mama and papa at play. Watseka goes inside for the bridles, loops one around the nose of Armonía, and throws one brown leg over her back. I expect the worse for an unbroken horse, which is for Armonía to buck Watseka off. Miraculously, she simply twists her head back to appraise the lovely person astride her, as if it is the most natural thing in the world for her to expect a ride. Watseka tosses me the other bridle. I rub the sleek black neck of Canción, now nearly full grown at two-years old. "Come, son of Cantante, are you ready to give his brother a ride?"

Canción nickers and tosses his noble head. I give his white star a quick scratch, slip the bridle over his nose, and climb on. He snorts and backsteps nervously for a moment, but Armonía whinnies as if to admonish him. Within no time at all, our two fine friends are galloping within the surf, manes flying, tails held high.

What a day, Luisa, but what a night to come.

April 2, 1524

Dear Luisa,

Stuffing clothes into bags and food into pots by the dim light of the dying fire, all while Watseka writhes in pain within our bed, I run around the shelter, my heart thudding within my chest as if it is the bloody hoof of a horse attempting to kick a hole through my ribs. She woke this way within the dark of night, and I am readying us to travel to the village near the two rivers. By my count, she still has a month before the birth of our child, and I am frightened out of my head with thoughts of losing them.

I pause to appraise her. Her belly looks as if she has swallowed a huge cannonball. She puffs between pains and arches forward to groan when another one comes. I jump over the flames to the corner where my clothes are and start tossing things. My shoes, where the devil are my shoes? I need my shoes if I am going to travel a fifteen-day journey as if the hounds from hell are on my heels.

"Carlo, Carlo."

I whirl. Watseka waves me to her side and I take her hand. "What, love, what can I do?"

As I wipe beads of sweat from her forehead, she gives me a reassuring smile. "Pain better."

"Really?" Nearly collapsing with relief, I stiffen my spine before I fall on top of her. "Really? Are you certain?"

She nods, no doubt reading the concern within my eyes and within my voice, and places my hand to her belly. I feel nothing at first, until either a foot kicks or a fist punches, drawing a smile from my tightened lips. "We have a fighter on our hands, my love." Her eyes squint at my unknown words. I make fists and punch the air, and she gives me a knowing grin.

I offer water, which she sips. She gives me the cup, heaves a huge cleansing breath, and her entire body relaxes, free from whatever was causing those dreadful pains.

Idiot, I tell myself. Juliana had those same pains, something the nun who was looking after her called "false birth." Satisfied with the cause my memory provides, I lie down and close my eyes.

Watseka soon sleeps, her breaths soft and slow. I roll facing her, then try my back. Unable to sleep, I face the fire. The warmth upon my cheeks and brow takes me back to the night of Luisa's birth.

How long ago was that exactly? The days, weeks, and years stumble within my mind like a drunkard. Luisa is … I do not remember her current age? Well, if I can recall the first date I wrote in the journal, that would help. No … no … I cannot even remember that. Perhaps it is my worry over Watseka and our child. She screamed so terribly only moments ago, similar to the screams of Juliana that night.

I reach back, casting a gossamer web to catch a memory as if it were a fish within the Rio Tinto.

Yes, oh yes, I remember. It stormed that night, lightning and thunder as ferocious as that which occurred during the night when Watseka knelt by the bones of her husband. Wind whistled and roared around the corners of the house, and I feared the window panes would burst. I had sent word to the mama and papa of Juliana, but the storm's fury kept them away.

She cried so for her mama. My mama patted her hand and wiped her brow, until the nun said to boil water and gather clean rags.

I paced from the fireplace to the door, from the door to the fireplace. I wrung my hands to where I expected my skin to fall off like that of a snake. Papa said little, for we both knew those wrenching screams did not bode good fortune. Even Cantante leapt his corral and came to a window, to peer inside with huge eyes, lashes blinking, rain in runnels down his white star. Thunder rattled the windows each time lightning cracked, but he never left. It was as if the rain were his tears of sorrow at what was about to happen.

Beatriz came from her bedroom and held my hand wordlessly, eyes red from weeping. Except for the crash and roll of thunder, the rain pounding the windows, and the screams reverberating from Juliana within our bedroom, Silence lay her lonely head within our home, bidding Death to gallop here upon a pale horse, to carry either my wife, my child, or both into the hereafter.

Beatriz squeezed my hand. "Carlo, if you play your flute, might it calm Juliana? You know how she loves your music."

At the window, Papa turned. "It is worth the attempt, my son." He takes my flute from his pocket and presses the warm wood to my palm. "I thought you might want to play for your comfort." He rubs my shoulder. "But I believe we all can use some comfort, yes?"

"Go to her bedside where she can hear you," Beatriz says. "Papa and I shall stand within the doorway and listen."

Sitting upon the bed, the nun concentrates on the bloody ruin of the birth canal, while Mama, on the other side of the bed, holds the legs of Juliana open.

Mama looks back at me with downcast eyes. I expect her to wave me out but she does not, perhaps sensing how I should say goodbye.

When I reach the bedside, my vision blurs from the tears filling my eyes. I shove them away with the heel of my hand but they return, an unleashed waterfall of heat.

Before me, Juliana wavers. Either a spirit or my wife, she wears a white nightgown drenched with sweat. However, ghosts do not breath huge gulping breaths. And ghosts do not have black hair, wet and dripping, plastered to their cheeks. And ghosts do not ignore their husbands because their backs are arched, their teeth are clenched, and they scream the screams of the damned.

Try as I might, I cannot contain my sobs. Papa and Beatriz come to stand with me. Mama goes to the other side of the bed and wipes tears. "I see you have your flute, Carlo. Play that song … what was the name? You played it that evening she and her papa came."

"The Song of Cantante," Beatriz whispers. "She loved it so."

Watseka murmurs in her sleep. A horse nickers outside and I turn to see Canción stick his head through the door. My mouth falls open. Is this a bad omen, like Cantante coming to the window that terrible night was a bad omen? No no no, it cannot be. Watseka is strong and brave and everything I am not. Our child shall be born healthy and squalling, ready to kick and punch this island of ghosts and misery to pieces, ready to love us and be loved.

Canción withdraws his head. The embers of our fire crackle and pop. I close my eyes, but I know I shall not fall asleep. Regardless of my hopeful thoughts, fear rends my very bones with dread at the coming birth.

June 4, 1524

Dear Luisa,

I may have miscounted the months, for Watseka is larger than I ever thought possible. My poor dear can hardly stand in the morning, much less go outside to relieve herself, which is quite often. She slaps my hand when I try to help her as she waddles toward the thicket. Her swollen belly bulges from beneath the unbuttoned bottom of my old cloth blouse. Her hands press into the small of her back. Her shoulders arch rearward for balance. Her tiny feet shuffle forward, leaving streaks within the sand. Muffled groans of exertion issue forth with every sliding step.

Worrying constantly about the possibility of the birth going terribly wrong, I keep one of the leather bags packed with clothing and another packed with smoked deer and fish in a clay pot, including another clay pot with several water skins within the same bag.

How a baby so large can come from a woman so small, I do not know. Luisa did not near this size, and Juliana was as small as Watseka, so my fears about losing both her and our child have haunted me for every minute since she experienced her false birth pains.

With my last journal entry concerning your mama, Luisa, it should be clear how you were born and how she died shortly after. Please, if you hear my thoughts or read these words, perhaps within that misty morning place where dreams give way to wakefulness, know her death was not your fault. Regardless, and this does not place fault either, the nun said she bled to death from the damage done to her insides due to her narrow hips.

Are you there, Luisa? Are you there, Juliana? Have you both abandoned me?

Watseka sleeps soundly. I cannot, so I sit gazing into the embers of the fire, where shimmering crimson paints the circle of the stones as if they were bathed in blood.

Despite the warmth of this starlit summer night, whose glow is bright enough to illuminate the sailcloth above me, a sudden chill presses icicles of dread into the nape of my neck.

Yes, Death is stalking me—as it has since Mateo, Barros, Sancho and I washed upon this island—either Death or misery or both. I suppose I deserve no less for leaving my darling daughter in Palos de le Frontera so long ago.

My regrets—God in Heaven, how they weigh upon my soul—for I could not bear the sight of that square of black lace covering the ashen face of my love, put there to keep flies away from her mouth, nose, and eyes. No sooner than the first shovelful of soil thudded to her coffin, I collapsed to my knees and wept until my throat grew raw, ignoring the words of comfort from our families. Then, two years later, when I could bear my grief no longer, I took Luisa to Mama and Papa and Beatriz for a week-end, returning in the middle of the night to slip a note under the door to explain my leaving. At dawn the next morning, I galloped Cantante to the port on the Rio Tinto, where I begged to board the ship after purchasing the journal, along with too few quills and bottles of ink.

Watseka moans softly. Sweat beads upon her brow. Her hand moves to either a foot or a fist that shoves the taught skin of her brown belly.

It has begun.

I boil water with hot stones placed within the turtle shell, add strips of sailcloth, and sit to wait for the pains to awaken her.

We have decided to use one of two names from her people for our child—Kanti for a girl, Kitchi for a boy. Kanti means "singer," and I like it as a reference to Juliana. Kitchi means "brave," and I like it as a reference to both my families, who braved the loss of my dear wife much better than I.

I wonder if they forgive me for leaving them in such a horrendous manner? I know the answer before the question clears my thoughts, so I should not have asked it.

My God, why did I leave my home and all those dear to me when they, Luisa, and our Heavenly Father would have been my combined rock upon which to lean? Luisa, you brought me so much happiness, yet I still abandoned you as if you had never been born.

Upon the sailcloth roof, the starlight dims. I go out to see whisps of clouds pass, gray and ghostly. A few droplets of rain wet my face. Thank God it is not a storm. I have had enough of deathly coincidences—*quite* enough.

Still, I cannot rid myself of this melancholy, and the wise words of my Papa drift from my childhood … *Prepare, my son. Think ahead to what might happen. Prepare.*

From my journal, I remove the curl of hair I took from Juliana on the night she died and trim half the red ribbon from it. I then cut a lock of hair from Watseka and tie it with the ribbon, leaving it within my journal where I wish my two loves to reside after we three are gone. Doing this, a sudden surprise shocks me, for my hands do not tremble and I do not weep. Perhaps, I suppose, I realize I am never to be happy. Forever cursed … forever cursed.

But why? But how? What deeds lurk within my memory to make me feel this way? Yes, leaving Luisa is one such deed, but what others might reach toward me with oaken claws like those of the old men and the old women trees here, hunched over with windward suffering? I cannot recall mistreating Mateo or Barros, and although Sancho and I shared harsh words, we overcame them before he died. I certainly never mistreated Cantante, who gave his life for me, and whose son cares for me as much as his papa does.

Something twists within my mind, as if a waterspout is screwing itself into my brain.

Cantante *does* love me? Cantante *did* love me?

Oh, no, why think such a silly thing when Cantante is safe in his corral, loving me like always? What a brother he is to me, proven by how he saved my life during that sudden snowstorm all those years ago.

I fetch my flute from the fireplace mantle. Juliana shall enjoy a song during the birth of our child to ease her anxiety. No doubt it shall ease my own anxiety, as well as that of Papa, Mama, and Beatriz. This storm rumbling overhead, however, does us no good whatsoever. At least the fire crackling cheerfully within the hearth brightens the living area, where papa and I wait for the birth pains to strengthen.

I peek into the bedroom. Juliana lies still and quiet. Thank goodness the nun, who stands like a ghost within the corner, came quickly, although I cannot quite recall how she received word. How the mind plays tricks at these times of woe and want.

Juliana rises from the pillow, her features as drawn as a skin upon a drum. Patting her hand, I kiss her brow. "It shall be fine, dearest. Everything is prepared for our departure."

The cords of muscle within her neck bulge as the first true pain hits. She falls back to the pillow. Dark eyes widen. Teeth clench. A blue vein within her temple throbs.

Someone has placed a necklace of tiny shells around her neck. I do not recall who, but that is of no consequence. More tricks upon the mind, I suppose.

"Papa?"

Ah, the voice of our unborn child comes to me. I secretly desire a daughter to love, so I call her Luisa.

Carlo, my love, do not despair.

Ah, Juliana, you are always within my mind, even as I watch you struggle with your birth pains. We shall be together soon. Always and forever. No more suffering, no more pain. Our darling daughter shall hold our hands as we enter the gates of Heaven itself.

Mama bids me leave the bedroom. I go to the fireplace, to the door, to the window ... pacing … pacing. Hour after hour, lightning flashes, thunder crashes, windows rattle within their panes. Mama rushes from the bedroom to the kitchen, rushes back with more steaming rags. Beatriz likely prays within her room.

The screams begin, long and loud, shrill and reverberating. Death is arriving upon a pale horse. I am ready … I am ready.

Beatriz comes from her bedroom, eyes red from weeping, and holds my hand. Except for the crash and roll of thunder, the rain pounding the windows, and the screams reverberating from Juliana within our bedroom, Silence lies her lonely head within our home. Yes, Pale Horse, bear Death here to carry my wife, my child, and myself into the hereafter, where none of us shall ever suffer again.

Lightning flashes, revealing Cantante at the window, come to peer inside with huge eyes, lashes blinking, rain in runnels down his white star. Thunder rattles the panes each time lightning cracks, but he never leaves. It is as if the droplets of rain are his tears of sorrow at what is about to happen.

Beatriz squeezes my hand. "Carlo, if you play your flute, might it calm Juliana? You know how she loves your music."

At the window, Papa turns. "It is worth the attempt, my son." He takes my flute from his pocket and presses the warm wood into my palm. "I thought you might want to play for your comfort." He rubs my shoulder. "But I believe we all can use some comfort, yes?"

I do not understand how my flute was within his pocket. Did I not retrieve it from the fireplace mantle hours ago?

"Go to her bedside where she can hear you," Beatriz says. "Papa and I shall stand within the doorway and listen."

Leaving the puzzle of the flute behind, I shuffle to the door, knock and peek inside.

Sitting upon the bed, her body turned askew, the nun concentrates on the bloody ruin of the birth canal. On the other side of the bed, holding the legs of Juliana open, Mama looks back at me with downcast eyes. I expect her to wave me out but she does not, perhaps sensing how I should say goodbye.

When I reach the bedside, my vision blurs from the tears filling my eyes. I shove them away with the heel of my hand but they return, an unleashed waterfall of heat.

Before me, Juliana wavers.

Either a spirit or my wife, she wears a white nightgown drenched with sweat.

However, ghosts do not breathe huge gulping breaths. And ghosts do not have black hair, wet and dripping, plastered to their cheeks. And ghosts do not ignore their husbands because their backs are arched, their teeth are clenched, and they scream the screams of the damned.

Try as I might, I cannot contain my sobs. Papa and Beatriz come to stand with me. Mama goes to the other side of the bed, wipes tears, and kneels upon the bed to hold the trembling legs once again. "I see you have your flute, Carlo. Play that song—" A scream drowns out her words. She blinks repeatedly, and another tear runs down her cheek. The scream fades. "What was the name? You played it that evening Juliana and her papa came."

"The Song of Cantante," Beatriz whispers. "She loved it so."

Flute upon my lower lip. Playing now. Can barely manage it. Screams echo.

Juliana, my Juliana, I love you so.

She goes rigid and convulses—convulses again and again. Her eyes are black holes within a skull covered with parchment-thin skin. Her screams are guttural now, head whipping back and forth, fists clenched at her sides.

"Fight, my love," I whisper, hot tears still cascading down my cheeks. "Please fight, please fight. I cannot—" I choke back a sob— "I cannot live without you."

As if she is breaking in two, her back arches to an impossible angle, until only the top of her head touches the pillow. A never-ending groan bursts from between her clenched teeth.

And then—oh my God and then—she collapses like a sail after a storm, leaving nothing but a final breath, which slowly wheezes from her, a death rattle that shall haunt me for the rest of my days.

Weeping terribly, Mama rises from the bed and turns away. Papa goes to her side. Beatriz softly sobs into her hands. The nun marks herself and prays, leaving a bloody cross upon her white apron.

Juliana and our child are gone. I wanted a daughter so badly, but she is trapped within the small body. No foot kicks. No fist strikes. The taught, rounded belly is smooth and still.

I glare at the flute within my hands. Music? What need have I of music ever again? I snap it asunder and run from the house into the storm. The shrubs I planted scratch my arms. The soil beneath my feet squeezes between my bare toes. I fall down the mound of earth hauled in for a garden for Juliana. Upon my feet again, I run toward the corral of Cantante. The rain pounds relentlessly, thudding into the ground with a roar not unlike the sea. The droplets transform into mist wetting my lips with—

—salt?

As if it had never been birthed from the horizon, the storm vanishes, replaced by a black sky with so many stars, surely God has spread them from the east to the west, from the north to the south.

What madness is this? Why I am not soaked from the rain? Why am I not blown by the wind? Why am not muddy from my fall and am sandy instead?

Behind me, Cantante nickers. He then walks to my front and nudges me with his nose back toward my home, but I step aside.

The broken pieces of flute within my hands …

How—?

My God, I have forced the memories of that night away, including the full reason of why I left my home.

I look to the heavens as the terrible truth descends upon me.

Not only did Juliana die that terrible night, Luisa died as well, and my tortured mind would not allow me to believe this tragedy beyond comprehension, which drove me away from home and all those I love.

And now I must bear the same tragedy all over again, for I watched Watseka and our child die—as I watched Juliana and Luisa die all those years ago. Perhaps she and Juliana were so much alike that my guilt drew me to the past, except the past occurred this very night, living again with the death of Watseka and our child.

Truth descends upon me further, shaking my soul to the very core.

On the day of the funeral, my love lay within her coffin, the black square of lace upon her face. God help me, her belly was still near to bursting from our child within her, covered with her wedding gown, now her shroud. The lid was closed, the coffin lowered into the dark hole. No sooner than the first shovelful of dirt struck with a hollow thud, I ran home from the church, saddled Cantante, and begged passage upon the ship, completely abandoning my family without a single word of goodbye.

If I am not cursed, I should be. What a wretch I am, damned to hell as sure as the day I was born.

More truth descends upon me.

I stand upon the beach of this accursed island, feet within cool sand. Similar to the crashing waves of the sea before me, crests studded with starlight, the truth of my guilt fully opens my eyes.

I killed Mateo, for I saw those blue fish that attacked him.

I killed Barros, for I should have seen the folly of trying to impale a deer with wooden spikes lashed to a tree limb.

Although I did not kill Sancho, I feasted upon his flesh, denying my sin by believing he was a pig, which had escaped from a ship without a single pig upon it.

And Cantante—my brother Cantante. I killed him by cutting the throbbing vein within his neck, as surely as I killed Watseka by falling upon her with lust, to thrust and thrust until my seed poisoned her, culminating with a child whose death I am guilty of as well.

"No, Papa. Cantante saved you like that night in the snow. Do you not remember?"

I wave the ghost voice away, a sign of my previous insanity.

"Please, Papa, try to remember. Cantante gave his life for you."

No, Luisa. It was I who—

"You could not do it and he raised up to cut the vein. You are not guilty of anything, Papa, except love."

Listen to her, my love. You loved Luisa and I to the point of leaving your family because of your grief. You loved your friends also. Mateo, Barros, and Sancho would have given their lives for you without question, as you would have for them. Do not dishonor them by thinking otherwise.

"Juliana?" I peer up and down the beach. "Is it really you?"

Look to the sky, my love. Recall how we treasured our starlit strolls. Recall how we loved one another amidst the call of crickets and the sighs of the night. Recall how we held each other until the dawn. Do you not see how love still awaits you?

Cantante nudges me toward the dune, almost as if he wants me to tend to my dead wife and child. No, this is Canción. Armonía stands nearby.

God help me. God help me. I have cried so many tears within my life, I am as empty as a shell upon this beach.

Go with him, my love. Go with him and see.

Nickering softly, Canción nudges me again. I hold the broken pieces of the flute within one hand, plunge my fingers into his thick mane with the other, and allow him to lead me to the shelter.

No, Juliana, there is nothing to see here. Nothing except more death.

Behind me, Armonía snorts with what I can only describe as derision.

Near the fork that leads to my small cemetery, which now awaits myself and my dead family, I jerk to stop and tilt my ear toward the shelter. Did I hear— No! Can it be? Can it really be?

I start to collapse. Daring to hope, I regain my legs to run as fast as I can to the shelter, where I fling the door open.

In her bed, Watseka clutches a baby, naked and wailing, to her breast. I fall to me knees beside them. "A girl, my love? We have a daughter?"

"Kanti," she says. She then points to a wrapped bundle at her other side. "Kitchi."

"A son? We have a son as well?" I take him into my arms and kiss his pink forehead, kiss her bloody forehead also and count fingers and toes. Thank you, God, thank you so much for their perfection.

Watseka raises Kanti toward me. "Clean her."

The boiled rags make quick work of the blood. Watseka has tied the cord and cut it, but the afterbirth still lies near her feet. I take it outside and return to clean Watseka while she nurses our children. That task done, I add sticks to the fire and water to the turtle shell. When it boils, I add the bloody cloths for cleaning and sit beside the fire, eyes focused upon my three miracles.

The stars illuminate the sailcloth roof again. Moments later they fade as the rising sun sends faint yellow rays through the cracks within my old wall, laddered with cuts that represent my days here. Three more months shall mark a total of three years since I arrived.

Unbelievable … amazingly unbelievable.

Since Juliana and Luisa died, how many times have I despaired? How many times have I prayed? How many times have I cried?

It is as Father Cristobal told us time and time again … "Now, children, you may pray for this and you may pray for that, expecting those prayers to be answered when you desire. However, God answers prayers in His time, not yours. Remember that as you grow and learn in this life, for it is the only one you shall have."

True words from my old teacher, one of the wisest men I have known.

And now, to my amazement, my prayers have been answered upon this blessed island, painted upon the sea with the finger of God, as natural a wonder as I have ever seen.

Thank you, Heavenly Father, for all your blessings. Thank you, Juliana and Luisa, for watching over me. Thank you, creatures of this island, be you great or small, flying or swimming, hopping or running, for keeping me company during my days here.

And to my brother, Cantante, thank you for saving my life, not once but twice. Without you, I would not be alive to know such blessings as Juliana and Luisa, or Watseka and our new family.

The babies grunt like tiny pigs feeding at a trough. Watseka looks up and smiles. I return her smile.

What trials lie before us? Our home shall not last forever, evidenced by the thinning and frayed sailcloth roof and the nails bleeding rust down the walls. Well, I never thought to be here forever, for I thought to be home by now.

Still, home is where a family abides. As long as I have our family, including our horse friends, happiness and contentment shall be my companions for the remainder of my life.

September 11, 1524

Dear Luisa,

A little over three months old, Kanti and Kitchi are as plump as can be, with dark hair quickly replacing the fuzz with which they were born. They nurse like two foals, suckling with satisfaction several times during the day and night. I never cease to enjoy watching their pink lips work in and out, in and out, or their tiny fingers with translucent nails closing and opening, closing and opening, or their dark eyes blinking slowly, until they close in blessed slumber. Changing the sailcloth triangles covering their bottoms, however, I can quite do without. Well, until they kick and squeal when I tickle their feet.

The nights are cooler now, but they still carry the hint of summer. The first flocks of those large honking birds flew over the island yesterday, winging their way south. I no longer hear loneliness within their song, but wonder instead. The gulls and backward-kneed birds, of course, never fail to amuse my family when we go to the beach, where I point out our feathered friends to the children.

This morning as they nap, and as Watseka and I cook our meal, she is silent. I wonder what she might be thinking but I shall not ask. It is best to wait, for she eventually tells me when something is bothering her.

The last bite done, she drinks water and sets the cup aside. Still, she does not speak, for even though we have learned many of our words since we met, she prefers to gather them within her thoughts first.

We wash our pots and cups by the light of a shimmering sun rising over the island, which bathes our clearing with golden light. Like always, gulls screech over our heads, while birds chirp and twitter within the trees. A rabbit crosses the path in a single bound. At the far edge of the thicket, Canción and Armonía browse upon vegetation. Their tails swish, manes shake. Canción drops brown balls of dung, steaming within the crisp air.

I cannot ask for a more perfect dwelling place. Nature, along with my family, is all I shall ever need. Still, the silent brooding of Watseka is a concern, and I am tempted to ask her what is the matter.

Done with the pots and cups, she hangs them upon limbs to dry. Then she goes to my chest and takes out my journal, which is something she has never done. At my side, she opens the cover and touches the curl of hair from Juliana. "Who is she?"

I kiss her forehead and lead her into our home, where our children nap upon our bed.

As we sit beside each other near the smoldering embers, it is my turn to gather my thoughts, until I recall how we have already had a version of this conversation.

I draw a line to represent land, include two stick figures, and point to one. "Carlo."

Watseka nods. "Yes."

I point to the other figure. "Juliana, my wife." To further explain, I draw a cross by the head of the second figure.

"Carlo wife …" The brow of Watseka knots above her eyes. "Carlo wife, spirit world?"

"Yes," I say, wiping the sand smooth.

"You miss fam … fam …"

"Family. Yes, but I have a family now." I realize how so many words at once may confuse Watseka, so I tap my chest with my fist. "Kanti, Kitchi." Then I take her length of straight hair from my journal and kiss it. "Watseka, Kanti, Kitchi. My family now."

I hope for a smile but I do not receive one. Instead, she draws the two rivers where her other people live, adds several stick figures and points to them. "Watseka family … Carlo family. We go?"

The question somewhat surprises me, although it should not. If anyone knows the value of family, I certainly do. Still, my language skills concerning the words of this new family are questionable, but Watseka shall help me along.

I nod to her. "Yes. We go."

October 4, 1524

Dear Luisa,

Having spent almost a month in preparation for our journey, this is my last entry into my journal. If you question why I do not take it with me, I prefer to leave it and my memories where some future wayfarer may discover it and wonder what manner of people lived here once upon a time, as well as the intrigue of the presence of Spanish horses. Also, I am using the last pages, the last bit of ink, and the last quill. God is good, is he not? After all, He allowed me everything I needed, not only to write our story, but to survive upon this island.

"But, Papa, how shall anyone find your journal when you have taken the shelter down and Watseka has taken the sail cloth and ropes to her vessel?"

I look up into the sky, supposing the imaginary voice of my daughter shall stay with me forever.

Imaginary, my love? Oh, ye, of little faith. If not for how Luisa and I watched over you from Heaven, you would have perished long ago.

Oh, ye, of little faith indeed, Juliana, for that is certainly myself. Forgive me, and thank you so much for watching over me.

"But, Papa, what about your journal? I was sleeping upon a cloud and did not see what you did with it."

I hear you, my darling girl. I have already placed my journal within a piece of cloth, rolled my broken flute within another piece of cloth, and placed both within my chest. A knotted rope secures the brass clasp, while within the center of our clearing, the sands of this island conceal it. How many years it may lie hidden, I do not know. Perhaps it is folly to think someone shall discover it, perhaps not, but it is a comfort to believe the story of myself and those I love may live on forever, waiting not far from Mateo, Barros, Sancho, Cantante, Uhanu, and the tiny, palm-sized infant born to Watseka.

Upon a fur nearby, Kanti and Kitchi lie facing each other, attempting to roll over. Both narrow their eyes with concentration before falling to their backs. Frustrated babbling follows, making me smile. Watseka made another set of tanned deerskin clothes for Kitchi, which he now wears. Thankfully, the babies were not overlarge when they were born. Their clothes have a bit of room to grow as well, and we shall have time once we reach the village beside the two rivers to make them new clothes before winter sets in.

Watseka comes up the sandy path from the calm water, where she has taken the last clay jar of food. Armonía, wearing her bridle, goes to her for a rub. Watseka gladly complies, scratching her neck and forehead.

I go to Canción, my brother who lives on through the bloodline of Cantante, and mount his back. The sun has warmed his coat, sleek and black. Watseka places Kanti and Kitchi within my arms, mounts Armonía, and I give her Kitchi.

We have planned our final ride upon the beach during our last days here. This is where we go now, as the dawn breaks over the sea, sending luminous rays of yellow and orange upward to brighten the sky, as well as our future.

The horses ease down the sandy dune and trot toward the surf. During the last months, both the northern and southern herds have managed to merge. Perhaps they know, as humanity should know, we are stronger when we stand together than apart.

They gallop toward us from the south, hooves flinging sand. Some break off for the surf, and foam bursts upward into clouds of spray. Tails drip water. Manes waggle. Snorts and whinnies permeate the air. They rejoin the other horses and trot past us, as if to acknowledge our departure.

Three years ... it is difficult to fathom how I have lived here for so long, including how I have lost my family in Spain and my friends from the ship.

I face Watseka.

But I have a new family now. Amazing. Astounding. Blessed beyond compare.

We leave the beach to ride up and over the dune and down the path to the calm water, where we dismount. With the babies secure upon their fur within the vessel, which I now know is called an aquointan, and the bridles from Canción and Armonía there also, we paddle toward the far shore.

Looking back, I wait to see if our practice of swimming the horses within the calm water shall have them follow us. They snort and splash, enter fully, and swim along, heads arching back and forth with ease, breaths puffing from flared nostrils.

Watseka has an idea to make a sort of wheelless wagon from two long poles tied together at one end, with the rope draped over the shoulders of one of the horses for pulling. Shorter poles lashed to the trailing ends will create a platform. Upon this we shall carry our supplies for the journey, letting each horse rest while the other drags it. If the platform proves sturdy, we may also use it to carry Kanti and Kitchi while they nap.

The sun rises above my island and those crooked trees, nearly blinding me with a sudden burst of golden illumination.

Farewell, Mateo and Barros. Farewell, Sancho and Uhanu. Farewell Cantante and child of Watseka.

A tinge of emotion catches within my throat, for I cannot say farewell to Juliana and Luisa.

As tears fill my eyes, I start to turn away from the island, but stop as a faint movement at the bottom of the sandy rise catches my eye. Of the many things the movement might be, such as marsh grass wavering within the breeze, a bird flitting amongst the greenery, a deer or a rabbit moving stealthily about, I prefer to believe my wife and daughter from Spain are waving, black curls falling about their shoulders, smiles gleaming, souls and hearts as free as those of the angels.

Love.

Does it not remain with us always, sealed deep inside to be released when we meet our families once again in Heaven?

Oh, yes, it most certainly does.

I wave to my two angels. All my love to you both, Julianna and Luisa.

Until we meet again.

Carlo Cipriani

Book Club Questions

1. In the first diary entry, we learn how Carlo's wife has died. Did you have any idea how that may have happened?

2. When you read how Carlo would never eat horse, did you think he might resort to that to survive in the future?

3. When you learned how the crew had discussed cannibalism, did you think Carlo might resort to that to survive in the future?

4. When Carlo thought he saw the horses to the north, did you think Cantante had survived?

5. For those who have never been to Corolla, North Carolina, it is a long, narrow strip of land, which a person unfamiliar with the area could mistake for an island. Did you think the aspect of starving and not having fresh water was accurately written?

6. There have been instances where bluefish, which is an actual fish, have bitten people wading in the surf. Did Mateo's death surprise you?

7. Whitetail deer, rabbits, and other animals live on the Outer Banks. Was it realistic how these men could not catch them, and how Barro's died from the attempt?

8. Although Sancho originally appeared to be a mean person, we learn how his father's treatment of his mother made him that way, including how it affected him to the point of killing his wife. Is it understandable to believe how a person's past can

make them do such things? Also, is it understandable how a person can see their mistakes and learn from them?

9. Carlo's mind is obviously being affected when he uses Sancho's body to survive. Do you think imagining the pigs was a way to cope with doing something he never thought he'd do?

10. Carlo's mind was again affected when he thought Cantante was a ghost, come to comfort him as he died. How did you feel when he discovered Cantante was real, and had come to save him like he saved Carlo from dying in the snowstorm?

11. When Carlo saw the native couple in their vessel, did you think he would ever meet either one of them again?

12. History teaches us how many cultures across the world have mistreated others, as well as their own people. When the native tribe across the calm water was attacked, how did you feel about it?

13. Did you empathize with Watseka when she changed her mind about making love to Carlo because she still loved her dead husband?

14. Did you think Carlos' reaction to Watseka's daughter's death happened because of how Luisa died?

15. Did the death of Watseka's daughter, including how it affected Carlo, hint at anything concerning Luisa?

16. When Watseka took Carlo to her village, do you think he imagined what had happened accurately?

17. Watseka loved her husband very much. When she brought him back to bury him, did you think she did that because she knew she was falling in love with Carlo and needed to move on from her husband's death before she could admit it?

18. Did the dual narratives of how Juliana died and of Watseka's pregnancy make you think Watseka might die too?

19. Did the dual narratives help you understand how Carlo relived the night when Juliana and Luisa died, including how he truly believed that Watseka and his child had died in the same way?

20. Were you surprised when Carlo ran back from the beach to discover Watseka had given birth to twins? From their talk of the village near the two rivers, did you think they might go there to live?

ABOUT THE AUTHOR

J. Willis Sanders lives in southern Virginia, with his wife, banjos, resonator guitars, and one acoustic guitar.

With ten novels completed and more on the way, he enjoys crafting intriguing characters with equally intriguing conflicts to overcome. He also loves the natural world and, more often than not, his stories include those settings. Most also utilize intense love relationships and layered themes.

His first novel (not this one, but he plans to publish it) is a ghostly World War II era historical that takes place mostly in the midwestern United States, which utilizes some little-known facts about German POW camps there at that time. It's the first of a three-book series, where characters from the first continue their lives.

Although he loves history, he has written several contemporary novels as well, and some include interesting paranormal twists, both with and without religious themes.

He also loves the Outer Banks of North Carolina, and he has written three novels within different time frames based on the area, what he calls his Outer Banks of North Carolina Series, this novel being the first.

Other hobbies include reading (of course), vegetable gardening, playing music with friends, and songwriting, some of which are in a few of his novels.

To learn of new releases, follow him on Amazon.com, Facebook.com, or https://jwillissanders.wixsite.com/writer.

Readers: to help those considering a purchase, please leave a review on Amazon.com, Goodreads.com, or wherever you bought this book.

Thank you.

CPSIA information can be obtained
at www.ICGtesting.com
Printed in the USA
BVHW071112180821
614612BV00010B/729

9 781954 763104